DARCY

AND

ELIZABETH

Frances Morgan

CENFAR BOOKS

Published by
Cenfar Books

ISBN 0-9544278-0-7

Typeset by MusicPrint, Warblington
Printed by RPM Print & Design, Chichester

*This book is dedicated to Suzie and
Sammy, who will always be in my
thoughts, and to Nigel for his patience
throughout this project.
My grateful thanks.*

INTRODUCTION

Jane Austen was born on the 16th December 1775, to the Reverend and Mrs Austen. Jane was their seventh child, and spent most of her early and teenage years at their rectory in Steventon.

In the eighteenth century, it was the custom of mothers of Mrs Austen's standard to nurse their new born babies for the first three months, then farm them out to the village ladies, only to be returned home when they were of a 'sensible' age. This custom, it is believed, had a profound effect on Jane. More so than the rest of her siblings.

Her life, apart from her writing, was uneventful. She never married, (although, she did, for a few short hours, become engaged to the brother of her dearest friend), but spent the majority of her life in the company of her parents and her sister Cassandra.

She started writing at an early age, and her first novel, Sense and Sensibility, was written when she was only eighteen. Pride and Prejudice was written at the age of twenty, and Mansfield Park shortly afterwards.

At the age of twenty five, Jane's parents made the startling decision to move from Jane's beloved Steventon to the city of Bath. This upheaval so disconcerted Jane she wrote nothing for nearly ten years. Her writing skills only flowed when she had the peace and security of a permanent home. Her life in Bath was not a happy one. The hustle and bustle of society was not suited to her disposition, and she was much relieved, when, after her fathers death, at the age of seventy, she settled down with her mother and sister, in a small house on her brother Edward's estate in Chawton, Hampshire

Settled at last, she took out the manuscripts that she had carried with her wherever she had lived, and made them ready for publication.

All three books took sixteen to twenty years to be published. Her first book, Sense and Sensibility, was published when she was thirty seven years old, with the author kept anonymous. A thousand copies were believed to have been printed and sold, bringing Jane the vast fortune of £140. This money was the first Jane had ever received that was entirely her own. It made the difference between relying on her family's charity and being an independent woman. When Pride and Prejudice was published in 1813, her publisher offered her £110 for the rights. Jane had been hoping for £150, but she settled for his first offer. Still keeping her name anonymous, Pride and Prejudice outsold Sense and Sensibility. By the time Mansfield Park was published, Jane had admitted to being the author, and was much in demand at gatherings and parties.

Emma was published in 1815, and brought in the princely sum of £221.6.4d. She dedicated this book to the Prince Regent, who wished it, and in those days, a wish was more of a command.

Persuasion followed in 1817, but Northhanger Abbey was not published until after her death in 1817.

Jane was ill for close to a year before her death at 4.30am on the 18th of July 1817. She was only forty two years old. What she died of was not know at the time, but many years later, in 1964, Sir Zachary Cope believed that she had died from Addison's disease. This disease is of the tuberculosis strain and results in vomiting, dehydration and skin discolouration. She was buried in the Cathedral at Winchester on the 24th of July 1817, although the register records the date as the 16th. Her mother outlived Jane by ten years, dying in January 1827 at the age of eighty seven.

Jane's stories, although sympathetic with the time, did, very rarely call on actual situations for their ideas. It is thought that at one time Pride and Prejudice was a much longer novel. She talks of cutting parts out to make a more concise story and it leaves one thinking how marvellous it would be to see these discarded pages.

Pride and Prejudice was by far Jane's favourite book, and Elizabeth Bennett her favourite character. She spoke many times to her friends and relations about the characters in this book, so it makes one wonder if there was more than a little of the true Jane Austen in the character of Elizabeth. Maybe not in real life, but how she would have wished her life to be.

All Jane's stories revolve round small family units, usually of three or four children living on the edge of high society. Their parents, not having enough wealth to live in the top society, were financially sound enough to keep servants and enjoy a full and satisfying social life.

In Pride and Prejudice she has cleverly constructed a romantic attachment between two people that is as relevant today as it was back in 1789. All her characters are colourful, animated and believable and deserve, in my opinion, to live on.

Pride and Prejudice is a beautifully written story revolving around a small family living in a house called Longbourne in the very heart of

Hertfordshire.

Mr and Mrs Bennett have five daughters, all of marriageable age. Miss Jane Bennett, the eldest, is fair haired, quiet, sensible and gentle. Elizabeth, who is a renowned beauty, spirited and intelligent, and Mary, who has little time for society, preferring to read her way through the contents of her father's library. The two younger Miss Bennetts, Kitty and Lydia, think only of the enjoyment they can extract from life. Men, especially the regimental kind, are treated to much flirting, so doing, brings much talk to the family.

When a single man of good fortune by the name of Bingley moves into the neighbouring estate of Netherfield, it is more than Mrs Bennett can do to conceal her excitement.

"He has five thousand a year. Just think Mr Bennett, he may very well marry one of our girls," she exclaimed in delight.

Owing to the fact that they had not produced a son and heir, Mr Bennett's estate, on his death, would be entailed away to a cousin by the name of Mr Collins, who had taken up the calling of the church.

It was therefore Mrs Bennett's sole aim in life to see her five girls married off, to, if possible, rich young men.

At an assembly in the nearby town of Meryton, Mr Bingley introduces the daughters to his two sisters, Caroline, who is to keep house for him, his married sister Mrs Hurst, and his good friend, the tall, elegant, handsome, Mr Darcy.

Mrs Bennett is beside herself with delight at another gentleman being introduced into their circle, but it did not take many minutes to reveal that Mr Darcy truly believed that he was in company much below his own station in life, and deemed it insupportable to stand up and dance with any of the ladies in the room. Mr Bingley's sister's were of the same opinion.

Much put out, and to the embarrassment of her daughters, Mrs Bennett voiced her opinion loud enough for everyone to hear.

"What if he is the richest man in Derbyshire, his manners do him no credit at all. Not at all like his amiable friend Mr Bingley." Unfortunately Mrs Bennett's disposition was one of vulgarity and stupidity.

Although it did not suit Mr Darcy, he found himself continually attracted to the dark-haired Elizabeth Bennett, but his outward countenance relayed no such feelings.

Mr Collins, whose father had been estranged from Mr Bennett, arrives at Longbourne with the proverbial olive branch, and with every intention of securing one of Mr Bennett's daughters as his wife. His preference at first was Jane, but of being told of her impending engagement to Mr Bingley, he very quickly transfers his favours to Elizabeth. On his proposal of marriage, he explains that his gracious benefactor, none other than Lady Catherine de Burgh herself, who was also Mr Darcy's aunt, had suggested that it was time he took a wife, and he believed it would greatly add to his happiness.

Mr Collins was a simpering, pathetic figure who repulsed Elizabeth. Her refusal to marry him incurred the wrath of her mother. Mr Collins, however, soon forgot the pain of rejection and married Elizabeth's best friend, Charlotte Lucas.

The younger daughters were by this time totally engrossed with the militia who were passing the winter in town, especially a young handsome officer called Wickham. Both Elizabeth and Lydia found themselves attracted to this handsome newcomer. Further conversations revealed that he had been the prodigy of old Mr Darcy, but on his death, the young Mr Darcy had flatly refused to honour his father's wishes for Mr Wickham's future, leaving him to make his own way in life. He further informed Elizabeth that Mr Darcy had a sister, much younger than himself, who was of the same proud disposition. This new information only went to reinforce Elizabeth's mind that her first impressions of Mr Darcy were correct.

"I did not believe Mr Darcy to be as bad as this," she exclaimed when told, "but it does not surprise me. His manner is such that I believe him to be capable of anything."

Mr Wickham had much charm, and was totally believable.

Mr Bingley, who had been much attracted to Jane Bennett, had been told quite forcefully by his two sisters, Caroline and Mrs Hurst, that Jane was not a suitable match for him, and with the backing of Mr Darcy, he was persuaded to go back to town where Mr Darcy wished him to be in the company of his own sister, Georgiana. His hope was that, a match would be made between his sister and his closest friend.

Jane was heartbroken, so after Christmas it was suggested that she go and spend some time with her aunt and uncle Gardiner in Cheapside, a part of London, although respectable, was not frequented by the upper classes. When she was in town she visited Caroline Bingley at her home, and was left in no doubt that her brother, Mr Bingley, knew of her being in town, but was much engaged with Mr Darcy's sister. She had to then admit to herself that Mr Bingley no longer cared for her.

Elizabeth, who had gone to visit her newly married friend Charlotte and Mr Collins in Kent, was invited many times to dine at Rosings Park, the home of Lady Catherine de Burgh. Elizabeth's first impressions were that she was a very formidable lady, who liked the distinction of rank preserved. She was definitely not a woman to be crossed. Her daughter, however, was of a sickly nature, pale and delicate, but it was Lady Catherine's wish that she would in time become the bride of Mr Darcy.

During Elizabeth's stay with her friend, Mr Darcy and his cousin Colonel Fitzwilliam came to stay with Mr Darcy's aunt Lady Catherine at Rosings. Colonel Fitzwilliam was a very pleasant gentleman and Elizabeth spent many hours walking with him in the park.

You can imagine Elizabeth's surprise when, alone one evening after dinner, Mr Darcy arrived unannounced in a much agitated state, and declared his deep regard for her. He explained to her that although her relations were far beneath his own, and that he was going against his better judgement, it could not be helped. His feelings would not be repressed. Her fervently begged her to become his wife.

Elizabeth was most surprised as she was of the opinion that Mr Darcy disliked her as much as she disliked him. The thought of marriage to this proud, disagreeable man, was something she did not even want to contemplate. In her opinion he was arrogant, conceited and had a selfish disdain for the feelings of others, but at the same time she was well aware of the honour he was bestowing on her.

On her refusal to accept his proposal, his reaction was one of disbelief, and although he controlled his anger very well, it was visible in every line of his features. For someone of Elizabeth's birth to refuse a man of his stature was beyond belief.

The reasons she gave for refusing him were his part in the break up of relations between Mr Bingley and her beloved sister Jane, and his treatment of Wickham.

Informing her that she had said quite enough, he left the house totally confused that she could have formed this opinion of him. Her suggestion that she may have had different feelings if he had acted in a more gentlemanlike manner tortured his very sole.

He spent the whole night writing a letter to Elizabeth, informing her of the true facts of his dealings with Mr Wickham. How he had preferred, and was given the money instead of a living, and that he had, in the recent past, attempted to persuade his sister Georgiana to elope with him. He assured Elizabeth that his version of Wickham was the correct one, and Colonel Fitzwilliam could vouch for every word.

By the time she had returned to Longbourne, it was evident to Elizabeth, that she had been most deceived by Mr Wickham's version of events, and felt embarrassment and guilt at her treatment of Darcy.

Her aunt and uncle Gardiner invited her to join them on a holiday on the peaks of Derbyshire, and she was most concerned, but interested when one of their excursions took them to the great estate of Pemberley. Mr Darcy's ancestral home. They were assured by the housekeeper that the family were away from home, but Mr Darcy had returned early, and a confrontation between Elizabeth and Mr Darcy in the garden was most embarrassing.

His manner towards her was nothing but polite and friendly, which surprised Mrs Gardiner, who knew only Elizabeth's opinion of the proud Mr Darcy.

By accepting an invitation to dine at Pemberley with Georgiana, Mr Bingley and his sisters gave Mr Darcy hope that Elizabeth's feelings may have changed.

Before he could pursue this new turn of events, Elizabeth received a letter from her sister Jane, informing her that their youngest sister Lydia, had run away with Mr Wickham, and they were now living, unmarried in London.

Elizabeth was distraught. This act of her sister's would bring disgrace and dishonour to the whole family. No respectable man would ever seek their company again.

Mr Darcy, who happened upon Elizabeth a few moments after her discovery, was shocked and grieved. Although he offered his sympathies, it was not many minutes before he left her, stating that she must have been long wishing his absence. As he left the room, Elizabeth was convinced that she would never see him again.

Her whole family were much distraught with the actions of Lydia, and Mr Bennett, with the help of Mr Gardiner, set off to London to discover their whereabouts.

Unknown to Elizabeth, Mr Darcy had also gone to London. He had an idea who, if anyone, would know where the couple were staying.

On discovering their hiding place, he visited Mr and Mrs Gardiner, and explained that if he had exposed Mr Wickham's character when he tried to elope with Georgiana, this situation could not have come about. He felt it was his responsibility to put right the wrong that had occurred.

A new situation was secured for Wickham in a Northern Regiment, his debts were paid off, and the couple were made to marry.

Mrs Bennett was beside herself with delight that one of her daughter's was married at last. Mr Bennett however was not of the same opinion. He knew that a great deal of money had been laid down to bring about this favourable end. He believed that he owed a great debt to his brother in law, Mr Gardiner, and had no idea how he would ever repay it.

When Lydia returned for a visit to Longbourne, she unintentionally let slip that Mr Darcy was at her wedding. This was a great shock to Elizabeth, who could not understand Mr Darcy's involvement in all this, so she wrote to her aunt Gardiner for an explanation. On discovering that Mr Darcy was responsible for putting her youngest sister's life back on the right path, her feelings towards him grew stronger, and more ardent. It pained her greatly to know that her chance of happiness with Mr Darcy had slipped through her fingers, and it was all of her own doing.

A few weeks later news came to the village that Mr Bingley was returning to Netherfield. Mrs Bennett was delighted, Jane disconcerted, and Elizabeth confused. It took several days before Mr Bingley paid a visit to Longbourne, and to Elizabeth's delight, he was accompanied by Mr Darcy.

It was evident that Mr Bingley still had feelings for Jane, she Mrs Bennett took every opportunity possible to leave the two alone together.

Mr Bingley, who had no wish to go against the advice of his friend, was most surprised when Mr Darcy, admitted that he had been wrong in his judgement of the situation, and gave Bingley his blessing to go ahead and marry Jane. Bingley wasted no time in making his proposal to Jane, and it was accepted without hesitation. No-one could have been happier.

During the following week Elizabeth received a most unexpected visit from Lady Catherine de Burgh. She announced that she had come to lay to rest the rumour that Elizabeth was to marry her nephew Mr Darcy. It was out of the question. To marry so far below his station in life would bring disgrace to the whole family. She would not allow it to happen. Mr Darcy, she informed Elizabeth, was to marry her daughter Anne. As Elizabeth was not very forthcoming with her information, Lady Catherine demanded to know if she was engaged to Mr Darcy.

When she admitted she was not, Lady Catherine demanded a promise from her that she never would be. This Elizabeth was not prepared to give, so Lady Catherine departed threatening that she knew what to do about the situation.

Her disclosure to Mr Darcy of the events at Longbourne had quite the reverse affect to which she had hoped. If Elizabeth had refused to promise not to marry Mr Darcy, it could only mean that she had not rejected his affections forever.

His hopes raised he revisited Longbourne and discovered that Elizabeth's feeling had changed so drastically towards him, she was now as deeply in love with him as he was with her.

To the delight of her parents, the two sisters shared the same wedding day.

"Three daughters, all married. God has been very good to us," Mrs Bennett exclaimed.

"He has, my dear." Mr Bennett was already mourning the loss of his two eldest daughters. He knew that from this moment on, no sense would be spoken in the Bennett household, ever again.

In this book, Darcy and Elizabeth, I have carried on the story a few months after the marriage of Elizabeth and Jane, to Mr Darcy and Mr Bingley.

It progresses through the following twelve months, and discloses, what, in my opinion, may have indeed happened to the many characters in the book.

Jane Austen's character are colourful, animated and believable, and deserve to live on. She did, in fact, during the final chapter of her novel, suggest ways in which some of the characters could continue.

The characters in Pride and Prejudice touched the hearts, hopes and dreams of many of us, and indeed, if you think as I do, you will wish to discover what in my opinion befalls them.

Darcy and Elizabeth was written by me with much pleasure, and in the hope of giving enjoyment to you.

Chapter 1

It is certain that there are some things a man of good fortune cannot buy, such as love, friendship, happiness and an heir to his fortune.

At first the size and the history of the state of Pemberley had overawed Elizabeth, but after a few months of marriage, she was at last starting to look on the great house has her home. Life was extremely good, Mr Darcy was more attentive and loving than she could ever have desired. He showered her with gifts, of jewels, carriages and fashion that, in all her wildest dreams she could not have imagined. What pleased her most, was the fact that he was now far less proud, more approachable and decidedly less harsh in his thinking than he had been in the early days of their acquaintance. Their marriage, had been so far, an extremely happy one. Though the breach it had made in the extended Darcy family was yet to be resolved. Lady Catherine de Burgh, had flatly refused to accept Elizabeth into the family. Her absence from the wedding was noticed and much talked of. There had been no communication since, and although Elizabeth disliked the woman intensely, it pained her to know her happiness had caused the breakdown of relationships between Mr Darcy and his aunt. Many times she had broached the subject, only to be met with Mr Darcy's insistence that his aunt should make the first move to reconciliation. She eventually came to the conclusion that they were both of the same temperament, and indeed it would take a great deal of persuasion on her part to break down the barriers. At one time she had considered writing to Lady Catherine, but the consequences if Mr Darcy disapproved were so daunting, she shield away from the prospect. She had discussed it with her sister Jane, who was also of the same opinion. "If Mr Darcy wishes to reconcile with his aunt, Lizzie, I am sure he will do so in his own time," she had told Elizabeth. "Think back, Lizzie, to the things she said. It will take a lot of forgiveness on both sides to mend this breach. Mr Darcy has been very hurt by her remarks about you, and he is so violently in love with you I think, he will find it difficult to forgive anyone who slights you."

Jane was right, as always, and Elizabeth lent on her sister's sensible reasoning very often.

Elizabeth pushed the thoughts to the back of her mind and concentrated on more pleasant events. Her beloved father was due to arrive at Pemberley later that afternoon, for his first visit, and Elizabeth could not wait to see him. She had missed him dreadfully since her marriage, and thought of him often. There were no worries that Mr Darcy would be offended by Mr Bennett's visit, Elizabeth knew that both parties would go out of their way to try to get along. Her mother was altogether a different prospect. Unfortunately she spoke without thinking, and there had been many times in the past where this had caused Elizabeth to colour with embarrassment. Her mother, as yet, had not been invited by her daughter to visit Pemberley, but Elizabeth knew that out of obligation alone, she would have to make the offer soon, and she dreaded it. The thought of Mr Darcy being made to feel uncomfortable in his own home, by her mother's verbal ineptness, made Elizabeth cringe.

It was nearing four in the afternoon when Mr Bennett alighted from his hired carriage in the driveway at Pemberley. He was greeted with delight and love from his daughter, and with genuine respect from his son in law.

"I am extremely happy to welcome you to Pemberley," Mr Darcy said as he bowed to his father in law. "I wish you to feel that this is your home for as long as your visit extends."

"You are extremely kind, sir," replied Mr Bennett. "I have to congratulate you on your most happily situated accommodation. It is, sir, I may say, most magnificent and imposing."

"I thank you, sir," Mr Darcy bowed once more then led the party inside the house.

After refreshments had been served, Mr Darcy retired to his study leaving Elizabeth to talk to her father in private.

"Is your chosen partner everything you wished for Lizzie?" Mr Bennett inquired.

"More than I dared hope for father. Truly I am the happiest woman alive. I have to remind myself sometimes that I am not dreaming."

"Then I am happy for you my child. It is a great responsibility that you have taken on. I dare say this house needs a good deal more attention than Longbourne."

Elizabeth laughed. "It does indeed father, but Mrs Reynolds the housekeeper is very kind."

"I can see you are happy Lizzie," Mr Bennett frowned. "and a great deal luckier than your poor sister Lydia. I do believe things are not all they should be in that quarter."

"O no father. What is the matter. Is Mr Wickham not proving to be a good husband?" Elizabeth spoke with concern. "Surely after so short a marriage, there cannot be anything amiss?"

"I fear there is child. Since the birth of their daughter in March, Mr Wickham spends a great deal of his time in London or Bath. This I fear does not please his wife."

"Surely that is acceptable in marriage, father. Lydia knew that he liked to socialize before the marriage took place."

"Maybe so my dear, but knowing is one thing, living with it quite another, as I have found to my cost."

"What is to be done? Is there anything to be done to help the situation?"

"I fear not my child. This is something Lydia is going to have to sort out for herself."

"Poor Lydia," sighed Elizabeth. "She is so headstrong."

"She is indeed, and nothing will change the matter. She is still one of the silliest girls in England."

Their conversation lasted until Mr Darcy joined them for dinner.

"Your wife is in good health?" Mr Darcy asked. "and your daughter?"

"I am afraid they are, Mr Darcy. One talks all day and the

other buries herself in the library. Life has little to offer either of them that they haven't enjoyed already."

"One finds happiness in many quarters, father."

"They do Lizzie, and I shall find mine in the peace and quiet of my study."

Elizabeth smiled lovingly at her father, he bore his misfortune with honour and silence. Mrs Bennett could be very wearing at times, and she often wondered how her father bore it with so much forbearance.

"You must feel happy to shoot, fish or walk anywhere you will at Pemberley during your stay, sir." Mr Darcy offered. "Elizabeth or myself will assist you with any questions you may have. Our home is yours to use as you choose. We are both delighted that you could spend some time with us. It has indeed given Elizabeth much joy."

"I am deeply honoured, Mr Darcy, and delighted to find my favourite daughter happy, content and radiant. I fear this is more down to her life with you than my arrival, sir."

"Our life here is everything I wished it to be," Mr Darcy smiled across the table at his wife. "If you would permit me, sir, I would very much like to show you around the estate tomorrow."

"Will it be completed in one day, sir?" Mr Bennett asked with a twinkle in his eye. "By what I have seen so far it is extensive indeed."

Mr Darcy recognising his father in law's humour smiled good naturedly. "I think we may cover the majority of it, sir."

"Then I shall look forward to it."

The following days were taken up with much conversation, shooting and taking in the delights of Pemberley.

"I will go to visit Jane tomorrow for a few days," Mr Bennett announced over dinner on the fourth evening of his visit.

"But father, you have only just arrived. Is your visit to be this short?" exclaimed Elizabeth in disappointment.

"Are you unhappy with Pemberley?" Mr Darcy asked.

"Not at all. I have been made very comfortable here, but Mrs Bennett does not enjoy her own company for too long. If I do not return within the next week, I fear she may come looking for me."

Elizabeth laughed, but the thought of her mother arriving unannounced filled her with dread.

"Why do you not accompany your father to Southview, Elizabeth? I am sure you would like to see Jane." Mr Darcy suggested.

"I would, very much, but I have things to attend to here, and Jane has only moved into her new home a few weeks. It would be presumptuous of me to burden her with extra worries at this time. The place will be in uproar and I would feel uncomfortable."

"You may be of great assistance to her, Elizabeth," Mr Darcy argued. "As she is with child, she may well tire easily, and as I have to go into town on business for a few days, you may find the lack of company distressing."

"You are probably right, my love. I will do as you suggest and accompany father to Southview."

It was settled. Darcy smiled at his wife and Mr Bennett experienced a glow of pride, that his second daughter was at last in the company of a man she could respect.

Jane was extremely pleased to see her father, but her joy was twofold when she saw he was accompanied by her beloved sister.

"Lizzie, father, I am so pleased you could find time to visit," she said as she greeted them. "I have so much to show you. The house and grounds are so much larger than Netherfield. I am convinced I shall get lost, never to be found again. Come inside, you must be tired after your journey."

"It's only thirty miles, Jane, what is thirty miles of good road," Elizabeth laughed, remembering a previous conversation she had enjoyed with Mr Darcy.

"How are you feeling, Jane?" Elizabeth asked once they were settled. "You look very well. Being with child suits you

I think."

"O Lizzie, I am so happy, and Mr Bingley is beside himself. Truly Lizzie I am the happiest woman alive."

Mr Bennett laughed. "That is the second time I have heard that remark in this last week. My dears you will have to sort out between you who is the happiest. I would not like to see it end in conflict."

"Both daughters laughed. "We are both happy in our separate ways father," smiled Elizabeth.

Once Mr Bennett had stated his intention of walking the grounds, and the two girls were alone, Elizabeth's face became suddenly serious.

"I am beginning to think that I will never give Mr Darcy a son and heir to secure the future of Pemberley, Jane. It is above six months now, and there is no sign of me producing a son."

"You worry too much Lizzie. It will not help, and besides, what is six months. It is nothing for couples to go several years without a child."

"Yes, but is that by design," sighed Elizabeth. "I am concerned, Jane. It keeps me awake some nights. What if I can't give Darcy a son? He may very well tire of me and look elsewhere for his comfort."

Jane smiled at her sister. "O Lizzie, he isn't likely to do that as you are well aware. Mr Darcy is so very much in love with you I think. You know he is Lizzie. Be sensible. All this distress will only delay what you crave the most. Try to relax Lizzie, all it can do is help. You are happy are you not?"

"More than I could ever dream possible. Mr Darcy is so loving and attentive, it is difficult to believe it will always be like this."

"Enjoy it while you can Lizzie. You will only spoil things by worrying so much. You will have a son. I am sure of it."

"O Jane, I wish I was more like you." she looked across at the face of her sister with deep affection. "You have heard that my good friend Charlotte Collins is to give birth in August."

"Yes, I did hear. There you are, Lizzie, she has been married a year above you, and is only now extending her family. Truly Lizzie you worry too much."

"I cannot still believe that Charlotte could marry such a man, Jane. Mr Collins is so very different from her, and I am convinced in my own mind that she could have done much better for herself."

"Maybe she could, Lizzie, but we are all different. I believe Charlotte wished only a comfortable home. Mr Collins is after all unlikely to cause her discomfort. He has much regard for her I believe."

"You are probably right, Jane, but to settle for material comforts is intolerable."

"For you and I, Lizzie, but we are not all the same. I am sure she is content with her situation."

Elizabeth changed the subject. She frowned deeply. "What do you think of father's news about Lydia, Jane?"

"I don't know what to think. It is distressing indeed. Poor Lydia, she married in haste without thinking of the future. Do you think Wickham is very bad, Lizzie?"

"I am afraid I do. Nothing he does will ever surprise me again."

"I know father says that Wickham spends a great deal of his time away from home, but he does always return to Lydia. There must be some affection for him to do that, surely, and he did marry her for love, I am sure of it."

"Are you, Jane? I fear I am not. I think he married her for the money Mr Darcy offered him, and very little else."

"No, I am sure you are wrong, Lizzie," Jane reflected. "He could have married someone else if it was only money that enticed him. No. I truly believe he married her for love. Maybe not as you and I are lucky enough to know love, but I think he had deep affection for her."

"He wasn't thinking of her welfare when he persuaded her to run away with him," Elizabeth persisted. "He could have ruined our whole family, and he would not have cared."

"That is just it, Lizzie, he didn't have to marry her, he could have refused."

"If his intentions were honourable, Jane, he would have gone to father in the proper fashion to ask his consent, not take her to London. Still it is all in the past. We will just have to watch over her, and help where we can. I would invite her to Pemberley, but I know Mr Darcy is not at all keen on the prospect, and he will never allow Wickham under his roof, I am sure of that."

Jane sighed. "I feel so sorry for her, Lizzie. Do you think if I invited her here it would help. Mr Bingley would have no objection.

"Let us see how things go, Jane. I wouldn't like Lydia to think we are being presumptuous about her marriage, She may not think that there is anything amiss, and we would only put her in an uncomfortable position if we question her."

"She writes to me to assist her with money, so all cannot be well," Jane confided. "O, Lizzie I do worry about her, she is still so very young."

"She writes to me also, but they are both of a frivolous nature I fear they will always outspend their income, and as father says, she has to learn to manage her own life," replied Elizabeth. "We are not responsible for her, Jane, we can only help so much," After a few minutes of silence Elizabeth continued. "Do you see much of Caroline and Mrs Hurst?"

"They visited a few times at Netherfield, but so far she has not sought an invitation here. Although I am sure it will not be long until she does. I confess, Lizzie, I cannot help but still think very ill of her. She was the instrument of much distress to Mr Bingley and myself."

"You sound bitter, Jane. This is indeed not your disposition." Elizabeth said.

"O, Lizzie I do not seem able to forgive her for what she did. Imagine if Mr Darcy had not owned up that he concealed my being in town from Mr Bingley. I may still be broken hearted and living at Longbourne. I have to accept her as my sister for Bingley's sake, but I must confess I have great difficulty in being even polite to her. My thoughts of her are very ill indeed."

Before Elizabeth could answer, Mr Bingley entered the room.

"Mrs Darcy," he exclaimed. "I am delighted to see you again. You look very well. Are you in good health?"

"I am, sir, thank you," Elizabeth replied.

"I see that you are. And Mr Darcy, is he in good health?"

"Very well, sir."

"How well do you like living at Pemberley. Have you found your way around all the rooms yet?"

Elizabeth giggled. "Just when I think I may have done, I find another wing to investigate. Truly it is the most amazing house, but Mrs Reynolds is much help. She has much patience."

"How long are we to have the pleasure of your company at Southview?"

"A few days, sir. My father insists he has to return to Longbourne before the end of the week. He fears my mother will embark on a rescue otherwise."

"Well I am very pleased to see you. We don't see enough of you. Now we are settled much closer you and Darcy must make us a visit as soon as it can be arranged. It seems a long time since we sat down to dinner together."

"It is above four months, since you came to Pemberley." replied Elizabeth. She loved her sister's husband dearly, he was so open and friendly, it was infectious.

"How ever long it is, it is too long. Tell me, is your father resting?"

"No, sir, he insisted on walking the grounds. He enjoys the solitude I believe."

"You are also a great walker as I remember." Bingley said.

"I do enjoy the woods and groves very much. I only wish I had enough time to get to know the grounds at Southview."

"I hope ... I am sure, there will be many more occasions

when you can stay longer and investigate every inch."

"I am sure you are right Mr Bingley. Pray tell me, how are your sisters?"

"In perfect health I believe," he smiled. "They are very much hoping to visit shortly."

The remainder of the stay was passed with much pleasure, so when Elizabeth returned to Pemberley she felt refreshed. Jane always had a good affect on her, and she missed their late-night conversations very much.

As the carriage turned in through the gates, Elizabeth's heart gave a little flutter. She couldn't wait to see Darcy again, and hoped with all her heart that he had returned from London.

He wasn't waiting on the steps, so she inquired from Mrs Reynolds the housekeeper the whereabouts of her husband.

"He is out riding ma'am." Mrs Reynolds replied.

"Will he be long do you think."

"His intentions ma'am were to return before your carriage arrived from Southview."

"Then I'll just go and freshen up before his return." Elizabeth said. Mrs Reynolds had been a good friend to Elizabeth since her marriage. The management of a house the size of Pemberley was daunting indeed, and without her help Elizabeth doubted very much if she would have managed at all. She had heard of cases in the past when a long standing housekeeper had made things very difficult indeed for its new mistress. Mrs Reynolds had been employed by the Darcy family above twenty years, and in sole charge since the death of old Mr Darcy six years before. She had every reason to resent Elizabeth's presence, but there had been no sign. Quite the opposite in fact, she had been nothing but helpful, and given Elizabeth every kind of support.

The hour for dinner was approaching and there was still no sign of Mr Darcy. The heavens had broken with a sudden summer thunderstorm that hadn't been experienced for some time, and Elizabeth was concerned. It was not like Mr Darcy to stay out when his intention had been stated that he would be at Pemberley in time for Elizabeth's expected return from Southview. If he had come back to the house and gone straight to his study, she was sure she would have been informed of it.

She rang the bell for the footman.

"Has Mr Darcy returned from his riding yet?" she asked.

"No ma'am."

"Thank you Dawson. Would you be so good as to ask Mrs Reynolds to come here."

He bowed low and left the room.

"Mrs Reynolds," Elizabeth said as her housekeeper entered the room. "This is most unlike Mr Darcy to be so late. It is not his behaviour at all. Have you any idea where he might be?"

"No ma'am," the housekeeper replied. "My only thought is that he may have taken shelter from the storm."

"But the rain has stopped above an hour now. It concerns me very much Mrs Reynolds."

"I am sure it does ma'am. To be so late is not like the master at all."

"Have you any idea in which direction he may have travelled?"

"No ma'am, he could be anywhere on the estate. Do you wish me to send someone to find him?"

"Good gracious no," Elizabeth exclaimed. "Mr Darcy would not be pleased at my interference. Thank you Mrs Reynolds, would you be so good as to tell cook that we will wait dinner until my husbands return."

"Very good ma'am."

Before she could leave the room there was a commotion in the hall. Mrs Reynolds went to see what all the noise was about.

"It's Mr Darcy ma'am," the footman informed the housekeeper. "He has taken a fall from his horse, and lies in the woods. Mr Daniels the gamekeeper found him, we are taking a dray to recover him."

"Is he very much injured?" Mrs Reynolds asked in alarm.

"I fear so, ma'am. Mr Daniels says his eyes are shut, and

there is blood coming from his head."

"God forbid," Mrs Reynolds threw her hands up to her face. "Make haste and help him. I will go and inform the mistress."

On hearing her husband had been injured Elizabeth became distressed. "I must go to him. Where did they find him?"

"There is nothing you can do, Mrs Darcy." Mrs Reynolds tried to console her. "The grounds men are at this moment aiding his return. They have taken a dray to transport the master home."

"Send for the doctor Mrs Reynolds, we must have him here for when Mr Darcy returns. O dear God, I pray he is not badly injured."

Although it was less than half an hour before the servants brought Mr Darcy back, it seemed an eternity to Elizabeth. She remained the whole time on the steps to Pemberley, scanning the early evening darkness for the first sighting of the dray. As soon as she saw it in the distance she ran towards it.

She was beside herself. Her beloved Darcy was lying very still and motionless on the flat bed of the dray. His eyes were closed, and there was blood seeping from a wound to the right cheek. The men had covered him with blankets and an icy chill ran down Elizabeth's spine.

"Get him inside at once," she cried. "Mrs Reynolds, is Dr Williams here yet?"

"No, ma'am."

"Send him straight to Mr Darcy's apartments when he arrives." she ordered.

Mr Darcy was duly installed in Elizabeth's own bed, and once the doctor had seen him, it was confirmed that Mr Darcy was indeed suffering from severe concussion, and his wrist was broken. The wound to his cheek, although deep, would heal quickly. Providing it was kept free of infection.

"I have made him as comfortable as I can Mrs Darcy, but I fear it is now a case of waiting. He should start to show signs of recovery very soon now. Do you wish me to stay?"

Silent tears were running down Elizabeth's cheeks as she looked down at her husband, lying so helpless in her bed. His face drained of all colour.

"I need you within calling distance at all times Dr Williams, I thank you," she said very quietly.

Once the doctor had left the room Elizabeth sank to her knees beside the bed, and taking Mr Darcy's uninjured hand in hers she let the tears flow, and prayed most fervently that he would recover quickly, and be returned to her.

Elizabeth continued to sit by her husband's side throughout the night, watching the face she loved so dearly for signs of recovery. It was many hours before the first sign came, and then it was only a very faint flutter of the eyelashes. Elizabeth's heart skipped a beat, she watched to see if it would be repeated. When it was she sent for Dr Williams immediately.

"It is a good sign Mrs Darcy. I can see now that he is sleeping and not unconscious," he smiled encouragingly at the distraught woman standing wringing her hands. "Trust me ma'am, everything will be well I assure you. Keep him warm and resting, and you may rest with ease that his recovery will be swift."

Elizabeth smiled weakly. "I thank you for your trouble Dr Williams, and I pray that you are right in your assessment."

"Trust me my dear, I have been a doctor a long time, and Mr Darcy is of a strong constitution." he bowed and left the room.

Sinking down into a chair next to the bed Elizabeth let her eyes close, and was only awoken by the movement and sound of a low moan coming from the patient. She was instantly awake and stood up abruptly, knocking the chair over as she did so. She brought the candle closer to Mr Darcy's face. He was sweating profusely, and turning his head from side to side, his eyes still closed.

Panicking, Elizabeth ran out into the corridor, calling for Mrs Reynolds as she went. She was surprised, but pleased to find her devoted housekeeper asleep on one of the settees in the gallery outside the door.

She immediately jumped up on the sound of Elizabeth's call.

"What is it, ma'am? Has my master taken a turn for the worse?"

"I fear he has, Mrs Reynolds." exclaimed Elizabeth. "Send for Dr Williams at once." The distress in her voice was profound.

"He has caught a fever, Mrs Darcy, we must take great care of him. Bring some water so that we may bathe his forehead ." Dr Williams ordered as he bent over the bed. "I fear that the time he spent in the thunderstorm is now taking its toll."

For three days and nights together Mr Darcy remained in a dangerous state of fever. Elizabeth did not leave his bedside. His every need was attended to by her with prodigious care.

"Mrs Darcy, you cannot go on like this," Dr Williams insisted. "If you carry on in this vein, I am sure I will have two patients to watch over and not one."

"I cannot leave him, sir, he is everything to me, and I must make sure that very good care is bestowed upon him."

"And will be, I assure you," Dr Williams was adamant. "You must rest Mrs Darcy. Your actions are doing no good to anyone. Mr Darcy would be most displeased if he thought you were being treated in this manner."

"I am sure you are right Dr Williams, but I cannot forsake his bedside," Elizabeth said. "I would not rest, it is better that I am here. The fever may break at any time, and I wish to be with him when it does."

"Then permit the servants to have a bed made up for you in here. You must consider your own health."

In the end Elizabeth condescended to do as Dr Williams suggested, she would not leave Mr Darcy's side.

It was the following afternoon when the fever broke, and for the first time in four days Mr Darcy opened his eyes. The relief was too much for Elizabeth, she broke down in floods of tears and collapsed to the floor.

As the week progressed, to everyone's relief Mr Darcy's health continued to improve. He was very weak from the lack of nourishment, but apart from the bandage on his wrist, and the scarring to his cheek there were no outward signs of his ordeal.

Chapter 2

"You are truly a great nurse, Elizabeth," Mr Darcy exclaimed on his first evening downstairs. "I dare not think how I would have managed without you these last days." He paused for a moment and then continued. "After all the effort you have afforded to secure my welfare, I feel very humble knowing I have another request to make of you."

"If it is in my power to grant it," replied Elizabeth with a smile. "I shall be more than happy to do so."

"I have been corresponding with my sister Georgiana over these last few months, and it has become apparent to me, that there is nothing she would like better than to make Pemberley her home. I have taken it upon myself to promise her that I would seek your agreement."

"You have no need, sir, this will always be her home, for as long as she wishes it. Indeed it is my wish also."

"My dearest, sweetest Elizabeth, it often escapes me how I managed for so long without you in my life." The expression in his eyes as he gazed across at his wife, was one full of love.

Elizabeth ran to him and knelt down by his chair. "You have made me the happiest woman alive. I am truly content."

"Then if I have your blessing I shall relay the good news to her at once. We may expect her arrival shortly afterwards. She is indeed very eager to join us."

"Then I shall instruct Mrs Reynolds to prepare her apartments first thing tomorrow."

Mr Darcy was right. Georgiana was not long in accepting the offered invitation.

Elizabeth looked forward to her homecoming with much pleasure. She knew that the one thing dearest to Mr Darcy's heart was that his two most favourite women should become as close as real sisters. In this Elizabeth was determined to do everything in her power to achieve. She already loved Georgiana, and she was convinced that this was one of the ways in which she could repay Mr Darcy for his generous nature. Besides it would be nice to have another women in the house.

As the carriage rolled up the drive Mr Darcy and Elizabeth stood on the steps and awaited its arrival.

"Georgiana, I am delighted to see you again," Elizabeth exclaimed as she greeted her sister in law. "I have been looking forward to this day for so long. My dearest wish was that you would want to return to Pemberley, but I had not the right to suggest it."

Mr Darcy, who was standing a few feet behind the two women, felt such a surge of love and pride when he heard these words, he wanted to gather Elizabeth up in his arms and hold her forever. Instead he greeted his sister with pleasure, then taking his wife's arm he escorted them inside.

"Elizabeth, I am so happy to be here." Georgiana said as they walked. "I have longed to return, but I feared you would be offended by my presence. Well, that is," she faltered a little. "So soon after your marriage, I mean, it is not…I didn't think…"

Elizabeth took her arm and laughed. "Georgiana, nothing could make me happier than to have you here with us. Your company will be most beneficial. Especially when Mr Darcy is away from home. This is a very large house you know, and I am not acquainted with it all as you will discover."

"You are so good to me, Elizabeth, I am sure I will be happy here."

"I shall make sure you are. Now no more concern, this is our home."

Georgiana had only been at Pemberley but two weeks, when she tapped on the door of Elizabeth's bedchamber before breakfast.

"What is the matter, Georgiana, you look very out of spirits this morning?" Elizabeth asked with concern.

"I am finding it very difficult to understand the way you speak with my brother. I have not heard him spoken to in such a manner before. I am indeed greatly puzzled by it."

"My dear Georgiana," smiled Elizabeth, as she took both of the girls hands in hers. "There are many ways, and indeed many things a wife may say to her husband that would not be tolerated from anyone else. Including a very beloved sister."

"Then you are not quarrelling?" the young girl seemed to relax a little.

"You are happy with my brother?"

"Happier than I deserve. You were right when you told me last year in Lampton, that you could never find a kinder or better brother. I now know how you felt. Truly Georgiana he is the best man I have ever met. You must not mind my teasing Mr Darcy, it is done purely out of love. Indeed it is."

A broad smile spread over Georgiana's face. "Please forgive me Elizabeth. I think I have a lot to learn about two people being married."

"It is unfortunate that you lost your dear mother at an early age. If she had continued to live you would, I am sure, have heard similar conversations between your own dear parents."

"I trust you, Elizabeth, and I would hate for my brother to be offended in any way."

"Then we are both of the same mind. I also would not like to experience a time when I intentionally caused Mr Darcy grief. Now come, we will take a stroll in the garden before breakfast."

Talking and laughing together they descended the stairs, but before they could gain the liberty of the garden, Mr Darcy appeared in the hall. His face was dark and serious.

"May I speak with you, Elizabeth," he asked.

"Is there something amiss, sir? Have I in any way offended you?" Elizabeth was very much upset. She had not seen this serious side of Mr Darcy for many months now. "Tell me, sir at once so that it may be rectified.

"My dearest Elizabeth, how could you possibly do anything to offend me," he smiled down at her, and taking her arm escorted her through the door to the garden. "No my dear, I am, unfortunately the carrier of some grievous news that will sadden you greatly."

"Are you unwell, sir, have your injuries been the cause of more discomfort? Pray tell me at once."

Darcy gently took her arm and led her to a seat beneath an arbour. He felt proud that her first thoughts were for his welfare. "No, I am well, there is nothing the matter with me. I fear my news is connected with your own family."

"Jane! It is, Jane! The baby, is something wrong with the baby?" Elizabeth was most agitated.

"I have received a letter from your father…"

"He is unwell." she stood up abruptly. "I must go to him."

"Please calm yourself Elizabeth," Mr Darcy urged. "It is not your father, or Jane. Now let me speak."

Elizabeth sat back down on the seat.

"It is your mother Elizabeth that has been the victim of ill health. Your father writes that after receiving some disturbing news your mother suffered a seizure and the doctors are most concerned."

"Then I must go to her. She will need me." Elizabeth was worried for her mother, but much relieved the news had not been of her father. Her feelings caused her much guilt, but her father was so very dear to her. "What news did she receive that would bring on such a serious discomfort., sir?"

Darcy gently took her hand. "Please try not to distress yourself any further Elizabeth, but the letter concerned your sister Lydia."

"Lydia, what has she done now?" Elizabeth was most surprised.

"She writes and informs your parents that Mr Wickham, (he almost spat the words out) has abandoned his wife and child, and left for Paris. His companion is believed to be a widow of much fortune, and the news so shocked your mother that it brought about the seizure. I am afraid Elizabeth your father fears the worst."

"Gone to Paris," Elizabeth was full of disbelief. "How can he do that. He has a wife and child? Who is the woman?

Does my father say?"

"No he does not mention a name, but you can be quite sure that Mr Wickham is capable of anything. In his search for the easy life, I fear he will stop at nothing."

"How can such a man continue to live in society?" asked Elizabeth in exasperation. "Poor Lydia, she does not deserve such treatment."

"She does not, but I think your mother is, at this moment more in need of your concern."

"O yes," Elizabeth stood up again. "I must go to her." She turned to her husband. "Jane, has Jane been informed? She must not be distressed at this time. Her confinement is imminent."

"I am sure Mr Bingley will take great care of her," Mr Darcy replied.

"I am sure he will. O I must go to my mother."

"Do you wish me to accompany you Elizabeth? I would be more than happy to travel to Longbourne with you."

"You are not fully recovered from your fall, sir, and although it would give me much pleasure to have your company, I would not like to be the instrument of any reoccurrence in your ill health," exclaimed Elizabeth.

Darcy laughed at her anxiety. "Believe me Elizabeth, I am quite well. The journey will be most beneficial to me. I am sure your company is all I need to recover quickly."

She took his arm and held it tightly as they walked back towards the house.

"Do you think mama is in very great danger, sir?"

"I have no wish to concern you my sweetest Elizabeth, but I fear she may be. Your father's letter was directed to me, which make me think he is very concerned indeed. He trusted me to relate the news to you in a sensible way. A way that would cause least harm and distress."

"Then we must leave at once, she will need me," Elizabeth quickened her stride.

"Pray take control of your feelings my love. If you were to become ill with the distress of your news, then you would be of no assistance to your mother." Darcy smiled down at her. "Besides I am sure your sister, Jane, will also need your support."

"You are so very kind to me, sir."

Within an hour Mr Darcy and Elizabeth were on their way to Longbourne. The journey appeared to take much longer than Elizabeth remembered. She prayed that her mother would make a full recovery, and she was more than grateful for the support, and company of her dear husband.

By the time they reached her parent's house Jane was already there. She looked pale and concerned.

"Is mama, very ill, Jane?" she asked as she greeted her sister.

"O Lizzie, I am glad you have come. Mama lies so still, and her colour is all gone." Jane held her sister close for a few seconds.

"Has the doctor been summoned. What did he say? Where is father?

"The doctor has gone away just now. He states that there is nothing to be done. O Lizzie, I am so worried, what if she does not recover?"

"Please do not distress yourself, Jane. It will not be of help to you at this time. Indeed you should not have travelled so far."

"I am well Lizzie, but father sits by mama's bed day and night. He will not leave her, and he speaks very little. He is besides himself with concern, I fear he may become ill too."

While the girls had been talking, Mr Bingley had emerged from the house and was deep in conversation with Mr Darcy. They had strolled a little to one side and were out of earshot.

Elizabeth was shocked when she saw the state of her mother. It was difficult to distinguish the colour of her mother's face from the bed linen. Her father did not stir on her entrance, he sat close to the bed, his face was devoid of expression. A broken man.

"Father, Lizzie has come," Jane told her father quietly. "Please come and rest. Let Lizzie and I watch over mother."

Mr Bennett turned to look at his favourite daughter. "She was always worrying about what would become of her when I departed this earth Lizzie. Now I fear the tables have been turned."

"Is it so very bad father?" Elizabeth went to her father's side. "What are the doctor's predictions? Is there hope for recovery?"

"I fear there is very little my dear. Mrs Bennett has not moved once since the attack came upon her. I am very concerned indeed," He spoke very quietly and there was a resigned note in his voice. "In the five and twenty years I have known Mrs Bennett, she has never been this quiet. I confess I am already pining for her poor nerves."

Elizabeth could not help but smile. Her mother's nerves had been part of their lives ever since she could remember.

Mrs Hill then entered the bedchamber with a message from Mr Darcy.

"I beg your pardon, sir, but Mr Darcy and Mr Bingley are in the drawing room, and they are asking your permission to send for a doctor from London."

"Thank you Hill. I will go down and speak to them directly," Mr Bennett replied.

Mr Bennett held Elizabeth's hand and Jane's for a few seconds, then he passed silently out of the room.

"Mr Darcy, Mr Bingley. It is very good of you to come."

"Mr Bennett we are shocked and saddened by the news in your letter," Mr Darcy said. "I would indeed deem it an honour if you would permit me to send for my own physician from town. We must, as you will agree, do everything in our power to bring your wife's health back as it should be."

Mr Bennett walked across the room and sank down into one of the fireside chairs. His face was grey and strained, his manner resigned.

"Your intentions are honourable, sir, and I thank you, but I fear there is nothing to be gained. Our own doctor is of the opinion that Mrs Bennett's attack will prove fatal. It is just a matter of time."

"Sir," Mr Bingley stepped forward. "Far be it from us to go against your wishes at this time, but I am sure by obtaining a second opinion we would all feel as though we were helping."

"You are both good men, I am prodigiously proud of you," Mr Bennett said. "If it will lay your concern then you have my consent to do everything in your power to attain the services of a doctor who will restore Mrs Bennett to health."

"I thank you, sir. I shall leave immediately for town," Mr Darcy bowed and left the room.

Mr Bingley followed his friend out into the hallway.

"Do you wish me to travel with you Darcy? I would be more than happy to."

"I think you would do better to remain with the ladies," answered Mr Darcy. They will need much support I fear."

Elizabeth heard the carriage depart and guessed that Mr Darcy had gone for further medical assistance. She experienced a surge of pride, that after all the insults her mother had directed at her husband, he was still prepared to help in any way he could.

"Has word been sent to Kitty and Lydia, Jane?" Elizabeth asked her sister.

"I am sure father would have written to us all on the same day," replied Jane. Kitty went to Lydia as soon as she heard of Mr Wickham's actions, so she would not have been here when poor mama had her attack, Nothing is known of Lydia's condition, no-one had heard anything from her. I am sure they will come as soon as they are able. They do have a greater distance to travel than we did."

"She is so very selfish, Jane. I doubt very much that she is even thinking of poor mama at this time," Elizabeth spoke with irritation.

"Lizzie that is unkind. Lydia has not had an easy time with Mr Wickham I think."

"She insisted on marrying him, Jane, when all her relations

were of the adverse opinion. Mr Darcy told me himself that he had spent over an hour in her company trying to dissuade her on the matter. And just think, Jane, she could have cost both of us our marriages and happiness. Not to mention Mary, and Kitty's future."

"She was in love Lizzie. Surely you can understand that," Jane smiled at her sister. "Common sense does not play a great part when you are in love, and she was only sixteen you know."

"Dear Jane, I wish I could think so well of people as you do. You always see the best side of their character."

"Poor mama. Do you think she is in great danger Lizzie?"

"Mr Darcy seems to think that she is. Poor father, it is very hard on his feelings. Do you think I ought to go down to him?"

"He is with Mr Bingley Lizzie," Jane replied. "Maybe he needs a man at this time. I would give them a little more time. He needs to rest, he has been with mama day and night since she took ill. He will come back soon I am sure."

Mr Bennett had fallen asleep in his chair from pure exhaustion and was not awakened until two carriages pulled up in the driveway. One bringing the doctor and Mr Darcy, the other Lydia and Kitty.

"I really don't need this," Lydia cried as she entered the hallway. "My dear Wickham has been taken from me by some woman who has designs on him. What am I to do Lizzie? He had no wish to go Lizzie, he was taken without his consent."

"Lydia!" exclaimed Elizabeth in horror at her sisters selfish nature. "Mama is seriously ill and may never recover. Do you always have to put your own feelings uppermost?"

"It is all right for you Lizzie, Mr Darcy never leaves your side, and you do not have children to worry about," Lydia protested. "You never understand Lizzie. Only Kitty knows what I am suffering."

While this conversation was occurring Mr Darcy and the doctor had gone into the study where Mr Bennett had just woken up.

"I am indeed grateful that you could attend Mrs Bennett at this time," Mr Bennett said. "Our own doctor, does not, I fear, have any hope for her continued recovery."

"Shall we go to see the patient, sir," the doctor suggested. "There are many advances in medicine that have not, unfortunately reached the outskirts of town. I will see if I have anything that will benefit your wife."

As they left the room Lydia was still protesting of her husband's misfortune.

"I think you had better calm your temper Lydia. Father is much distressed at this time, he has no wish to hear your problems as well." Elizabeth was starting to get angry with her younger sister. "You can go and see mama directly the doctor has finished his examination of her."

"I have to see to my child first. It has been a long journey and she needs to rest." Lydia flounced off in the direction of her old bedroom.

"I cannot believe that she could be so selfish at this time, Jane. Does she not think of anyone except herself?"

"She is young Lizzie, and very upset," Jane tried to sooth her sister's temper. "Wickham has hurt her very badly. Imagine how we would feel in her position."

"But mama could be dying and all she thinks of is herself. It is not to be tolerated, Jane."

"Give her time Lizzie. Her whole world has fallen around her," Jane persisted. She paused for a few seconds as something occurred to her. "O Lizzie, Mary. Where is Mary? Have you seen her since your arrival?"

"She is resting," Mr Bennett spoke behind them. "She's a good girl, and has been with her mother most of the night. I have sent her to rest. As for Lydia Lizzie, do not let it worry you. She has many concerns of her own at the moment."

"Father...I didn't mean...It is just that she acts so selfishly at times." Elizabeth coloured up with shame that her father had overheard her comments.

"I know my dear," Mr Bennett replied patting her arm. "Is

the doctor still with Mrs Bennett?"

"Yes father."

He slowly climbed the stairs, and then the two girls heard the bedroom door open then close.

Mr Bingley came out into the hallway followed by Mr Darcy.

Elizabeth ran to her husband and held his arm. "Is there anything your doctor will be able to do for mama, sir?" she asked.

"Do not distress yourself Elizabeth. Everything that can be done for your mother, will be. I assure you."

"With your two younger sisters in the house, Jane," stated Mr Bingley. "I suggested to Darcy that the four of us could overnight at Netherfield."

"I cannot leave mama, sir," Jane exclaimed. "She may need us, and father is so very tired. We are going to have to insist on his resting. No I shall remain here so that I may be of help when it is needed."

"Then I shall stay also," confirmed Mr Bingley.

"There is no need to inconvenience yourself, sir," Elizabeth joined the conversation. "Jane and I will be perfectly happy to keep mama company. No, you have done our family a great service this evening, it is only right that you should retire in comfort. We may be in greater need of your support shortly. Go to Netherfield if you wish and return in the morning refreshed. I am sure it would be far more beneficial to all parties."

"Then I insist you send word to us any time of the night if you wish us back again," urged Bingley. "I have no wish to leave your side at this time, Jane."

"There is nothing to be done, sir," Jane smiled at her husband. "Lizzie and I will be quite content to sit with our dear mother. Father may have a greater need for your services tomorrow, and it would be of more use if you are rested."

It was settled that after the doctor had attended Mrs Bennett, the two men would travel the three miles to

Netherfield, and return the following day.

Before the doctor had finished his examination of Mrs Bennett, Mary arose from her sleep and joined the rest of the party in the drawing room.

"Mary you must have been through so much," Jane greeted her sister.

"At this time my dear sisters," she spoke as she entered the room. "We must draw on each other's strengths, and turn our feelings into the heart of our family. Outside influences, I believe, should be cast aside, and all our strength must be pooled to support our dear father."

"Mary you must have suffered much pain I think," Jane stood up and crossed the room to her sister. "Being all alone when illness struck our dear mother must have caused you much distress."

"In your absence," continued Mary in a cool detached tone. "I have been my mother's companion. I sit by her bed and read, being ever aware of any change in her condition. I have, I believe, been of much support to our father."

"I am sure you have Mary," Elizabeth said. "Tell us what happened when the seizure struck mama. Did she suffer much pain?"

"No, I do not believe she did," Mary sat impassive on a high-backed chair. "She read the letter that Lydia had been selfish enough to send. It stated that her husband had left her for sexual excitement with an older person, and that she wished our mother to go to her at once. When papa was informed of this news he forbade Mrs Bennett to travel to her aid. He informed our dear mother, that Lydia had to start to face up to her own actions. He did however allow Kitty to travel north to be with her sister. Our aunt, Mrs Phillips was sent for, and spent many hours in mama's company. After dinner I took mama her tea, and she went on at length about the condition Lydia had now found herself in, and how vexed she was that our father would not allow her to go to her. "If anything should happen to my dear Lydia I shall never forgive him Mary, and

Wickham! Well I always knew he was no good. To entice my dear girl into marriage, just to have position in society, it is not to be born. O Mary, what are we to do, your father has a will of iron. He will see her ruined, you mark my words." These were the last words mama spoke. Her eyes closed, her head and shoulders dropped to one side, and she never moved again. Our father has been beside himself with concern. Lydia has caused our family much distress, and I, myself, hold her fully responsible for our mother's condition."

"You may be right in your thinking Mary," Jane said softly, "but what you are suggesting is too high a price for Lydia to bear. She has enough problems in her own life without having to accept the ones you are imposing on her."

"We must all be brave enough to face the consequences of our own actions, Jane," Mary insisted, " and therefore Lydia must be told of her folly."

"Mary, I forbid it!" exclaimed Elizabeth. "How can it possibly help the situation at all. You may keep your own thoughts on this matter, but I beg you not to voice them to Lydia. Surely Mary's father has enough to occupy his mind."

Before Mary could answer, Mr Bennett and the doctor entered the room.

Elizabeth ran across and took his arm

"What news, father? What did the doctor say? How is mama? Tell us at once."

He patted Elizabeth's hand and gently extracted it from his arm. Silently he made his way to his own armchair and collapsed very heavily into it.

"The news is much the same child. Mrs Bennett is in the hands of God. Her condition is such that she may remain with us for many months, or she may depart this life at any time."

"O father, is there nothing to be done?" Jane asked with tears in her eyes.

"No my dear, Jane. It is I fear a matter of waiting. The doctor has been good enough to administer a potion that he is convinced will aid Mrs Bennett's recovery, but only time will tell."

While the remaining party were talking, Mr Darcy and Mr Bingley held deep conversation with the doctor. Their faces were grave, and Elizabeth's heart sank as she watched them. Mr Darcy then shook the doctor's hand, bowed and returned to Elizabeth's side.

She looked up at him hoping for a sign of encouragement, but he did not look at her. His face remained dark.

Lydia and Kitty now entered the room. "Can we go to see mama now?" Lydia asked. "The baby is sleeping, it will not need attention for an hour or two. I have told Hill to listen for her."

"Lydia, you do not tell Hill anything, you ask her," Elizabeth was disgusted with her sister's attitude.

"Stop picking on me, Lizzie. I shall go and see mama," she left the room with a deep scowl on her face.

Kitty followed her without saying a word.

"I cannot understand Lydia at all," Elizabeth was exasperated. "Her manner is bordering on insolence."

"Leave her, Lizzie," Mr Bennett instructed. "Sometimes it is better to say very little I think."

"Maybe you are right father, but she should have more consideration for mama's condition."

"I think you should rest now father. Lizzie and I will watch over our dear mother. Indeed we are as troubled about your health as we are about our mother's," she looked at him with concern. "Please rest father, we will send word if there is the slightest change in her condition."

"You are good girls," Mr Bennett replied. He kissed them both on the forehead and left the room.

Elizabeth looked across at her sister. "In your condition, Jane, I think you should be resting also. I can stay with mama."

"I could not rest, Lizzie. Even if I retired to bed, I would not sleep. No truly, Lizzie, I will be all right. I would much rather be here with mama. The worry would be too great if I were not."

"Take care, Jane. This is a time when you must, for once, put your own condition first," Elizabeth urged.

"I am well, Lizzie, believe me. If I feel the need for rest, I will tell you."

The two sisters talked as they kept watch by their mother's bedside.

"What do you think father will do if mother does not recover?" Elizabeth asked Jane.

"I do not know, Lizzie. It does not bear thinking about," she replied. "I know mama has driven him to distraction at times, but he has great regard for her I think. If you had seen his face, Lizzie, when Mr Bingley and I arrived, it was so strained, I feared for his own health."

"It is difficult to think of the future without mama," Elizabeth sighed deeply, then after a short pause she continued. "O Jane, I feel so ill that I have never had the courage to invite mama to Pemberley. I have put Mr Darcy's feelings before that of our dear mother."

"Do not blame yourself, Lizzie. Mr Darcy has suffered much at the hands of mama. Indeed she has a way of causing offence when it is least needed. He has been most generous towards her, but she insists on causing him distress."

"You are right, Jane, but the knowing of it does not make me feel any better. No, I promise you, Jane, if mama does recover, I will take her to Pemberley." Elizabeth stated.

"She would like that Lizzie. There is nothing more she enjoys, than to boast of her children's achievements."

All of a sudden there was a movement under the bedclothes, and both girls jumped to their feet.

"Mama, mama, can you hear me," Jane exclaimed. "Dear mama please open your eyes. It is me, Jane, and Lizzie is here also. Please, mama." There was another small movement.

"I will go and fetch father." Elizabeth headed for the door.

"Shall we wait a while, Lizzie?" Jane asked. "There is nothing of substance to show him yet. Shall we not wait until she opens her eyes?"

"But we promised to inform him of the slightest change Jane."

There was a quiet moan coming from the direction of the bed.

"You go, Lizzie. I do believe mama is coming back to us." Jane's smile lit up her face.

Mrs Bennett moved again, this time more decisively than before, and her eyelids started to flicker.

Mr Bennett was but two minutes before he entered his wife's bedchamber. He crossed to the bed and took hold of her hand. "Mrs Bennett, you have had us all beside ourselves," he spoke quietly. "Is this your new way of claiming our attention?" There were tears in his eyes and a look of love on his face. "If it is, Mrs Bennett, then I must say you have excelled yourself."

Mrs Bennett moved again.

"O mama, please come back to us," Jane urged. "Papa, has been without mind over your illness. He is truly distressed."

The eyelids flickered again, and this time they fully opened. Jane started to cry, and Elizabeth collapsed into one of the chairs.

Mrs Bennett's eyes moved slowly round the room until they rested on her husband's face. There was no recognition in them for quite some time, then slowly, very slowly a dawning expression spread over her face.

"Mrs Bennett, it has been so quiet these last few days, I confess I have had difficulty living with it." Mr Bennett told his wife.

"Shall we wake Mary, Kitty and Lydia?" Jane asked.

"There is no call to disturb them, Jane," replied Mr Bennett. "Your mother, I feel is now on the road to recovery. No Jane, let them sleep till morning. There is nothing to be gained by waking them now."

"Jane, my dear Jane," Mrs Bennett's voice floated up from the bed. It was slurred, quiet but distinguishable.

"O mama," cried Jane kneeling down my her mothers bed.

"We have all been so worried. I am glad you have come back to us. Lizzie is here, and so is Mary, Kitty and Lydia. Lydia has brought your granddaughter to visit you."

A slightly twisted smile crossed Mrs Bennett's face.

Elizabeth crossed to the bedside and kissed her mother gently. "Dear mama we are so pleased to have you back with us."

"Come Lizzie, let father have some time alone with our dear mother," suggested Jane. "The dawn is only now breaking, we will walk in the garden."

As they descended the stairs Hill came from the room she used in the back of the house.

"It is good news," Jane said as she saw the worried look on their faithful housekeeper's face. "Mama has come back to us. She opens her eyes."

Hill collapsed into floods of tears. "Forgive me, ma'am. I have been so dreadfully worried for you all."

"It is all right, Hill. I am sure everything will be well now." Jane put out an arm to comfort the distressed woman.

"O Lizzie," Jane exclaimed as they walked. "I am so relieved our dear mother is returned to us. I feared that she would depart this world, and father would be consumed with guilt over his refusal to allow her to go to Lydia. I confess I did think it was very wrong of him."

"That maybe Jane, but Lydia has caused him great concern these past two years. She has to learn to deal with her own life," replied Elizabeth. "Indeed Jane, she is a wife and mother now, she must learn to take on her own responsibilities. We cannot always be there to pick up the pieces."

"You are right Lizzie, I know, but she is still so very young. What do you think she will do now. If Wickham has gone, then she will have no money to support herself and her daughter."

"It is a worry Jane, but I am sure between us and father we can ensure her comfort. She is such a silly, headstrong girl. If only she would listen to reason, most of her concerns could be avoided."

A carriage came round the corner of the drive, and the two sisters seeing it was their husbands, ran to meet it.

Both men were surprised and delighted to see the change of emotions in their wives.

"Our mother has come back to us," Jane said breathlessly. "She opens her eyes, and speaks to us."

"I am delighted to hear it," Mr Darcy smiled. "Is the doctor still in residence?"

"He is, sir," replied Jane, "but we have not woken him with the news yet. It is only the matter of an hour since Mrs Bennett showed signs of recovery. Do you think it would be wise to summon him?"

"I do indeed. Confirmation from an experienced man always holds more weight I believe." explained Mr Darcy.

"Then I shall go to him at once." Jane turned and went into the house.

"Do you still fear for our mother's health, sir?" Elizabeth asked her husband.

"It is good news indeed that your mother had improved, but the doctor's predictions were so severe yesterday, it surprises me that Mrs Bennett has recovered so quickly."

"You fear that there will be a relapse, sir?" Elizabeth's voice was full of concern.

"I do not know," replied Mr Darcy. "It is better to await the doctor's examination. Your mother's condition is such that it causes much concern Elizabeth. There is not enough known of this illness as to be absolutely sure of the outcome."

"I pray you are wrong Mr Darcy. The relief to my dear father when mama opened her eyes was a delight to my heart."

"I also pray I am wrong Elizabeth. I am indeed concerned that you are no more saddened."

"Your support is of great comfort to me, sir." Elizabeth smiled up at her husband. His concern for her since their marriage was a constant source of surprise to her. She took his arm and they followed Mr Bingley into the house.

Mr Bennett greeted them in the hallway. The strained look had disappeared from his face, and he was smiling.

"I am deeply indebted to you Mr Darcy," he said. "I have no notion what your physician prescribed for Mrs Bennett, but it has had amazing results."

"I am very pleased to hear it," Mr Darcy smiled slightly. "Would you be so kind as to permit me to consult with the doctor before he leaves Mr Bennett?"

"Don't say you are going to take ill Mr Darcy, my poor nerves cannot take any more."

"I assure you, sir, I am quite well."

"I'm pleased to hear it. By all means go talk to your friend. I believe he is at this moment in the study."

Mr Darcy was absent for quite some time, and Elizabeth was concerned. She was unsure whether he was consulting the doctor on his recent fall, or gaining information on Mrs Bennett's condition?"

By the time he returned the room was so full of people talking she had little opportunity to speak with him alone. Several times she tried to catch his eye but he was very careful to avoid her attempts. Lydia was in full flow over her recent betrayal, and Kitty was hanging on every word.

"Mr Wickham did not want to go to France Lizzie. He was lured there against his will," Lydia stated.

"In that case Lydia he should return home as soon as he can extract himself from his abductor's clutches." Elizabeth said a little sarcastically.

"I am sure he will. He has no wish to stay away from his daughter any longer than he has to. He will come back Lizzie. Take my word on it."

"Then I am pleased for you. Have you been in to see mama this morning Kitty?"

"I don't know why you pick on Lydia so Lizzie, she is most upset at this time." Kitty defended her sister.

"I am sure she is Kitty, but mama is most unwell and

deserves all of our attention. Have you seen her this morning?"

"Lydia and I went in before breakfast. I was very surprised to see her awake. Last night I feared she may leave us forever."

"Don't be so silly Kitty," Lydia scolded her. "If mama was going to die, she would have done it when she had her attack. Not waited until now."

Jane looked at her youngest sister with horror. "Lydia, that is most disrespectful. How dare you talk about mama in that fashion?"

"Well none of you understands the stress I have been under since my poor Wickham was taken away, and I have a baby to look after as well you know."

Elizabeth could stand it no longer. "No-one takes an adult person away without their consent. If Wickham has gone to France with this woman, then he went willingly."

"How can you be so cruel Lizzie. You were always jealous of my Mr Wickham. You wanted him for yourself at one time, well you cannot have him. He is mine."

"I have no wish to relieve you of your husband's company Lydia. If I never saw him again I would not think twice about it."

"Lizzie you are horrid," Lydia stood up and rushed from the room, almost knocking Hill over as she did so.

"I know what you say is true Lizzie," Jane said quietly, "but surely if Lydia wishes to believe Wickham went against his will, that cannot be so wrong."

"My dear Jane, she has to realize what a person Wickham is. This is not the first time he has caused her concern, and it will probably not be the last."

"You have no idea how upset Lydia is over her husband leaving her Lizzie." Kitty interrupted. "She does have a child to consider you know."

"And we are very concerned for her Kitty," Elizabeth replied, "but holding ideas that are not true will serve no purpose to anyone. Wickham left because he wanted to, that is all."

"Elizabeth, would you honour me with your company in the garden?" Mr Darcy spoke to his wife.

Elizabeth flushed slightly knowing she had been a little too outspoken. Mr Darcy opened the door and she passed through.

"How long do you wish to stay at Longbourne, Elizabeth?" he asked when they were out of earshot of the building. "Now your mother is starting to recover, I wondered if you still wished to be with her?"

"I think another day or two will assure us of our mother's recovery, sir. Do you have business elsewhere?"

"Not urgent business, my love, but I do need to attend to a few things." He was quiet for a few moments, then he said. "Do you wish me to go to France and see what Mr Wickham's intentions are, Elizabeth?"

"It is very good of you to consider it, sir, but we cannot keep returning Lydia's husband to her." Elizabeth frowned. "I am very vexed that she should act in this way when poor father is suffering so much."

"Your youngest sister has a lot of maturing to do Elizabeth," Mr Darcy said. "It does not help her progress when your mother encourages her to act in this manner. I fear she will remain in constant turmoil."

Mr Darcy's remarks shocked Elizabeth. It was not like him to slight any of her family. Although they had, at times caused him discomfort, he had always remained impartial.

"You think mama is responsible for Lydia's actions, sir?" she asked.

"I am afraid I do. She was not checked at an early age, and is now paying the price."

There was silence for several minutes while Elizabeth digested this new turn of events, then she changed the subject. "Did your conversation with the doctor enlighten you to mama's condition may I ask?"

"It did my dear. Although Mrs Bennett has returned to the world, she has not recovered. Her condition remains uncertain.

Dr Edwards informs me that your mother Elizabeth is without motion on the one side of her body, and he cannot rule out the arrival of another seizure. From today onwards she must be attended to with great care. I will talk to your father in regard to obtaining a nurse."

"You are very good, sir. My family are so very indebted to you, I have no idea how we can ever repay your kindness."

"Your family owe me nothing, Elizabeth. I think only of your comfort."

Elizabeth held her husband's arm even tighter as they made their way back towards the house.

"Lizzie, come quickly," Jane met them at the door. "Mama sits up and is aware of us." She frowned slightly. "Although dear Lizzie, I should make you aware that she is not fully herself. Her one arm is of no use to her at all, but I am convinced it will come back in time."

"O Jane, you always look on the positive side of life. I wish with all my heart I could be more like you." Elizabeth took her sister's arm and they mounted the stairs together.

Mr Darcy and Mr Bingley went in search of Mr Bennett, and found him in the study.

"Please forgive us Mr Bennett, we have no wish to invade your privacy," Mr Darcy spoke as they entered the room, "but we wish to consult you on the practise of engaging a nurse to attend your wife. We both feel that this would lighten the burden of your family considerably."

"Your thoughts do you justice, and I thank you, sir, but I am sure Mary and Kitty will manage very well. Mrs Bennett is not the easiest of women to attend to."

"That is why we suggest a nurse, sir," Mr Bingley spoke for the first time. "The stress on your two younger daughters would soon become unbearable."

"Maybe you are right, sir. I confess I am not thinking as I should be at this present time."

"That is understandable, sir," replied Mr Darcy. "May I suggest we engage someone for a short duration?"

"I know the perfect one," announced Mr Bingley. "Leave it with me, sir. I will send for her directly."

"You are both good men. My daughter's have been most fortunate in their choice of husbands." Mr Bennett spoke without looking up. He knew without anything having been said, that both men understood his financial situation. He felt both embarrassment and gratitude, but most of all he felt extreme pride in his two son in laws.

With Mrs Bennett now showing strong signs of recovery, it was a much happy party that enjoyed several hours of cards and music that evening.

Chapter 3

"Lizzie! Lizzie! "Kitty knocked on Elizabeth's bedroom room before breakfast the following morning.

"What is it Kitty. Has mama been taken ill again?" Elizabeth's voice was full of concern.

"No Lizzie, I have not seen mama this morning. It is Lydia," Kitty was most distressed and waving a piece of paper in her hand. "She has run away I think. She says she has gone to find Mr Wickham."

"Kitty come in and keep your voice down, you will wake mama. Now tell me quietly, what is the matter?"

"O Lizzie, I heard the baby crying for some length of time, and as no-one attended it, I went to see what the matter was. Lydia was not in her bed, so I went to the baby's cradle. There was a note pinned to the covers. It says she has gone to Paris to find Mr Wickham. And Lizzie it must be true, some of her clothes have gone as well."

"Good God. Let me see the note, Kitty."

Taking it from her sister she read the note with mounting alarm.

Dear Kitty,

By the time you read this letter I will have left Longbourne in search of my dear Wickham. I know you will understand Kitty as Jane and Lizzie will not. Wickham has been taken away against his will, and he is in need of my help I am sure.

I am leaving my dear Lucy for you to take care of Kitty. She is a good baby, and will cause little concern. Do not tell mama, as I will return as soon as I find my dear husband.

Lydia.

"Stupid, stupid girl! How can she be so selfish at a time like this. To leave the baby? This is intolerable Kitty. O where is Jane? I must speak with Jane."

"What about the baby Lizzie? It is still crying. and I am sure I know not how to care for it."

"Go and fetch Hill, Kitty," Elizabeth ordered with more than a little exasperation in her voice. She hurried from the room in search of Jane.

"O Lizzie, is this true? Has she really gone to Paris? Jane asked once she had heard the news.

"I fear she has, Jane. This letter says so and Kitty is convinced there are clothes missing from her room."

"What can be done? How long has she been gone do you think?"

"I do not know, Jane, but we must tell father. It pains me to distress you further at this time. You should be free of care in your condition, but I fear we cannot keep this a secret."

"No indeed, but do not concern yourself over me Lizzie, I am well. Do you wish me to go and tell father?"

"If I go to father, can you help Hill with Lucy?" Elizabeth asked.

"I will go directly. O Lizzie, how can Lydia be so stupid. To go alone is beyond comprehension."

"She thinks only of herself, Jane. She has no thought for poor mama," Elizabeth was most upset. "Lydia has always had her own comfort as her first concern."

"That is unkind Lizzie, she is much troubled I think."

"Maybe so, Jane, but to add to father's troubles at this time is intolerable."

"You are right Lizzie, but she must be very concerned for her future. I will go to Lucy and see if I can help."

Mr Bennett was shocked when informed of the situation. "What can be in her head Lizzie? Does my youngest daughter take a delight in running away?"

"I do not know father, but she thinks only of herself I believe."

"You are probably right Lizzie, but she has many concerns of her own at this time. The thoughts for her own future must be uppermost in her mind I think."

A message was duly sent to Netherfield to inform Mr Darcy and Mr Bingley. Lucy was fed and settled and Mr Bennett started his preparations for his trip to Paris.

It was less than half an hour before the two men arrived from Netherfield.

"What is the situation Elizabeth? What is being done?" Mr Darcy asked as he entered Longbourne.

"My father is preparing to travel to Paris, sir," Elizabeth replied.

"I must speak with him."

"I believe he is still in his study, sir."

The two men went directly to Mr Bennett.

"I have no wish to interfere, sir," Mr Darcy said. "but my horse is faster, and I believe, my knowledge of the area is more recent than your own may be."

"You could be right Mr Darcy, but this situation I fear lies squarely on my own shoulders," Mr Bennett replied. "I understand your wish to be of assistance, but you have had the misfortune of retrieving my daughter in the past, and I will not live through another occurrence of that nature. No, sir, this is of my concern alone."

"But your wife, sir," Mr Bingley joined the conversation. "She is in great need of your support."

"She is indeed, sir, but I am convinced that my four daughters will supply any support Mrs Bennett may need. I cannot, and will not shirk my responsibilities again."

"I perfectly comprehend your feelings, sir," Mr Darcy argued. "but if my friend and myself leave immediately, I am sure we can intercept Mrs Wickham before she reaches her destination."

"I am sure you would, sir, but my mind is made up." Mr Bennett was adamant. "This is my responsibility, I must be allowed to have it."

"Your intentions are clear, sir," Mr Darcy replied. "May myself and my friend have the honour of accompanying you?"

"It appears Mr Darcy that I have no way of dissuading you, so I will welcome your company."

"We are indeed honoured, sir," Mr Bingley said. "In which direction do you presume your daughter travelled?"

"My belief is, from town she would have gone directly to Portsmouth."

"Her length of departure," Mr Darcy asked. "Is there some indication?"

"Her bed has been slept in," Mr Bennett sighed. "I believe her to have walked to Meriton in the early hours, where she would have secured a carriage for herself. As none of the servants heard her departure from Longbourne, I believe her journey to be started on foot."

"Then we must make haste," Mr Bingley suggested. "We may yet be in time to intercept her journey."

A more comfortable and faster carriage was secured from Netherfield, and the three men departed in the direction of town. Mr Darcy enraged at the stupidity of Lydia, Mr Bennett despondent that his youngest daughter could cause so much concern, and Mr Bingley hopeful that everything would turn out well.

Their journey was fast and direct. They reached town in good time and with little interruption.

"If you will permit me, sir," Mr Darcy said as they stopped to change horses. "I believe it will do as well to inquire around town as to which route Wickham has taken. We are all guessing that it is to Portsmouth he was heading I think."

"We are indeed, Mr Darcy. Do you propose that there may be another purpose to his intent?" Mr Bennett seemed most puzzled.

"I do, sir," replied Mr Darcy. "To be as sure as to state his intentions, begs me to think he had designs of another nature. I have known his character for a good many years."

"Good God Darcy, I believe you are right," exclaimed Mr

Bingley. "Are you of the opinion that he may still be in town?"

"I think it possible Bingley."

"Then I shall go directly to the places I would suppose him to be," Mr Bingley stated.

"I fear it will not be that easy Bingley. You forget he is at this time excluded from society by his actions," Mr Darcy reminded him. "We must search out new accommodations. There are people who, I am sure, will know of his whereabouts."

As Mr Bennett would not hear of his son in law's taking full responsibility on their own. Mr Darcy, against his better judgement, agreed that they should search together.

It was several hours before the whereabouts of Mr Wickham was discovered, and the circumstances in which he was found, were alarming indeed.

The situation was a run down boarding house, in the more seedy part of London.

"Good God, Darcy, whatever is amiss?" Mr Bingley exclaimed.

A great commotion was unfolding in the entrance to the boarding house, with Mr Wickham at the centre.

The look on his face when he recognized Mr Darcy was a cross between pure shock, and alarm. But then seeing it could be his salvation, his expression changed.

"Darcy, I am delighted to see you," he exclaimed with as much dignity as he could muster in the circumstances. "These men are trying to arrest me with charges I have no knowledge of. Tell them Darcy that I am a close acquaintance of yours."

Mr Darcy stepped forward. "Pray tell me, sir, what has this gentleman done, that it needs the law to settle it?" he spoke directly to the constable restraining Mr Wickham.

"I am not sure, sir," the constable replied. "I was just instructed to apprehend this gentleman, and take him to Bow Street Station."

"This is outrageous." Wickham was still trying to release himself from the constable's grasp. "Unhand me this minute."

"You must have some indication of his offence?" Mr Darcy argued.

"I believe it is a question of theft, sir." the constable replied. "Now if you please, sir, I'll get on with the job in hand." With that remark the policeman deftly manhandled Mr Wickham into a carriage that was waiting by the kerb, and galloped away.

Mr Bennett, who had been totally speechless throughout, now spoke.

"For the love of God, what has that fool son in law of mine done now?"

"It appears, sir that he has stolen something." Mr Darcy replied.

"God Darcy, what is to be done?" Mr Bingley was most agitated.

"We shall have to go to Bow Street, and try to discover the exact nature of his crime." Mr Darcy's face showed no expression.

"But what of Mrs Wickham?" Bingley asked. "Shall we not continue to Portsmouth?"

It will take but an hour to discover the exploits of Wickham. If there is nothing to be done, then we will carry on our journey towards Portsmouth."

"Now we know the whereabouts of Wickham, Darcy, surely it would be more beneficial to apprehend Mrs Wickham before she can board a boat for Paris? This is very dire Darcy, upon my word." Mr Bingley was most distressed.

It is my opinion that Mrs Wickham has not reached her destination at this time. She then has to secure a passage, and I doubt very much that ships leave everyday for Paris. No Bingley, I believe we have time to discover Wickham's crimes."

"Mr Darcy, your intentions are most honourable," Mr Bennett said. "but I believe it is my responsibility to extract Mr Wickham from his follies."

"If the charge is theft, sir, I doubt very much that there is anything, anyone can do." Mr Darcy replied. "My opinion is, that we should all travel to the police station and ascertain the extent of the charges."

On entering the station Mr Darcy was shown much respect, so it did not take long to discover the charges against Mr Wickham were grave indeed. He was charged with taking money, and jewellery from a Mrs Henrietta Wilkinson. The total in question was above six hundred pounds.

"Whatever lengths will the man go to," Mr Bennett exploded. "He is indeed the most devious son in law to be burdened on any family."

"The charges are grave indeed," Mr Darcy said. "I have asked the Inspector if we may speak with Wickham, to obtain his version of events."

"His spell in prison could be of some duration I believe," Mr Bingley sighed. "Not to mention the shame it will bring."

"Let us find out more information Bingley," Mr Darcy suggested. "It is too early to speculate."

The three men were installed in a small room to await the arrival of Mr Wickham.

"Darcy!" Mr Wickham said as he entered the room. "These charges are false, at the very least."

"Mr Wickham," Mr Bennett stepped forward. "What disgrace have you brought on my family now?"

"It is all a falsehood, sir, you have my word on it," Mr Wickham spluttered. "These charges have been brought about most unjustly."

"Your word, sir, I believe it counts for nothing at all," Mr Bennett was beside himself.

"Sit down Wickham. This is no time for falsehoods. If you wish us to help you with this situation, the truth must be told at once." Mr Darcy's face had grown dark with temper.

"I have done nothing to bring about this situation I find myself in," Wickham insisted. "It is all an untruth. Believe me Darcy."

"I do not believe you," Mr Darcy spat out the words. "We have pressing business in another quarter, and have very little time to waste on your exploits. Tell us the truth at once, or we will leave you to rot in your own mess."

The tone of Mr Darcy's voice left Wickham in no doubt that he meant what he said. His shoulders dropped, and an expression of resignation spread over his face.

"Did you take the property the police are accusing you of?" Mr Darcy asked.

Upon my honour Darcy, I did not acquire the possessions by theft," Mr Wickham was still on the defensive. "They were a gift."

"If this is true Wickham, what brought about these dire circumstances?"

"Have you not heard of poor losers Darcy. Surely this must come as no surprise to you?"

"Nothing you do ever surprises me." Mr Darcy's temper had receded a little. "Now tell us the extent of the charges before you."

After some persuasion, Mr Wickham admitted to an attachment, with the lady in question, and offered the information, that the items were given to him as a gift, then the money was gambled away at the casino. On discovering what he had done, Henrietta Wilkinson, stated that she wished him out of her life, then accused him of theft.

"You have to secure my release Darcy, I have no charges to face, and my dear wife, will be most distressed to discover my circumstances."

"Your wife, Mr Wickham, is the sole reason we are here," Mr Darcy almost spat out the words. "If it was not for the shame you continue to bring to my family, I would not waste my time on you. Even taking this into consideration, I am still of the mind to leave you to your own devices."

"It is a misunderstanding, sir," Mr Wickham pleaded. "I must be given the chance to amend my actions."

"You have been given more chances than you deserve Wickham. Tell us the whole truth, or we will abandon you to your own fate." Mr Bingley spoke for the first time.

"It is a mistake, sir, believe me."

"I will ask you for the last time Wickham, were these items acquired by honest means? Only the truth will help you now." Mr Darcy asked.

"They were a gift, sir. I would stake my life on it." Mr Wickham replied, but the colour that appeared in his cheeks belied his words.

"That is about what you will be doing." Mr Darcy replied. Then he left the room, closely followed by his two companions.

"The man is a menace to society," Mr Bennett exclaimed, once they were outside. "He does not deserve any help from anyone."

"Indeed he does not," Mr Darcy replied, "but to leave him there would bring much shame to his relations I fear."

"What are your proposals Darcy?" Mr Bingley asked. "My opinion is that he is guilty indeed."

"You are probably right Bingley, and the repercussions are dire indeed."

"Leave him to his own devices," Mr Bennett suggested. "A term in goal may well bring him to his senses. I am sure my daughter will bear the shame with much emotion."

"Our penal system is such that removing property that is not your own, carries a high sentence indeed." Mr Darcy explained.

"Such as, Mr Darcy?" Mr Bennett inquired.

"Larceny, of a much lower nature, has resulted in many men losing their lives to the noose."

"Good God, Darcy, you can not be serious?" Mr Bingley was aghast.

"You know full well Bingley, that is the law."

"What is to be done? Is there anything we can do?" Mr Bingley was now most upset.

The life of his former friend repulsed Mr Darcy to the very soul, but if, by his actions, he caused Elizabeth distress, he was prepared to do anything to contain the situation. "I will address my attorney, and acquire his view on the matter.

In the meantime, I suggest Mr Bennett and yourself take some rest. We still have Mrs Wickham to find."

"I cannot allow you to go to such lengths on behalf of my family Mr Darcy. Your generous nature has been exploited in the past. I will not stand by and see it happen again." Mr Bennett was adamant.

"Time is of the essence, sir. With every respect, I must be allowed to over rule you on this matter. I will go to my attorney directly, then join you at my house. Mr Bingley, would you be so good as to escort Mr Bennett to my accommodations?"

"I will Darcy," Mr Bingley replied. "but do you not wish company on your journey?"

"It would serve no purpose Bingley, besides it is but a short journey to my destination. I shall join you directly."

As there was now no room for argument, the party went their separate ways.

It took little under an hour for Mr Darcy to contact his lawyer, and to instruct him to discover the truth of Wickham's arrest, and if at all possible arrange his release, at whatever financial cost it may incur. He then returned to join the rest of his party.

In the very early hours of the following morning, Mr Darcy was visited by his attorney, with the information that, unless the lady in question removed all charges, nothing could be done.

"Then I shall visit her at once," Mr Darcy decided. "Her home is in London I believe?"

"It is, sir," replied his friend. "I will accompany you myself."

By the time Mr Darcy returned to his home, Mr Bingley and Mr Bennett had breakfasted, and were ready for the day.

"Darcy, where have you bee?" Mr Bingley greeted him. "We were at a loss to explain your absence. Have you any news for us?"

"I have indeed," Mr Darcy replied. "My attorney has had the good fortune to arrange the release of Mr Wickham. He will be here directly, then we may proceed with the rest of the journey."

"Mr Darcy, my family are once again in your debt. Tell me, sir, how are we ever going to repay your generous nature?

"It is done, sir. We will speak no more on the subject."

The conversation was interrupted by the arrival of Mr Wickham.

"Mr Darcy, I am indeed in your debt," he announced as he walked into the room.

Mr Darcy totally ignored his comments and spoke directly to his lawyer.

"All is well I take it?" he asked.

"It is, sir."

"You have my grateful thanks."

Mr Bennett spoke to his wayward son in law. "Mr Wickham," he declared. "If the punishment was left entirely in my hands, I would have you flogged to your very last breath, but unfortunately it is not so. My youngest daughter, has an attachment to you that appears to be unbreakable. She is the only reason I do not raise my hand to you at this very moment."

"I cannot account for my behaviour, sir," Mr Wickham simpered. "To bring concern to my wife is grievous indeed. I can fully understand if your wish was to see me out of your sight."

"It is indeed Mr Wickham," Mr Bennett was beside himself with anger, "but my daughter is at this very moment on her way to Portsmouth in search of you. Thanks to your selfish actions, she is most probably in great danger."

"Then I must go to her." Mr Wickham gave a good impression of someone greatly concerned.

"No, sir," Mr Bennett was adamant. "You will return to Longbourne in the company of one of us, while the rest of us continue our journey to Portsmouth. I have much to say to my daughter before she is again in your company. Mr Bingley, would you be so good as to escort Mr Wickham back to Longbourne."

"I will indeed, sir, if it is your wish," Mr Bingley agreed.

"Your wife may be in need of your support. It is only right that you should be with her at this time." Mr Bennett suggested. "Now get along with you. Get this man out of my sight." He went to walk away but turned back abruptly. "If, Mr Bingley, by some fortunate turn of fate, you should encounter a sharp bend close to a deep slope, I would not be at all surprised if your travelling companion met with a slight accident."

Mr Bingley was shocked at this suggestion, then realizing Mr Bennett was not entirely serious he said. "I am sure I have heard of such a thing happening on many an occasion, sir."

Mr Bennett turned to Mr Darcy. "Mr Darcy, would you be so good as to accompany me on the remainder of our journey?"

"I would be honoured, sir."

An overnight stay in an Inn was necessary before their journey could progress, so it was evening on the following day before their destination was reached.

"The port is busy and extensive, sir," Mr Darcy said. "May I be so bold as to suggest that one of us should attend the port office, to see if Mrs Wickham has secured a passage, while the other makes a search of the dockside. I believe, sir, our actions would be reinforced in this way."

"You are probably right Mr Darcy. I must confess I have no knowledge of the workings of a seaside port."

"Then I will attend the offices, sir, if you would be so good as to survey the dock."

It was less than half an hour before Mr Bennett caught sight of his wayward daughter. He wanted to go to her and tell her he was glad she was safe, but his frustration at her actions took over.

"Lydia!" he exclaimed. "Have you no thought for yourself or your family. To take on so and put us all to great inconvenience. With Mrs Bennett in her sick bed. This is not to be tolerated."

Lydia whirled round at the sound of her father's voice. She was both surprised and angry. "You had no need to follow me father," Lydia stepped back and looked as though she would take flight, but her mind was changed. She pulled herself up to her full height and faced her father. "I am going to see Wickham, and you cannot stop me. He is my husband and my place is by his side. I am determined to go father."

"Have reason child. You do not understand the dangers you are putting yourself in by travelling alone in this way."

"I will not go back with you. I want to see Wickham." There were tears in her eyes, but her spirit remained intact.

Mr Darcy, who had seen the reunion, remained a few feet away as not to interfere.

"What in the world is he doing here?" Lydia demanded when she caught sight of him.

"Why does he keep trying to stop me seeing Wickham. Well, he will not this time. Wickham has been taken against his will, and needs my help. I will go to Paris and help him."

Mr Darcy stepped forward. "I have no wish to change your direction Mrs Wickham, but if you will attend your father, you will discover that your husband, is at this moment at Longbourne."

Lydia's face was full of disbelief. "You are lying to me," she screamed. "He has gone to Paris, he said so in his letter. I will not go back with you, and you cannot make me."

"Lydia," Mr Bennett was now very angry with his daughter. "What Mr Darcy tells you is the truth. Your husband was discovered in London, and has return to Longbourne in the company of Mr Bingley."

Lydia thought for a while, then thinking she had caught them out in a lie she said. "That cannot be so. If Mr Wickham was in London, and I doubt for one minute that he was, he would have come to Portsmouth with you. He would not have gone off in another direction. That proves you must be lying to me."

"As there is no ship leaving this port before the morning tide, may I be so bold as to suggest we retire to the comfort of an Inn," Mr Darcy suggested.

Lydia looked at him with distrust, until, seeing the sense of his suggestion. she agreed. There was no way she would admit to either of them, that she had been too frightened to enter an Inn by herself to eat. In fact, she had not had a decent meal since the evening before her departure from Longbourne.

Once settled at the Inn, it took over an hour to convince Lydia of her husbands follies, and that Wickham was in fact at Longbourne and not Paris.

"I do not believe my dear Wickham would steal anything from anybody," Lydia defended her husband." I will go back with you but if, father you are lying to me, and my dear Wickham is not where you say he is, I will return here and carry on my journey to Paris."

"That my child will be entirely up to you. Now I suggest you rest. You are a great concern to your parents."

With Lydia retired to her bed Mr Bennett allowed himself to relax. "Mr Darcy, I am again indebted to you. Indeed, the inconvenience my family have caused you lies heavy with me, sir. I have not the slightest idea how I can ever repay you."

"You owe me nothing, sir," Mr Darcy replied. "You have given me your daughter, and I cannot be more blessed. She has made a difference to my life that is beyond description. My debt is to you, sir."

"You are a good man Darcy. I have to admit that I have not always thought so. On first acquaintance I believed you to be most unpleasant."

"I am sure you did, sir," Mr Darcy laughed. "My conduct to everyone on my first visit to Hertfordshire, fills me with shame. My pride and conceit overruled my intentions."

"Well, well, it is all in the past." Mr Bennett smiled. "It is best that we let it remain there I think."

******

Back at Longbourne, the fact that Lydia had run away again, had been kept secret from Mrs Bennett. Her condition, although improving slowly, was still of much concern.

Jane and Elizabeth were at a loss to know how they could be of assistance. Apart from spending many hours in Mrs Bennett's company. all they could do was watch and wait.

"Jane, how can Lydia possibly think that she could travel to Paris, and leave the baby in the care of Kitty? I must confess my thoughts for her are very ill indeed."

"She is very much troubled I think." Jane replied quietly. "Her mind is only on her own concerns."

"But to go off in the middle of the night, telling no-one, Jane. No I think she is a selfish, stupid girl, with no thought for others."

"I am inclined to agree with you Lizzie, but what is some misfortune overtakes her. To travel so far alone, it is dangerous indeed. The people she will meet will not be of our standing I am sure. And Paris! O Lizzie, she has no knowledge of the area. How will she direct her enquiries? It troubles me very much."

"I had not thought of it in that respect, Jane," admitted Elizabeth. "It is of much concern. O poor father, whatever must he be feeling?"

Jane sighed heavily. "If anything befalls Lydia, I cannot think how it will affect mama."

"No indeed. I fear it does not bear thinking of." Elizabeth stood up and started to pace the room. "How can she be so selfish, Jane? I cannot comprehend it at all."

"Father looked so defeated when he left Longbourne, I do hope Mr Bingley can be of some help."

"Poor father. Mr Darcy and Mr Bingley will be of great comfort to him I think. To travel so far alone with such concerns, would not have been advisable."

"Mr Darcy has shown much respect for our family, Lizzie. To think I used to imagine he was cold and aloof. I confess, I am now ashamed of my feelings."

Elizabeth laughed. "You have no need to be my dear, Jane. Mr Darcy has changed much since our acquaintance first began. He admits himself that he is quite another person."

"We have been very fortunate, Lizzie. Sometimes I fear for my own happiness. It is great indeed."

"And to soon be blessed with a child. I do envy you, Jane."

"You too will know the same joy, Lizzie. I am sure of it."

Elizabeth did not wish to dwell on her own concerns at the present time, so she said. "If mama were to discover Lydia's actions, I am convinced it would be the source of another attack on her health."

"I fear it would, Lizzie," Jane sighed. "We must at all times keep her in ignorance."

"How long will the journey to Paris take do you think?" Elizabeth asked.

"I do not know, but I fear it will be of some duration," Jane replied. "Perhaps they will discover Lydia before she can reach Plymouth.. I do hope so, Lizzie. I would wish...I would very much like, for Mr Bingley to be here for the birth of our child."

"I am sure he will be, Jane," Elizabeth sat next to her sister and took her hand. "This must be a very troubled time for you. The confinement so near, you should have no worries at this time."

"Please do not concern yourself, Lizzie, I am well. It is just that I would like Mr Bingley to be the first to see his new child. They could be away above a month, and that I fear would be too long."

"They will be back, Jane, I am sure of it." Elizabeth's tone was more positive than her thoughts on the matter. To travel to Paris, then search for Lydia could be above six weeks duration. "It troubles me that Mr Darcy has not recovered from his fall in full. For my family to cause him so much inconvenience at a time when his health is not of it's best, concerns me deeply."

"I am sure Mr Bingley will take care of them both, Lizzie. Did Mr Darcy suffer much injury from his fall?"

"I confess I was in fear for his very life for above two

days, Jane."

"Dear Lizzie, if only you had sent word, I would have come to you."

"Your goodness is too much, Jane. You must now put your own concerns first."

"I am well, Lizzie. Do not concern yourself."

*****

It was two days before Mr Bingley returned with Mr Wickham.

Elizabeth and Jane rushed out to meet the carriage, in the hope of seeing their husbands.

Elizabeth was shocked to see Mr Wickham, and disappointed Mr Darcy and her father were not in his company.

"Where is Mr Darcy?" She asked with concern.

"Your father Mrs Darcy," Mr Bingley explained, "has travelled to Portsmouth in the company of your husband, in the hope of recovering your sister Lydia."

"Then you did not go to Paris Mr Wickham?" Elizabeth was much confused.

"No indeed ma'am. I fear I have caused your family much distress.

"You have indeed, sir, and with dear mama still in ill health, you have been most unjust."

Mr Wickham looked suitably abashed.

"And Lydia has gone to Paris alone," Jane exclaimed. "Whatever will become of her? Poor Lydia, she is in great danger I think."

Mr Bingley went to his wife's side to give her comfort.

"Do not cause yourself distress, I beg you," he said. "I am sure Mr Darcy and Mr Bennett will recover Lydia long before she can embark on a sea voyage. She cannot be too far ahead of them I believe."

"Your words give me comfort Mr Bingley," Jane smiled up at her husband. "But my concern for my sister is great I fear."

"All will be well, Jane, I am sure," Mr Bingley consoled her. "How is Mrs Bennett's health? Does she continue to improve?"

"She does indeed, sir. We are not informing her of Lydia's misfortune at this time."

"My feelings are most humble for the inconvenience I have caused your family Mrs Bingley," Mr Wickham addressed Jane. "Indeed I cannot account for my actions, they were selfish indeed."

"They most certainly were Mr Wickham," Elizabeth rebuked him. "If any injury should befall Lydia, Mr Bennett or Mr Darcy through your behaviour, I am sure Paris will not be far enough away for you to hide."

"Mrs Darcy," Mr Bingley was most concerned, he knew of Elizabeth's temper, and feared for it. "The success of their journey is assured I believe. I have every reason to believe that they will reach Portsmouth and discover Mrs Wickham before anything ill can befall her."

"I hope you are right Mr Bingley," Elizabeth replied, then turning on her heel, she returned to the house, her emotions in turmoil.

*****

Within three days Mr Bingley's hopes had been confirmed. A carriage carrying Mr Bennett, Mr Darcy and Lydia arrived at Longbourne.

"Leave it now, Lizzie," Mr Bennett anticipated Elizabeth's concerns. "Your sister has indeed been through much."

Mr Darcy greeted his wife with much pleasure and relief, then followed Mr Bennett into the house.

"Don't look at me like that, Lizzie," Lydia said as she held on to her husband's arm with such a grip he feared it could not be released. "I had to find my dear Wickham, no-one else gave three straws for his situation."

"Nor you for your child Lydia. To leave a child so young without a mother, is disgraceful indeed."

"Kitty was to care for it. She is the only one who understands."

"You are both selfish, stupid people. To cause our dear parents so much concern at this time is intolerable."

"It is all right for you, Lizzie, you have no concerns," Lydia said defiantly. "Mr Wickham is my husband, and he needed me."

"And mama, did she not need you?"

Before Lydia could answer, Jane put a hand on Elizabeth's arm. "Do not distress yourself, Lizzie. Lydia is back with us unharmed. Surely that is our main concern."

"She has caused our father and Mr Darcy much inconvenience, Jane, and she shows no sign of repentance."

"Give her time, Lizzie," Jane tried to console her sister. "She has had much concern, and is now rejoicing in her good fortune. I am sure in time she will see the error of her actions."

"She will not, Jane, as you are very well aware," Elizabeth replied stubbornly. "Her thoughts are for no-one but herself."

"You may be right, Lizzie, but it does no good to dwell on it."

"You are too good, Jane. Your goodness is far greater than my own."

Two days passed before Mr Darcy suggested that a return to Pemberley was imminent.

"I have no wish to hurry you Elizabeth. If your wish is to remain with your mother a little longer, you have my consent," he said.

"My mother grows stronger by the day, sir. I truly believe that she is now on the way to recovery." Elizabeth replied. "With the new nurse that Mr Bingley engaged and Hill she wants for nothing." She paused for several seconds and then continued. "Mr Darcy you have shown nothing but kindness to my family, and indeed we are all greatly indebted to you. It pains me to impose further on your good nature."

"You have a request to make Elizabeth?"

"It concerns me greatly that Lydia's actions will infect

those of my sister Kitty. If she could be taken away to a different society, I am sure she could be saved."

"Your wish is that she resides with us at Pemberley?"

"I have no wish to impose upon you, sir, but my concerns are great indeed."

"Then she will return with us, and remain until such time as you are fully satisfied with your intention."

"I thank you, sir, you are indeed generous. Do you think Georgiana will have any objections to Kitty's arrival."

"I would hope not. It could turn out to be an advantage to you both. I am sure Georgiana would be more than happy to help you further Kitty's education."

"Thank you, sir."

"Is it only Kitty you have concerns for? Not your sister Mary?"

Elizabeth laughed. "I believe Mary is quite capable of putting Lydia in her place, sir. Mary only has interest in books."

Chapter 4

On their return to Pemberley Elizabeth was delighted to see Georgiana well and more settled.

"I have missed you so much Elizabeth," she announced as they entered the house. "Everything has been so lifeless without you."

"I am pleased to see you also," Elizabeth smiled at the young girl. "I hope you did not pine too much and miss out on the delights Pemberley has to offer at this time of year?"

"I am afraid I have taken up your pastime, and taken to walking the woods and groves."

"A very pleasurable and beneficial pastime I can assure you." Elizabeth laughed, she was very pleased to be back in her own home.

"Your mother is she now fully recovered." Georgiana asked.

"A little better, I thank you. Mrs Bennett has a long way to go before her health makes a full recovery, but I am convinced she is now on the right path."

"It makes me very happy to hear it."

"Georgiana, I would like to introduce you to my sister Kitty. Mr Darcy has graciously agreed to her staying with us for a few weeks. I am relying on you to help her with everything from music to fashion."

"I will be happy to help, Elizabeth. It will be of great pleasure to me to have another sister." Georgiana curtsied to Kitty then escorted her into the music room.

"My sister is at last happy thanks to you my dearest sweetest Elizabeth," said Mr Darcy. "I fear, with the loss of her dear mother at an early age, she has been sadly neglected with female company."

"With all these ladies in your household Mr Darcy, you are, I fear in great danger of becoming out numbered." laughed Elizabeth.

"Then I shall have to rely on you to invite guests that will hold the balance," he laughed back. "Now, however, I have much work to do in my study. I will see you at dinner, Elizabeth."

The following few weeks were such as Pemberley had never seen before. Its rooms were full of music and laughter, the gardens full of young women playing and walking. Both Georgiana and Elizabeth spent a great deal of time coaching Kitty in the finer points of high society. She was an apt pupil and learned very quickly. Mr Darcy had gone to town for several weeks, and Elizabeth was determined to show him, on his return, that at least one of her younger sisters could be in company without embarrassing him. Elizabeth wished to show off the transformation of her sister Kitty, at the Grand Summer Ball, that was arranged for the end of July. This was held every year, and was a very illustrious affair indeed. The cream of society would be present, not only from the Derbyshire area, but from the courts of London. It had been known, in the recent past, for Lord North, the Prime Minister, or even the Prince Regent himself to attend.

Elizabeth tried not to dwell on the standing of her guests too much, it only made her unsettled. She just prayed that she would not embarrass Mr Darcy in any way.

A letter had arrived for Elizabeth informing her that her sister Jane had given birth to a daughter. Both parties were in good health and Mr Bingley was the proudest father in the world. The birth, Jane informed her, had not been so arduous as she had been led to believe. Although Jane's letter filled Elizabeth with delight, it also brought to the forefront of her mind, her own condition. It pained her greatly that she had not, as yet, given Mr Darcy his own child. Preferably a son to secure the future of Pemberley. It was a major disappointment to Elizabeth, and it gave her many sleepless nights. Although Elizabeth would have dearly loved to visit her sister and newborn niece, she knew it was impossible with the responsibilities before her. She had never organized any on a scale such as this, and the arrangements had to be right.

Mrs Reynolds was Elizabeth's right arm. How she would

ever manage without her she had no idea. The time passed very quickly as the house was made to look very grand indeed.

It was two days before the summer ball was due to happen, Mr Darcy arrived back from town. Elizabeth was determined to keep the education of Kitty a secret, until, dressed in the latest fashion, she was presented at the ball, as a complete transformation. Georgiana was a great help in this, by keeping to their own apartments, it was less likely that either of them would accidentally come into contact with Mr Darcy.

"Are our sisters away from Pemberley?" Mr Darcy asked at dinner that evening.

"No, sir. I believe they are being discreet, and giving us some time alone together." Elizabeth smiled.

"Then I shall be ever indebted to them," Mr Darcy smiled back. "We do not have enough time to ourselves. How are the arrangements for the ball finalizing? Is there any way I can be of assistance?"

"I thank you no, sir." Elizabeth replied. "Mrs Reynolds has been most helpful. I believe Lady Catherine will be greatly missed this year."

"Elizabeth we have talked many times on this subject. My aunt made her own decisions at the time of our marriage. She was very hurtful in her opinion of you, and I leave it up to her to mend any breach in our relations."

"I do understand, sir, but Lady Catherine is a very proud lady, and may be suffering greatly from this breach."

"Then she only has to send a letter Elizabeth."

"Would it be so very hard to invite her to the ball. Our guests will be expecting to see her there." Elizabeth coaxed.

"You, as the mistress of Pemberley, may, if you so wish, extend an invitation to my aunt. That is an end to it Elizabeth." Mr Darcy's face had darkened, so Elizabeth knew she had gone as far with this conversation as she dared.

"It will be nice to see Jane again," she deftly changed the subject.

"It will indeed. She has fully recovered from childbirth?"

Mr Darcy asked.

"She is very well, sir, and looks forward to the ball with anticipation."

"And are we to be honoured with a view of Bingley's new daughter?"

"No, I fear not. It is as yet too young to travel. I hope it will not be long before we are invited to Southview. Jane must be a very happy woman."

"Indeed she must."

The rest of the evening was passed in a pleasant, relaxed atmosphere. Elizabeth with her embroidery, and Mr Darcy with his books.

After a great deal of deliberation Elizabeth decided against inviting Lady Catherine to the ball. She felt, that an invitation at this late hour of the proceedings, may give Lady Catherine the opinion that she was an after thought. There had been enough bad feeling between them without adding further offence. Besides, there was no way of being sure that Mr Darcy would speak to his aunt if she did arrive. It would be a grievous insult indeed if no word was spoken between them. No it was best to leave the reconciliation between nephew and aunt.

The following day was spent with Mrs Reynolds supervising the arrangements for the ball. The housekeeper was the rock that Elizabeth leaned on. Without her, Elizabeth knew she would not manage.

"If you ever left us Mrs Reynolds," Elizabeth said to her. "I am sure I would have to leave also. You have made my life very easy here. I am convinced I cannot manage without you."

Mrs Reynolds blushed deeply. "You are very kind ma'am. I am sure you would have managed very well. You are a natural to Pemberley Mrs Darcy, and if I may be so bold, I would just like to say, that I have never seen my master so happy and content, as since his marriage to you ma'am."

"I thank you Mrs Reynolds," Elizabeth smiled. "From one who knows my husband far better than I do, I take your words as the highest compliment."

This was the first large event Elizabeth had arranged at Pemberley, and she wanted everything to be perfect. Mr Bingley's sisters were coming, and she knew from previous experience, that they would be looking for the smallest of faults. Caroline Bingley would never forgive Elizabeth for taking the man she had set her heart on, and she would do everything in her power to show up Elizabeth's lack of breeding.

The guests that were staying at Pemberley started to arrive around lunchtime. To Elizabeth's great joy, her sister Jane and Mr Bingley were among the first to arrive.

"Dear Jane, you look so very well. How is your daughter? Who does she look like? Have you fully recovered?"

Jane laughed at her sister's excitement. "O Lizzie, she is the tiniest thing. I am sure I shall drop her. She is so very beautiful."

"Bingley, I congratulate you on the birth of your daughter," Mr Darcy greeted his friend. "I hope all is well."

"Darcy she is the prettiest thing you ever beheld. I pray she will grow to be the image of her mother."

"If you wish it, I am sure it will be so."

"That is one thing you cannot do for me Darcy. Although I am quite convinced you would try be it possible."

The bond between the two men had not changed since their marriages, and it pleased Elizabeth no end to see Mr Darcy relax amongst his favourite company.

"Caroline and Mrs Hurst will be here directly, Lizzie." Jane explained. "They were not quite ready when we left."

"They will be here too soon for me I think," Elizabeth pulled a face.

"Lizzie that is unkind, you know you do not mean it," but both girls laughed.

The next to arrive were Elizabeth's aunt and Uncle Gardiner. These were very dear to both Elizabeth and Darcy, and they greeted them with much pleasure.

"We are delighted you could come," Mr Darcy said. "I

hope your journey was without mishap?"

"It was indeed Mr Darcy," Mr Gardiner bowed to his host. "My wife and I are indeed honoured to be invited to such an auspicious occasion."

"I hope it will be the first of many visits, sir. You have not yet emptied my lake of fish." Mr Darcy replied, and his words gave Elizabeth much pleasure.

"I shall look forward to doing just that." Mr Gardiner beamed with delight.

Colonel Fitzwilliam entered the hall. "Darcy, Mrs Darcy, I am most pleased to be invited," he announced. "You both look decidedly well I see."

"Fitzwilliam," declared Mr Darcy as he moved forward to greet his oldest friend. "You are invited every year, how is it you sound so surprised?"

"Now you are a married man Darcy, I have to wait an invitation." both men laughed.

"Colonel Fitzwilliam, I am so pleased you could come," said Elizabeth. "I hope I have arranged everything to its usual high standard."

"I am sure you have Mrs Darcy. My anticipation grows by the minute. You know I am fond of lively music and good company."

"Then I hope you will find it in abundance at Pemberley, sir."

"I am sure I shall. I have never yet been disappointed."

Elizabeth suddenly realized that all her favourite people were now assembled in her home, and wished with all her heart that she could shut the door, and keep everyone else out. It was not to be, Caroline Bingley breezed in, and Elizabeth instantly felt the chill in the air.

"Mr Darcy," she said completely ignoring Elizabeth. "It is a pleasure to be at Pemberley once again. It holds so very many happy memories for me."

"Caroline, I am happy to bring you so much pleasure," Mr Darcy bowed slightly. "My wife is in full control of the arrangements for this evening, and I am sure she will make your stay a happy one."

Caroline looked at Elizabeth, and although she remained smiling the warmth of affection had disappeared. "Elizabeth, I am sure you have done your best, but this house has certain traditions that must be upheld. I am sure Mrs Reynolds has missed the expert advice of dear Lady Catherine. It must have been so dreadfully difficult for you Elizabeth, not being used to such immense gatherings."

"I do my best, Miss Bingley."

"I am sure you do Elizabeth, but you look so pale. I do hope the responsibilities you have taken upon yourself are not too much for you. The managing of an estate such as Pemberley, is a heavy mantle to carry, it must be quite wearing I am sure if you are unaccustomed to such society."

Elizabeth was determined that Caroline Bingley would not put her down in her own house. "I have generous support from my husband Caroline. He is ever careful that I do not tire myself too much."

The look Caroline bestowed on Elizabeth was enough to shrivel anyone's courage, but Elizabeth stood her ground.

"I think you will be pleasantly surprised at the arrangements this evening. Now if you will excuse me I must attend to my other guests. Mr and Mrs Hurst, you are very welcome to Pemberley."

"Thank you Mrs Darcy, we are so much looking forward to the amusements of this evening." Mrs Hurst curtsied.

Elizabeth was not sure which way to take this remark. Was the superior sister looking forward to the mistakes that would be made, or was she just being pleasant? The thoughts were pushed to the back of her mind, she was determined not to get paranoid.

"Where is dear Georgiana," Caroline's voice rose above the rest of the assembly. "I thought her duty would be here receiving her guests. You haven't banished her to the attics have you now Eliza?"

"Miss Darcy is at liberty to come and go as she chooses Miss Bingley. At present she is very much engaged with my younger sister, and their attire for this evenings ball."

"Your sisters, Eliza? Are they to be here too?" Caroline's tone was sarcastic.

"My sisters are always welcome under Mr Darcy's roof Miss Bingley.

Before the conversation could deteriorate any further Mr Darcy suggested everyone rested before the evenings events. Elizabeth walked the long gallery with Jane.

"She so infuriates me, Jane. How can she be so uncivil in Mr Darcy's own home?"

"Do not stress yourself, Lizzie. You know she wanted Mr Darcy for her own husband," replied Jane. "You have nothing to fear. Try to stay at a distance from her. Besides, Lizzie, there will be too many guests at the ball for her to cause too much offence."

"She will try, Jane, I am sure."

Jane laid her hand on her sister's arm. "If she can see her purpose is being achieved, Lizzie, it will give her much pleasure. You, Lizzie, are the mistress of Pemberley, not Caroline."

"My dear Jane, you are such a comfort. I do not know what I would do without your reason."

"Elizabeth," Georgiana had appeared at the far end of the gallery. "We are in great need of your assistance. May we beg a little of your time?"

"You can indeed, Georgiana. I will be there directly." Elizabeth replied. "Jane, you will be most surprised at the change in our sister Kitty. Miss Darcy has worked wonders with her. She is indeed a proper lady now. We intend to present her at the ball and give Mr Darcy much pleasure."

"Then I shall look forward to it with much anticipation, Lizzie. Away from Lydia's influence I am sure she is a very different person."

Elizabeth frowned. "Have you heard from Lydia since we

left Longbourne, Jane?"

"Not directly, but father informs me that she has gone back to the north with Mr Wickham.

"I hope all will be well with them now, Jane. I do not think father could endure any further adventures."

"No indeed. She is the cause of much concern to him I think."

"I will not detain you any further, Jane, you must indeed be very tired. I will go to Georgiana, and we will talk later."

Indeed there was no further chance of conversation with anyone before the ball started. Elizabeth spent time with Mrs Reynolds making sure that everything was as it should be. There was no way she wanted to embarrass Mr Darcy.

"Mrs Darcy, you show too much concern," Mrs Reynolds scolded her lightly. "My master will be more than pleased with the arrangements you have made. I am sure they are as good, if not exceeding those of other years."

"I thank you Mrs Reynolds, but this is the first time I have had to arrange such an occasion," Elizabeth frowned. "I would hate Mr Darcy to have to apologize for me."

"There will be no need for that ma'am I assure you. No-one could have worked harder, the house is a credit to you. Now go along with you and make yourself ready. You have many guests to greet, and if you do not hurry yourself, they will be here before you are ready.

Elizabeth relaxed a little. She took her leave of the housekeeper and headed for her own apartments to make ready for her first guests.

*****

"Elizabeth, you look exceptionally delightful this evening," Mr Darcy exclaimed as he entered his wife's bedchamber.

"I thank you, sir. I hope everything will be to your satisfaction this evening."

"I am sure it will be," Mr Darcy took her hand and kissed

it softly. "Come let us go down and start the festivities."

"Before we go, sir," Elizabeth said. "Georgiana has spent many hours at my sister Kitty's side helping her with the latest fashion and manner. I must confess the transformation is something to behold. She has gone to great lengths to keep the secret until this evening, I hope it meets with your approval."

"So this is why I have been deprived of my sister's company at dinner," he smiled. "I am sure whatever miracle my sister has performed on Miss Bennett, she will not compare in any way to the extraordinary beauty of my wife."

"I thank you, sir," Elizabeth blushed uncontrollably. These compliments from her husband always surprised and delighted her.

"I must say, your sister Jane looks exceedingly well this evening." Mr Darcy said has they descended the grand staircase.

"She does indeed, sir. I hope this evening's entertainments will not prove too much for her."

"Mr Bingley will take care of her I am sure. You cannot concern yourself about everyone's welfare. It is not possible."

"She is so very dear to me, sir. I would not like to see her distressed just to please me."

"I am sure she is wise enough to know when rest is needed," Mr Darcy replied.

"Darcy this is splendid," Colonel Fitzwilliam met them at the bottom of the staircase. "Mrs Darcy, you have excelled yourself, it does you much credit."

"Thank you Colonel Fitzwilliam. I confess it has caused me some sleepless nights."

"Well let me assure you, they were not suffered in vain," he continued. Upon my word I have never seen Pemberley looking so well. If your husband will permit me, I look forward to claiming one of this evening's dances with you Mrs Darcy. It is a delight I have not yet had the pleasure of."

"I am sure Mr Darcy will have no objections, sir,"

Elizabeth smiled at the handsome cousin of her husband. She liked Colonel Fitzwilliam very much. "Dancing is not one of Mr Darcy's favourite pastimes."

The ball progressed with much merriment. Elizabeth was congratulated many times on her excellent arrangements, and Kitty had the reception she had hoped for.

"I must say Elizabeth, your sister Kitty is indeed an outstanding beauty," Mr Darcy complimented his wife. "I am not sure how my sister Georgiana has managed this transformation, but she must be congratulated."

"I thank you, sir. It gives me great pleasure to know that it has had the effect it was designed for."

"Darcy, tell me at once," Colonel Fitzwilliam had joined them. "Who is that vision of delight talking to your sister Georgiana?"

"It is one of the younger Miss Bennett's Fitzwilliam. Elizabeth's sister Kitty."

"Then you must introduce me at once. She is, I declare, by far the prettiest girl in the room. I must have the honour of dancing with her, before I am passed all reason."

"Then we must relieve your suffering Fitzwilliam. I will introduce you immediately."

As soon as the introduction was completed Colonel Fitzwilliam took no time in claiming the following two dances. Elizabeth was proud to see her sister behaving as she wished her to. She stood watching them for some minutes and did not notice Caroline Bingley making her way towards her.

"Eliza, you have done very well," she announced. "You cannot have any hope of following in Lady Catherine's expert arrangements, but you have indeed surprised me with your efforts, I can see you have done your best."

"Thank you, Miss Bingley. Mr Darcy is happy with the arrangements, I am sure."

"Tell me, Eliza, how are you finding the living at Pemberley? You must find it a great change after the confines of Longbourne."

"Have you ever had the pleasure of visiting Longbourne,

Caroline?" Elizabeth asked in defiance.

"No," Caroline replied taken a little aback. "But Pemberley, Eliza, is like no other estate. It has a great many traditions to live up to. You cannot be expected to know them all."

"One gentleman's house is much like any other Miss Bingley. All be it on a larger scale."

"But the days, Elizabeth, must be very long when Mr Darcy is away engaged on business, and as for society, well you cannot possibly have made acquaintance with all of the Derbyshire's families." she sniggered into her hand.

"Mr Darcy rarely leaves my side, Miss Bingley," Elizabeth remembered Jane's words and stood her ground. "When he does travel to town alone, there are many delights at Pemberley that fill my day."

"How are you finding our society in town? It must be very different from what you have been used to."

"I find society very boring." replied Elizabeth, "Mr Darcy and I prefer our own company. Now if you will excuse me I have business with my sister Jane."

"Dear Jane," Caroline was reluctant to let Elizabeth go. "Tell me, how is she taking to motherhood. Mrs Hurst and I were so delighted when she married our dear Charles."

"It suits her very well I believe. Now I must beg your forgiveness, excuse me." Elizabeth made her way across to where Jane and Mr Bingley were sitting.

"Mrs Darcy, this is indeed excellent." Mr Bingley stood up. "Upon my honour, I have never seen Pemberley looking so grand."

"I thank you, sir. I confess without Mrs Reynolds I doubt if this ball would have taken place. She has been of great assistance."

"She is indeed a very able woman. If you will excuse me, I shall go and talk to Darcy while you sit with Jane."

"Lizzie, Colonel Fitzwilliam is paying Kitty a great deal of attention. This must be all down to you and Miss Darcy I think."

"She does certainly seem to have caught his eye. Georgiana has worked very hard with her indeed. Mr Darcy is most impressed with the transformation. O Jane, Caroline Bingley does not cease with her insults to me, in fact they are more direct now than before. How can you tolerate her with so much forbearance?"

"I am married to her brother, Lizzie. She has no authority in our household."

"If only I could feel the same way, but she is determined to belittle me in front of Mr Darcy."

"She may only achieve her purpose if you let her, Lizzie. Mr Darcy knows what she is I am sure. Believe me, the only damage she is doing is to herself."

"O Jane, you are so good. Have you seen mama since we left Longbourne together?"

"No, it was not wise for me to travel at this time, but I will make a visit as soon as I am able."

"Do take care, Jane. You are not yourself fully recovered."

"I am well, Lizzie, but I promise to be careful. I believe mama will very much miss my not being at Netherfield."

"It was not suitable to be settled so near Longbourne, Jane. Mama can be a very tiring visitor."

"She can indeed. Mr Bingley's patience was much tested." Jane sighed remembering her mother's frequent visits.

"Can I persuade you to take the next dance with me, Elizabeth?" Mr Darcy had appeared in front of them. "I notice your expected partner has found another distraction."

"He has indeed, sir. I fear he has not left her side since you introduced them." Elizabeth smiled then took the hand Mr Darcy was offering.

As they danced Elizabeth felt the eyes of many on them. She knew she would be the subject of much scrutiny this evening, and she wished to show everyone in the room, that Mr Darcy was still happy with his choice of wife.

"Miss Bingley offered me her condolences over the fact that my life has been much burdened since our marriage," Mr

Darcy said. "She is indeed a very offensive person."

"She is doing everything in her power to lower your good opinion of me, sir. I must confess it causes me much discomfort."

"You, my dearest Elizabeth are the only one who can achieve that demise. Her remarks are but a source of slight irritation to me."

The ball came to a close with no more unpleasant scenes. The guests who had been invited to stay gathered in the drawing room.

"Mrs Darcy, you did not tell me that you were hiding such a jewel within the confines of Longbourne," Colonel Fitzwilliam declared. "She is quite the most exquisite creature I have ever had the honour of dancing with."

"I thank you, sir. My sister is indeed blossoming into quite a beauty," Elizabeth smiled.

"Tell me," continued Colonel Fitzwilliam. "Is she to stay long at Pemberley?"

"Mr Darcy has been kind enough to offer Kitty an open invitation, sir. She is free to come and go as she pleases."

"I am delighted to hear it."

"Mrs Darcy," Mrs Hurst had joined them. "When are we to have the pleasure of your company in town?"

"I am not sure ma'am. I believe Mr Darcy wishes to spend the rest of the summer at Pemberley."

"It is a great loss to us, Mrs Darcy, that we are deprived of your company so very often. Society is suffering greatly I believe." Mrs Hurst said.

"I am sure Mr Darcy will return to town as often as business dictates Mrs Hurst, and we visit Southview often. Maybe we will have the pleasure of your company there in the not too distant future?"

"Dear Jane, to have moved accommodation, and given my brother a daughter, all in such a short space of time. It must be so very tiring for her. She is a dear girl."

"She is indeed, Mrs Hurst."

"Have you seen the new child yet Elizabeth?"

"Not as yet. I believe we are to travel to Southview at the end of the month."

"Such a dear child. My brother is delighted beyond all sense. I believe they are to call her Charlotte."

"I have not heard what her name is to be, but if it is to be Charlotte, as you inform me, then I am very pleased indeed." Elizabeth could not quite make out the manner in which Mrs Hurst was addressing her. It was indeed very friendly and open, not an insult to be heard.

"I trust you and your husband enjoyed the ball, Mrs Hurst?" Elizabeth inquired.

"We did indeed Mrs Darcy. Pemberley has always been a delight to me, and I can see that it will be more of a home than a house in the future."

"That is a great compliment, Mrs Hurst. I thank you." Elizabeth was more than surprised with this declaration.

"It must be beneficial for dear Georgiana to have a real home at last. I have always felt the loss of her dear mother to be a severe disadvantage to her."

"I am sure it was," replied Elizabeth. "Believe me Mrs Hurst, she will always have a home here as long as she requires it. She is very dear to me and I look on her as another sister."

"You are a good person Elizabeth. I extend my hopes and wishes that you will be very happy in your chosen life."

"I thank you," Elizabeth was more than puzzled by this change of attitude.

"Eliza," Caroline announced as she crossed the room. "I have just been talking to dear Jane about our niece. She sounds so delightful. Are you not intending to announce the arrival of an heir to Pemberley in the very near future?"

Elizabeth blushed with indignation. "When there is any news Miss Bingley, I am sure you will hear it through the usual channels. Excuse me Mrs Hurst." She turned and walked away. How could this woman be so openly insulting?

"Kitty and I would wish to play a duet we have been

practising Elizabeth," Georgiana intercepted her midway across the room. "Do you think it would be imprudent to play it now?"

"Not at all Georgiana. I am sure we shall all be delighted to hear it."

Elizabeth was grateful for this turn of events and went and sat on the settee next to her husband.

The piece was played beautifully, and without fault. It gave much pleasure to Mr Darcy and the remaining guests. Caroline Bingley, determined not to be outdone crossed over to the piano forte and struck up a tune that was both loud and out of context.

"That was very lively for this time of night Caroline," Mr Bingley said as the volume lowered.

"I thought everyone needed cheering up after this evenings entertainments," she announced without a blush of embarrassment. "We have, I believe, all missed the company of Lady Catherine. Is that not so Mr Darcy?"

"Until you mentioned it Caroline, it had not crossed my mind," Mr Darcy replied solemnly.

"This must be the first year she has not presided over Pemberley's summer ball," she continued.

As there was no answer, she stood up and walked in the direction of Mr Darcy. "I was telling Eliza earlier Mr Darcy, how very pale she was looking. I do hope the duties at Pemberley are not too much for her."

"Elizabeth is uniquely capable of managing Pemberley Caroline," Mr Darcy's face showed no expression. "Indeed her powers of organization are second to none."

"Mrs Reynolds must be a real treasure to you Eliza," she turned her attentions back to Elizabeth.

"She is indeed Miss Bingley. I am perfectly aware that I would not manage without her."

"It is time for us to retire my dear," Mr Darcy stood up. He had no wish to listen to Caroline's constant demoralization of his wife any longer.

"Eliza looks so ill, do you not think, Jane?" Caroline had no intention of changing the subject.

"My sister is very well Caroline, as you can see for yourself. I thought her exceptionally beautiful this evening." Jane replied. "Now I am in need of a good night's rest. Goodnight Caroline." She stood up, and followed by several other of the guests she left the room.

"Your sister is very ungracious towards poor, Lizzie," she said to her husband as they mounted the stairs.

"She is indeed," Mr Bingley replied with a deep sigh. "I do not know why she insists on doing it. It can only bring displeasure. Before Elizabeth married Darcy I could understand that it was maybe brought about by jealousy, but now? I have no idea what she hopes to gain through the way she expresses herself, Jane."

"May I be so bold as to suggest that you speak with her over this matter, and ask her to curb her displeasure. Even if only in society." Jane prompted. "I am convinced Mr Darcy will, in the future refuse to invite her to Pemberley."

"I will try, Jane," he sighed again. "but unfortunately Caroline listens to no-one."

When the guests had departed after lunch on the following day, Elizabeth took herself for a long walk around the many groves at Pemberley. She had missed her excursions over the past few days. There had been so much to attend to, she had not found the time to take her enjoyments of the gardens. She felt free and happy out here amongst the countryside, and at this time of year they were at their most pleasant. Her walk took her past a new plantation that Mr Darcy had designed. It was to hold trees from many different countries. Some had been given as presents, other acquired with great expense from far away places. It would be beautiful, she was sure. As she broke through the outer rim of the trees she was halted in her tracks. She could not believe what she was seeing. Gypsies had set up an encampment close to the river that flowed through the grounds. Although Mr Darcy had given his consent for the general public to walk or drive through the estate, Elizabeth did not think it extended to a whole camp full of people. No, she would have to report this finding to the steward. Her step quickened so she could be out of sight before any one of them noticed her presence. It wasn't that she was frightened, but the sight of the caravans did make her feel uneasy.

As she reached the safety of the immediate grounds, Elizabeth was surprised to see Mr Darcy walking towards her.

"Are you taking the air, sir?" she asked.

"No, not really Elizabeth. I wish to talk with you," he replied. "I have received a letter from Lady Catherine."

"O, sir, I am so pleased," exclaimed Elizabeth in delight. "I hoped she would mend the breach in your relations soon. I have always felt that I was the instrument of so much displeasure between you, and it has given me much pain."

Mr Darcy let Elizabeth finish her conversation before he continued. "It is not a letter of apology Elizabeth. It contains information that I fear will not lie well with you. It is of such a delicate nature, I can hardly bring myself to broach it to you."

"Whatever can it be, sir?" Elizabeth was most disconcerted. "Please feel at liberty to ask me anything you wish."

"The subject I have to address you on Elizabeth regards the heir to Pemberley."

Elizabeth felt her heart sink. It was as she thought, Mr Darcy had been expecting news of an heir for many months now, she was sure, and he was going to ask her why she had not produced one. But what had this to do with Lady Catherine? She felt her colour rise, but all she could manage to say was. "Oh."

"My aunt writes that a close cousin of mine is to return from the Far East, and wishes to visit us at Pemberley. It appears, by my aunt's letter that his parents have had a fatal accident, leaving him as sole beneficiary of their estates. His wish is now to return to England and make it his home."

"Then he will be most welcome, sir, but I cannot understand how this is related to the heir of Pemberley?"

"If anything should happen to me Elizabeth before a natural male heir is produced, then my cousin Edward Wentworth will, I fear, inherit the whole of the Pemberley estates."

This was not what Elizabeth was expecting to hear, a wave of relief flooded over her. "When...when do you expect his arrival, sir?" she asked in much confusion.

"The day after tomorrow, but do not distress yourself my love. On an estate such as this, precautions must be made," he had picked up on her discomfort, and it pained him that he had been forced to bring this subject to her attention at all. "It is of no reflection on either of us my dear. The Darcy estates are passed through the male line, and if we are lucky enough to have only daughters, then I feel we have to follow the lines of precaution."

Elizabeth knew that her husband was trying to make this conversation as easy on her feelings as he could, but the subject was very close to her heart, and she felt the insinuations keenly.

"I am sure in time we will have a male heir to take on the responsibilities of Pemberley, sir," she said at last.

"I have no doubt of it Elizabeth, but if anything unforeseen should happen to me before that happy event can take place, Pemberley's fate would be uncertain," he continued. "It is my duty Elizabeth to insure that my cousin is schooled in the business of the estate."

"Nothing must happen to you, sir. I know that I could not live without your company," Elizabeth was getting quite distressed.

"Think back Elizabeth to when I took a fall from my horse. My injuries could have been much more severe, and had it been fatal, the fate of these estates would have been left in the balance."

"I quite comprehend what you are saying, sir," Elizabeth started to calm down a little. "If you wish your cousin to visit Pemberley, I will make sure every hospitality is extended to him." It had dawned on her that her husband was struggling hard, between doing what he knew to be right, and trying not to discomfort his wife. Her heart went out to him in his discomfort. "I shall looked forward to his visit, sir with much pleasure."

"Thank you Elizabeth. I have no wish to upset you, but these matters must be attended to. I hope I have your understanding?"

"Indeed you do, sir."

"There is one other thing Elizabeth, Mr Wentworth brings with him a sister. She is, I believe Georgiana's age."

"Then I shall be more than happy to welcome her also. It will be much company for Georgiana and Kitty. Did Lady Catherine have any words of reconciliation in her letter, sir?"

"I am afraid not. It was a business letter, that is all."

"Maybe a reply would start to mend the wound, sir?"

"It may indeed. This rift between my aunt and myself is of great concern to you I fear."

"It is indeed, sir. It was, I believe our marriage that brought it about."

"If an answer to her letter will bring you pleasure Elizabeth I will attend to it."

"I thank you, sir, you are very kind."

They strolled back towards the house in silence until Elizabeth remembered the gypsy encampment. On relating her findings to her husband, she was much surprised to see he already knew of it.

"They camp here most years my dear. Apart from a little poaching, they cause very little damage."

"But are they safe, sir?" Elizabeth asked with more than a little concern.

Mr Darcy smiled. "What are you expecting them to do Elizabeth? Attack us in our beds?"

"No, sir, but we have always been taught to avoid any contact with gypsies."

"This family have been visiting the estate since my

grandfather's time. Trust me Elizabeth, they are quite safe, I assure you."

On entering the house they were met by Colonel Fitzwilliam, and Kitty.

"Darcy we are about to take a stroll of the gardens. I would ask you to join us, but I see you have already had the pleasure."

"We have indeed Fitzwilliam," replied Mr Darcy.

"The gardens are a sheer delight at this time of year Colonel Fitzwilliam," Elizabeth said. "I am sure you will get as much pleasure from them as we do."

"I am sure I shall Mrs Darcy, and may I say, this is turning out to be one of the most enjoyable of my visits. Music, dancing, lively conversation and good company, I am indeed fortunate."

"Then may it continue so," Darcy smiled.

"Is it the garden or your sister my friend finds so much pleasure in," Mr Darcy asked once they were out of earshot.

"The latter I am sure. Do you have any objections to the match, sir?"

"Not at all. They compliment each other very well. Indeed Elizabeth, you and Georgiana have created a very fine lady. Besides I have made a resolution never to interfere in the matters of the heart ever again."

"Thank you, sir, I am sure they will be very happy to know that they have your approval."

Mr Darcy retired to his study and Elizabeth went in search of Georgiana. She found her in the music room practising on the piano forte.

"Elizabeth," she exclaimed as Elizabeth entered.

"Please do not stop playing Georgiana. That piece sounded so very beautiful."

"I wish to talk with you over something Caroline said last evening."

"You look concerned Georgiana. I hope it did not cause you offence?"

"Not offence Elizabeth, but I am a little discomforted."

"What did she say to bring this about?"

"She suggested that I should not allow myself to be brought in on the conversations you have with my brother. The way you speak to him is not to be tolerated, she said."

"Did you ask her what her meaning was Georgiana?"

"I did and her reply was such that it confused me. She informed me that your way of talking was amusing to my brother at this time, but he would soon tire of it, and would then return to his equals. Time would put everything as it should be, was all she would say on the matter. What could she mean by it Elizabeth?"

"It must be very difficult for you Georgiana, but I think Caroline was very wrong to talk to you in such a manner. She wished, indeed I think expected Mr Darcy to take her as his bride. When this event did not happen, and his marriage to me took place, I believe she felt very deeply that your brother had married very much beneath himself. That is all."

"But my brother is very happy with you Elizabeth. He has told me so himself."

"I thank you Georgiana, I too have more happiness than I deserve, but Miss Bingley has not given up hope of securing your brother's affections. I believe she will do everything she can to achieve that purpose. She fears that myself and my relations will in time pollute the shades of Pemberley."

"That cannot be so Elizabeth. It makes me happy to see my brother so content."

"Then I assure you, I will do everything in my power to make it remain so. Now play me that wonderful piece again. I have a great yearning to hear it."

As Georgiana played Elizabeth tried to control her feelings. Caroline Bingley had no right to talk to Georgiana in that manner, it was not to be tolerated. She would speak with Mr Darcy over it. Caroline's jealousy must be stopped before it did some real harm. To involve Mr Darcy's sister in her spiteful revenge was unpardonable.

She mentioned it to Mr Darcy after dinner and was much

surprised at his response.

"Do not let it concern you Elizabeth. Caroline is indeed a bad loser, that is all."

"But to involve your sister, sir, surely this is not to be tolerated?"

"No, I admit she has gone too far there but I do not wish to enter into conversation with her on that level. We see her but rarely now Elizabeth, so I think we can overlook her discretions this once."

"As you wish, sir, but it pains me to see Georgiana so discomforted."

"Your feelings do you credit Elizabeth, but I am sure Caroline will soon see the error of her ways." Mr Darcy smiled at his wife. "You are the mistress of Pemberley now, and that is how I wish it to remain. Let Caroline take her pleasure at our expense, surely she can do but little harm."

The subject was dropped, although Elizabeth was not satisfied with Mr Darcy's views on the matter, she knew it would be of little use to continue the conversation. It would only invoke his temper, and this she wished to avoid at all costs.

Georgiana, Kitty and Colonel Fitzwilliam who had been amusing themselves on the pianoforte, choose at that moment to join their hosts.

"Darcy, I must say this house certainly has a different feel about it. Upon my word it defies explanation."

"For the better I hope?" Mr Darcy smiled.

"Indeed it is. There is a warmth about it that I have not encountered before."

"Then we must credit Elizabeth with the improvements," he smiled lovingly at his wife.

"I must say your arrangements for the ball were of the most excellent kind" Colonel Fitzwilliam continued. "Not a fault to be found."

"I thank you Colonel Fitzwilliam. I hope everyone was of the same opinion."

"I am sure they were. It was the most splendid evening.

Lady Catherine herself could not have done better."

Elizabeth spent the following morning at her desk writing letters to her mother and sister Jane. Her mother's condition was still causing much concern, and Elizabeth's thoughts were with her father, and Mary's future. If Mrs Bennett was to continue to be an invalid, then she was sure poor Mary's life would not be her own. She wrote as much in her letter to Jane, and touched on her promise to nurse her mother back to health at Pemberley. It was a promise made under the severest stress, and Elizabeth found to her discomfort, it was a promise she was not looking forward to full filling. The thought of Mrs Bennett under Mr Darcy's roof for many weeks was not one she wished to dwell on for too long. She felt very distressed that she could feel this way about her own mother, but if the past was anything to go on, the future did not bode well. Mrs Bennett's tongue had been the cause of much embarrassment to Mr Darcy. Pushing the thought to the back of her mind Elizabeth went in search of Mrs Reynolds.

"Do we have a room allocated for Mr Wentworth and his sister Mrs Reynolds?" she asked.

"Yes ma'am. The master has suggested the main bedroom in the west wing for Mr Wentworth, and the green room for his sister."

This surprised Elizabeth, as the bedrooms indicated were very regal indeed. This could only mean that Mr Darcy held his expected guests in the highest regard.

"I have promised Mr Darcy that we would extend every hospitality that Pemberley has to offer to his guests," she informed Mrs Reynolds.

"You can be assured ma'am that everything possible will be done to aid your guest's comfort."

"Thank you Mrs Reynolds. Do we have plans to open up the adjoining drawing room?"

"We do indeed ma'am. The master wishes Mr Wentworth especially, to have as much privacy as we are able to offer."

This information disturbed Elizabeth greatly. Was Mr

Darcy convinced in his own mind that they would never have a natural heir of his own, and was now going to spend time grooming his cousin for the future role as master of Pemberley?

Had there been more to the conversation they had shared in the garden, than was actually spoken? Elizabeth felt discomforted that her husband may be with holding the whole truth, all be it for her benefit. If only she could be with child, everything would be perfect.

Chapter 5

Mr Wentworth's appearance was not as Elizabeth had expected. Instead of muscular, and brusque, he was of slight build, a little shorter than Mr Darcy, quiet of manner and extremely elegant.

"I apologize profusely for invading your home in this way, sir," he said bowing low. "Lady Catherine would insist upon it, that I made this journey at this time."

"You are most welcome Mr Wentworth. May I introduce you to my wife Elizabeth, and my sister Georgiana."

"I am delighted to make your acquaintance Mrs Darcy, Miss Darcy. I hope my arrival has not disrupted your household too much?"

"Not at all Mr Wentworth," Elizabeth replied. "Indeed your arrival has been looked forward to with much pleasure."

"May I introduce my sister Sophia to you."

A girl of roughly eighteen years of age stepped from the carriage. She was dark haired and strikingly beautiful. Her smile lit up her face as she said. "My brother has told me so much about you I could not wait to see everything for myself."

"You are most welcome, Miss Wentworth," Mr Darcy bowed. "Please look on this as your home for the extent of your stay. This is my wife Mrs Darcy and my sister Georgiana."

After the introductions were completed everyone settled in the drawing room.

"You must find our climate very different after the Far East," Mr Darcy suggested.

"I do indeed, sir. I am decidedly grateful that England, at this time, is in full summer. Otherwise I fear we would not survive." he smiled, and the action transformed his face. He was indeed a very handsome young man. A few years younger than Mr Darcy, Elizabeth guessed, but he had that dark brooding look that was so prominent in her own husband.

"If you relate any preferences you may have to my wife, or my housekeeper Mrs Reynolds, they will be attended to at once." Mr Darcy offered.

"This is a warmer welcome than I had been led to expect. Indeed from Lady Catherine's account, I fully expected a more hostile environment."

"Lady Catherine has not visited Pemberley for quite some time. I doubt very much if she knows of the atmosphere here. I will admit after the death of my most excellent father, until the time my marriage took place to my dearest Elizabeth, Pemberley was not used as a home."

"It is far larger than my wildest dreams could imagine," Mr Wentworth continued. "On entering the grounds I feared for some time that we may never see the house."

Everyone laughed at this, and it brought back memories to Elizabeth, of the first time she had visited Pemberley, in the company of her aunt and uncle Gardiner, she too had had the same feeling.

"I know you have only this minute arrived Mr Wentworth, but Mrs Darcy and myself are due to embark on a two-day visit to the next county. It is something that I do not wish to postpone. May I beg your forgiveness, and suggest that you use this time to acquaint yourself with the geography of the building and grounds."

"That sounds most delightful, Mr Darcy. In fact I would prefer it this way. My sister and I will have plenty to occupy ourselves with, so please do not concern yourself."

"My sister Georgiana, and Miss Bennett, will remain if you have any concerns on any subject. Please feel you have the freedom to explore at will. I am sure my sisters will have much to talk of with your sister."

"I am sure they will. Sophia is very keen to learn of the latest fashions in England."

"I am, sir, and the ways of your society." Sophia's voice was soft and musical.

"Then we shall have much to do," Georgiana said. "I am sure your return will come before we are the least bit ready Mr Darcy."

"Then I am sorry I will not be missed," Mr Darcy feigned hurt. "Maybe I will not go after all."

"O but Elizabeth is so excited about seeing her new niece. You would not deprive her of that pleasure?"

"Then I shall have to go and risk being forgotten by my nearest relatives." Everyone laughed, and it pleased Elizabeth very much that Mr Darcy felt, at last that he could exhibit his sense of humour in public.

"We will be but two days, sir," she said. "I am sure no-one will forget you in that time Mr Darcy."

*****

"O Lizzie, I am so pleased you have come," Jane said as she greeted her sister. "I was sure Charlotte would have been too far grown before you have seen her."

"I doubt if I could have stayed away that long, Jane," Elizabeth hugged her sister. "Besides, it is less than two weeks since the summer ball."

"Come inside, Lizzie, you will love her as I do, she is the dearest thing."

As Elizabeth looked down into the cradle she experienced severe pains of longing. Why could she not have a child of her own. She felt tears of frustration spring to the back of her eyes, but quickly blinked them away.. "She is lovely, Jane, you are very lucky."

"I am, Lizzie, and Mr Bingley will not leave her side unless he has to."

"Mama will be delighted to see her. Will you be taking her to Longbourne soon?"

"I believe she will be able to travel in a month or two, Lizzie. Below that would be to risk her health. Come let us go down and join the others in the drawing room."

"Is our daughter to your satisfaction Mrs Darcy?" Mr Bingley asked with pride.

"She is delightful Mr Bingley. I congratulate you."

"You must see her Darcy, indeed she is the most beautiful

of all things."

"I shall very much look forward to the pleasure."

"I have been so bold as to invited some guests for dinner this evening Darcy, I would very much like your opinion on them." Mr Bingley became serious. "They are our neighbours here and have recently returned from France."

"Their name, sir? Do we know them through society?"

"Their name is Randal. Two brothers. One is a great deal older than the other. I do not believe we have ever met them before. Like I say they have been abroad for some years. Their father was Sir Elliot Randal I believe."

"Then I shall be happy to make their acquaintance." Mr Darcy frowned slightly. "I do believe our paths may have crossed some years before but I cannot bring the facts to mind at present."

"Their family estate goes back many years I believe, but most of their time is spent across the water." Mr Bingley explained.

"Then I shall be happy to give my opinion on them Bingley."

When the two guests arrived later that evening they caused quite an impression with the ladies. Their appearance was decidedly elegant, but more colourful than the usual attire of the gentlemen of England.

"We are most honoured to accept your invitation Mr Bingley," the older one spoke first. "My brother and I are not acquainted with the English way of life. Neither of us have ever set foot in this country before this month."

"You are very welcome, sir. May I introduce you to my friend Mr Darcy. Mr Darcy's estate is in the neighbouring county."

Both men bowed.

"I am delighted to meet you Mr Darcy. Indeed I have heard much of your family history. I believe my father and yours were acquainted before the move to France. He had much regard for your father I believe. May I introduce my brother

James."

The younger Mr Randal stepped forward and bowed, he was very different from his brother. His speech had an accent that was most attractive, and his air was far more confident.

"I am delighted to meet you Mr Darcy."

When all introductions had taken place everyone went into dinner.

"How long do you plan to stay in this country Mr Randal," Mr Bingley asked.

"The family estate has been shut down for over twenty years Mr Bingley, it is our intention to re-open the house and make it our home." Ross Randal explained.

"Then I shall look forward to introducing you into society, sir." Mr Bingley said.

"You are very kind. I believe we will find society very different from what we have been used to."

"What circumstance prompted your return to England after so many years, sir?" Mr Darcy asked.

"My brother has now come of age, and I felt it was time to acquaint him with the routes of his family."

"Have you cut all ties with France, sir or are your intentions to spend time there in the future?" Mr Bingley inquired.

"Our chateaux produces a very fine wine Mr Bingley; I would not like to sever a connection with such a source of pleasure. You must allow me to send you a selection for your opinion."

"You are most generous, sir."

The evening was passed pleasantly with music and much conversation. The younger brother entertained the ladies with stories of France, while Ross Randal held conversation with Mr Darcy.

"You will find society more restricted in England I think Mr Randal." Darcy suggested.

"That may not be a bad thing Mr Darcy. I fear my brother is a little too fond of the ladies. As your father was a friend of my own, I feel I am safe in explaining to you that my brother is, I fear a little wayward. I am of the opinion that, away from his preferred society, his character may be saved."

"This is disturbing news indeed Mr Randal," Mr Darcy frowned. "I hope your wish meets with success."

Mr Randal sighed heavily. "Society, in Paris is very free Mr Darcy, my brother, being both handsome and wealthy attracts many followers. It is not a good combination."

"You will find our society has much the same trend I fear."

"The short while it will take to acquaint ourselves with English society, will, I hope be enough to persuade my brother to act in a more gentlemanlike manner."

"If I may be of assistance in any way Mr Randal, I wish you to feel comfortable to call at anytime."

"You are most kind, sir. My wish is to restrain his interests within a small number of friends for the present, and hope he will attend to his ways."

"I hope your intentions are successful, sir."

*****

On their return to Pemberley Mr Darcy and Elizabeth were delighted to find everyone in good spirits. Mr Wentworth and his sister had acquainted themselves with the house, and the immediate grounds and were much impressed.

"This is indeed a very fine house Mr Darcy," Mr Wentworth announced. "My sister is of the opinion that once one strays from the security of the drawing room, there is a great risk that one will never be seen again. Their fate would be to wander the corridors in the hope of rescue."

"Then we must ensure that she is accompanied at all times until she feels confident of her position." Mr Darcy said solemnly.

"Your sisters have been delightful company. Indeed I cannot remember when I have felt so content." Miss Wentworth said.

"I am happy to hear it."

Over the next few days Mr Darcy spent his time, either in the study with Mr Wentworth, or riding through the estate.

The evenings were passed pleasurably with music, games and stimulating conversation. Indeed Mr Wentworth turned out to be a very fine musician.

Colonel Fitzwilliam had reluctantly returned to his many business interests, before Elizabeth had left to visit Southview, and it was with concern she noticed Kitty's change in attitude on her return. She was very quiet and reflective.

"Are you missing the attentions of Colonel Fitzwilliam Kitty?" she asked when they were alone together.

"O Lizzie, I confess he is so much in my mind, Truly he is one of the most amiable men I have ever met."

"I am very pleased to hear it Kitty, and I am proud of the way you have conducted yourself in his presence."

Kitty frowned. "I can see now what you and Jane meant about Lydia's behaviour, Lizzie. She acts very forward."

"It is all part of growing up Kitty. The likes of Colonel Fitzwilliam would not like a flirt for a wife."

Kitty blushed. "Do you think he likes me in that way, Lizzie?"

"You are definitely the reason for his extended visit. He likes you very much, I am sure."

"I do hope you are right, Lizzie, but he left without mentioning a return visit."

"He will be back Kitty, you may depend upon it." Elizabeth smiled at her younger sister's confusion. "Now Kitty there is a more serious matter on which I need to speak to you. I think one of us should pay a visit to mama. Father and Mary have had to shoulder the burden of Mrs Bennett's illness alone, and I feel we should offer them a little help in that quarter. With Mr Wentworth and his sister in the house, I feel under an obligation to support Mr Darcy at this time, and extend the hospitalities of Pemberley, so I fear the task will fall on you to visit mama."

"I do not mind going, Lizzie. When would you wish me to leave?"

Elizabeth marvelled at the change in attitude of her younger sister. "I think tomorrow Kitty, but please do not distress yourself that you are being sent away. Indeed your return will be much looked forward to. Mr Darcy is indeed very happy with your company, especially in regard to his sister."

"I like Georgiana, Lizzie, she has such an affectionate nature."

"She does indeed. I am now going for a walk in the garden Kitty, would you be so good as to inform Mrs Reynolds of your intended departure."

Elizabeth enjoyed a full hour wandering the garden of Pemberley, then on her way back to the house she encountered Mr Wentworth on one of the adjoining paths.

"Mrs Darcy, what a delightful surprise. I confess I am reluctant to wander too far from the house, in case I never find it again."

Elizabeth laughed, she liked this young man very much. "I encountered the same problem when I first came to live here, sir."

"May I be so bold as to inquire how long you have been married to Mr Darcy?"

"Above nine months, sir."

"He is the most agreeable of men I find," Mr Wentworth continued. "He has made my visit most interesting."

"Have you never met before, sir?"

"When I was but I child I believe. My memories of the meeting are not at all clear. Lady Catherine's views on Pemberley are far from what I am experiencing. Indeed she informed me in her letter that, standards of the Darcy estate had been much lowered in recent months. I do not understand her meaning. Do you have any idea what she could mean by that remark Mrs Darcy?"

"Lady Catherine feels that Mr Darcy married beneath himself when he made an alliance with me Mr Wentworth. My relations are not to the high standard she would have wishes for the Pemberley estates."

"I understand what you are saying Mrs Darcy. Is there a

sense of ill feeling between Mr Darcy and his aunt?"

"A little reluctance to accept me as Mr Darcy's wife, that is all. I am sure all will turn out well given time."

"With this turn of events, I find myself feeling much sorrow for Lady Catherine. She does not know the welcome she is missing."

"Thank you, sir, you are very generous." Although Mr Wentworth's presence at Pemberley disturbed her very much, Elizabeth found it increasingly hard to atone any blame to this pleasant young man.

"Pray tell me, sir, is your sister settling in to the ways of Pemberley?"

"She is indeed ma'am. Only yesterday she informed me of her great delight in being here."

"I am pleased to hear it." Elizabeth smiled. "I will talk with her directly and discover if she has any wish to go to town for a few days."

"I am sure she will be happy to involve herself in any plans you may have Mrs Darcy."

The following morning Elizabeth received a letter that shocked and grieved her. It was from her father informing her that her best friend Charlotte Collins had died in childbirth. Mr Bennett continued that Mr Collins was beside himself with grief, and Mary had immediately travelled down to Huntsford to offer any assistance that she could. The baby had fortunately survived, but Charlotte had succumbed to an haemorrhage and passed away the following day. Her father suggested that, if at all possible, a letter of condolence, or better still, a visit would be most beneficial at this time.

"O my poor Charlotte. My dear sweet Charlotte," Elizabeth exclaimed. "I must find Mr Darcy at once."

On relating this most distressing of news to her husband, she was much comforted to discover that he had every intention of travelling to Huntsford with her.

"This news is grievous indeed, but please my dearest sweetest Elizabeth do not distress yourself." Mr Darcy was full of concern for his wife's discomfort. "Georgiana, Edward and Miss Wentworth will all travel down to Huntsford with you. Indeed this may be the right time to visit my aunt."

"Thank you, sir, you are very kind."

They travelled to Huntsford the next day, and while Elizabeth and Mr Darcy went to visit Mr Collins, the rest of the party went directly to Rosings Park.

"Mr Darcy, my dear cousin Elizabeth," Mr Collins greeted them. "My poor dear Charlotte, taken from me in the prime of life."

"You have our deepest sympathy, sir," Mr Darcy said. "My wife is very much distressed by your loss."

"I do not know how my life will continue without my dear Charlotte for support. Indeed we were but one," Mr Collins continued. "She was the very essence of my being. Indeed she was."

"Your child survived Mr Collins," Elizabeth inquired.

"Indeed she did cousin Elizabeth. A little girl, the image of her dear mother." Mr Collins explained. "How Charlotte would have loved her, but it is not to be. My heart is broken, without hope of ever being the same again." He paused for a few seconds to steady his emotions before he had the voice to continue. "Lady Catherine has been kindness itself. Nothing has been beneath her concern. Indeed she is the rock on which I lean in these troubled times. She was so fond of my dear Charlotte. Cousin Elizabeth what will be my course of action now. A child hardly five days old, and no mother to comfort it."

"Mr Collins my heart goes out to you in your grief. Indeed Charlotte was the kindest, most generous, devoted friend one could have wished for," she was surprised how deep her cousins feelings were. By his face you could tell that he had spent many a night awake.

"Are there any arrangements we may have the privilege to be of assistance with Mr Collins." Mr Darcy asked.

"Your kindness does you much credit, sir. I am deeply

honoured that you hold my dear Charlotte in such high esteem as to lend your attentions to her at this time." Mr Collins replied.

"Your wife Mr Collins was the subject of much affection to Mrs Darcy."

"We … I am deeply humbled by your concern, sir. Indeed together with my most esteemed benefactor, Lady Catherine de Burgh. I am the most privileged of men."

"If we can be of any support at all, sir," Mr Darcy continued. "Our stay at Rosings will be settled for the foreseeable future."

"Your concern is more than I deserve, sir," Mr Collins bowed low.

"Is my sister Mary still a visitor in your home, sir," Elizabeth asked.

"My dear cousin attends to my daughter cousin Elizabeth. She has indeed been a great source of strength to me."

"May I visit with her Mr Collins?"

"You may indeed cousin Elizabeth. Lady Catherine has been so good as to engage a wet nurse for my daughter," he replied. "You will find all parties in the nursery."

Elizabeth climbed the stairs, her heart heavy and sad. Dear Charlotte, to pass away when one is so young. It was a bitter pill indeed.

Elizabeth entered the nursery to find Mary sitting near the cradle reading a book. "Elizabeth, it is good of you to come. I felt strongly that it was my duty to be with Mr Collins at this time. One does not know the sense of bereavement until one experiences it for themselves."

"Your probably right Mary. How is mama managing without you?"

"Kitty is there, with Hill and the nurse. One has to put priorities in there proper place Elizabeth."

"How long do you intend to stay at Huntsford Mary?"

"My presence here will be needed for some duration I think. Mr Collins was good enough to visit with us when Lydia ran away, so it falls on us to repay his generous nature where ever possible."

"I am sure it does Mary," Elizabeth said with concern, "but you have little knowledge of babies Mary, and Lady Catherine will, I feel sure, have matters well in hand. She will ensure the health and happiness of Mr Collins and his daughter will be uppermost in her mind I think."

"For all her good works Elizabeth, Lady Catherine is not a relation. It is up to his family to attend to his needs, and bring him comfort at this time."

"Do not take so much upon yourself Mary. You have your own life to consider you know."

"Mr Collins has been kind enough to extend an invitation to me, to enjoy the many books his library has to offer. Mr Collins is, Elizabeth, a great source of inspiration to my spiritual being."

"Take care Mary. This is not a game you are playing."

After looking at the small infant, and suffering pangs of longing for her own short comings, Elizabeth returned to the two gentlemen in the parlour.

"Cousin Elizabeth, my dear Charlotte has left me a living memory of herself. Indeed you must agree?" Mr Collins said.

"I do indeed Mr Collins. Your daughter is, as you say, a miniature of my dear friend. Are Sir William and Lady Lucas intending to pay you a visit, sir?"

"Lady Lucas is very much grieved by the death of her daughter, as indeed we all are. She is at this moment at Rosings Park being comforted by my gracious benefactor Lady Catherine herself. Dear Maria is with her and I fear in very grave spirits. My dear sister in law is beside herself with grief over this matter. She was so attached to her dear sister. Sir William remains by their side. This is a very sad time for us all cousin Elizabeth."

"It is indeed, sir. It pains me to see you so discomforted."

"He bowed low. "Your concern is of great comfort to me my dear young cousin."

"We will leave you now Mr Collins," Mr Darcy said. "Be sure to send word if there is anything we may assist you with."

"You do me great honour, sir."

Elizabeth and Darcy had just entered their carriage when Jane and Mr Bingley drove up.

"O Lizzie, I knew you would be here. I came to give you comfort at this time." Jane's face was full of concern for her beloved sister. "Charlotte meant so much to you I am sure."

"Jane I am so pleased to see you," Elizabeth said holding her sister for a few seconds." Indeed your presence at this time is of great comfort to me. Dear Charlotte, taken from us so young."

"My secondary concern was for the baby," Jane continued. "Has a wet nurse been found for her do you know?"

"Lady Catherine has been good enough to secure everything that is needed." Elizabeth smiled.

"I am sure she has," Jane smiled back. They were interrupted at this time by Mr Collins.

"Mrs Bingley." he exclaimed. "So very many illustrious personages visiting my humble abode. I am indeed overawed."

"Mr Collins, we are so distressed with your loss," Jane said. "We had to make this journey to insure that you, and your daughter were given every assistance."

"I am honoured indeed my dear cousin Jane, and you so newly delivered of a child yourself. It must give you much pain to be parted from it so soon."

"It does indeed Mr Collins, but I feel at this time, your own daughter should be at the forefront of all our minds."

"You are most gracious my dear cousin. My home will be made over to you for the duration of your stay."

"You are very kind, sir."

Mr Darcy and Mr Bingley were conversing not far from their wives.

"I say Darcy, this is the most devastating thing," Mr Bingley exclaimed to his friend. "I am at odds to think how I would feel had it been my dear Jane."

"It is a very sad time indeed Bingley. It brings Elizabeth much pain."

"Are you to stay at Rosings Park?" Bingley asked.

"Lady Catherine as been good enough to extend an invitation, but I fear the reception will be a decidedly chilly one."

"Up on my word Darcy, this must be a time for forgiveness. Even for Lady Catherine."

Darcy smiled at the earnest face of his friend. "Let us hope you are right Bingley. My aunt has been known to hold a grudge for many years, and her opposition to Elizabeth was great indeed."

"But surely now you are married, she must be settled in her own mind?"

"One would like to think so. My aunt has a tendency to prolong discomfort. Once thwarted her retaliation can extend for a considerable amount of time, and through many channels."

"Then let us hope this is not one of those times Darcy. Elizabeth has had much to suffer already."

Mr Collins now joined them. "Mr Bingley, I am indeed honoured. Your dear wife has offered to attend to my daughter. Believe me, sir, she does me a great service."

After further conversation Elizabeth and Darcy proceeded to Rosings, but not before they had promised to return shortly.

"Fitzwilliam!" Lady Catherine exclaimed on their entrance. "You do Mr Collins a great honour, but I suppose it is more to do with Elizabeth's feelings than the situation you find here."

"My wife is indeed distressed over this matter aunt," Mr Darcy replied.

"Dear Mrs Collins, she was such a genteel sort of person. Indeed this tragedy is not to be born." Lady Catherine stated. "You will find the house has many visitors Fitzwilliam. Dear Caroline Bingley and Mr and Mrs Hurst have endowed us with their company. Sir William and his family are in the drawing room.

Elizabeth felt her heart drop, Caroline Bingley was the one person she could well do without at this time. Up until this point Lady Catherine had paid her no attention.

"Elizabeth, I did not agree with your marriage to my nephew," she announced. "Indeed the manner of our last meeting left me most displeased, but it is done, and Pemberley will have to pay the price. It grieves me to see it."

"Elizabeth has brought much joy to Pemberley, aunt," Mr Darcy spoke in his wife's defence. "Indeed it has been remarked on by more than one visitor."

"It is your choice of life Fitzwilliam. I have no more to say on the matter. Elizabeth, the death of your friend must, I think, hang heavy on you."

"It does indeed, ma'am. I have never experienced so much grief, the pain is great indeed."

Lady Catherine's face softened a little.

"Eliza, we meet again, so soon." Caroline Bingley had entered the room. "Mr Darcy this is a most pleasant surprise."

"Caroline, we were not informed of your stay." Mr Darcy greeted her with distant respect.

"It was to be a surprise. We travelled down with dear Charles and Jane."

Elizabeth was convinced that Caroline had made the journey especially to see what reception Lady Catherine offered. If there was any possibility of putting Elizabeth in discomfort, Caroline was sure to be at the centre.

"It must be extremely daunting for you Eliza to be invited to stay in a house such as this. It cannot be at all what you are used to," she spoke quietly, well out of earshot of Mr Darcy.

"It is indeed Miss Bingley, but then I have your presence to guide me." Elizabeth was determined not to give Caroline any satisfaction.

This comment from Elizabeth temporally silenced Caroline, so she turned her attentions to Lady Catherine.

"To have so many varied personages under your roof at

the same time must be of concern to you Lady Catherine. Indeed it must make the entertainments very difficult indeed."

"I am used to entertaining heterogeneous gatherings Miss Bingley. My life has been far reaching and varied."

"I am sure it has Lady Catherine," Caroline smiled, she did not want to encourage Lady Catherine's disapproval. "There are few people who have the talent to preside over such gatherings."

Lady Catherine gave her a look that was a mixture of both perplexed and pleased.

"Mr Darcy, Mrs Darcy," Mrs Hurst was now in the room. "This must be an extremely sad journey for you to make. I was quite devastated when Jane told me."

"It is indeed Mrs Hurst," Elizabeth replied. "Charlotte was the most genteel person I have known."

"I had not the pleasure of knowing her for myself," Mrs Hurst continued, "but I did see her at a party Sir William gave. A very pretty girl, if I may say so."

"I thank you Mrs Hurst. She will be greatly missed."

"Mr Darcy," she turned her attention away from Elizabeth. "We were all most concerned when we heard of your accident. I do hope you are now well recovered?"

"I am indeed, thank you Mrs Hurst." Mr Darcy replied.

"Such an unfortunate happening, it must have caused Mrs Darcy much concern."

"Elizabeth was kindness itself. I have her to thank for my speedy recovery."

"Sir William and his party are about to return to the parsonage," Lady Catherine's voice rose over the hum of conversation.

"Then Elizabeth and I will accompany them," Mr Darcy replied.

"What, go back to the parsonage? I have ordered dinner for us all Fitzwilliam," Lady Catherine sounded put out.

"Mr Bingley and his wife have made a sudden visit," Mr Darcy explained. "I feel it only right that we should dine with them. This is, I believe their first visit to Huntsford."

"If that is the case, I will be very happy to receive them at my table. Send a servant with an invitation at once."

"You are very kind, aunt." replied Mr Darcy.

"Elizabeth, your sister I believe has recently been delivered of a child of her own?"

"She has indeed Lady Catherine. A daughter, less than a month old."

"Then she must take great care of herself. This travelling around the country will not be beneficial at all."

"I believe my sister travelled to be of comfort to me ma'am. She fully understands the relationship between Charlotte and myself."

"Her motives do her credit, but there are times when one's own condition must be paramount. Where is she staying."

"At the parsonage with Mr Collins ma'am. I believe, having just had a child herself, that she will be of assistance at this time."

"I am sure she will," Lady Catherine replied. "She sounds to be a very caring sort of a gal."

"She is indeed ma'am," smiled Elizabeth. "I believe I cannot think of a single time when a selfish word has passed her lips. She has the sweetest disposition."

"Then I shall be pleased to make her acquaintance," Lady Catherine made it clear that their conversation was at an end.

"Eliza," Caroline was back at her side. "It is such a fine evening, would you be so good as to take a stroll in the garden with me?"

This was one thing Elizabeth did not wish to do, but the thought of fresh air gave her the courage to agree.

"How are you finding Pemberley Eliza?" Caroline asked in a sickly sweet voice.

"I like it very well indeed," Elizabeth replied.

"It must be so very hard for you after Longbourne. The traditions and ways of Pemberley have been set for many generations. Only someone brought up in that social circle could possibly be expected to understand them."

"There is nothing wrong in change Miss Bingley. A fresh mind may, I believe prove to be nothing but beneficial."

"There are standards to be adhered to Eliza. The people on the estate expect Pemberley to remain unchanged."

"In essentials I agree with you," replied Elizabeth. "Progress however cannot be stopped. It is after all the very essence of our existence."

"Elizabeth," Mr Darcy had followed them into the garden. "I think you should rest before dinner. This has been a very tiring day for you."

"I was just saying to Eliza Mr Darcy, how difficult it must be to uphold the traditions of Pemberley," she smiled sweetly at him.

"Elizabeth will manage Pemberley as she sees fit Miss Bingley." replied Mr Darcy. "She has indeed been a breath of fresh air that has been badly needed on the estate for some time."

Caroline, not getting the reply she had hoped for, fell silent and followed Darcy and Elizabeth into the house, where Mr Bingley and Jane were waiting.

"Lizzie, you look so pale. Come you must rest," Jane said with concern.

"I have just suggested the same thing," Mr Darcy agreed. "Go with Jane to your room my love. Her company will be most beneficial to you."

The two sisters left the room, but before Caroline Bingley could attach herself to Mr Darcy, he addressed his aunt.

"I have need to talk with you, aunt. It is a matter on which I would value your opinion."

This seemed to please Lady Catherine, she rose and led the way into a small ante chamber.

"I wish to address you on the subject of Mr Wentworth and his sister, aunt, but before I proceed, I would like to clear up the matter of my marriage to Elizabeth. I know it was done against your better judgement, but it brings me great happiness. A happiness deeper than I have ever experienced before."

"That may be the case Fitzwilliam, but you have broken your own dear mother's heart. It was her dearest wish that you should be united to my own dear daughter Anne. It had been arranged since she was in her cradle. For Pemberley to have such relations attached to it is a disgrace. Your dear father would certainly not have allowed it."

"I perfectly comprehend your feelings, aunt."

"If that was so Fitzwilliam you would have taken my advice in the beginning. I cannot believe that you could bring such shame on the name of Darcy. Indeed it is most unsatisfactory."

Although Lady Catherine continued to slight his wife, Mr Darcy was determined not to make relations worse between them. "My marriage to your daughter was not one that I could in all fairness contemplate. Her delicate nature ruled out the prospect of her ever carrying the responsibilities that the mistress of Pemberley demanded. I would not have been able to bear the burden of putting my cousin Anne under a stress that would have undoubtedly added to her already delicate condition. No, aunt, it has been several years now since I realized that Anne required a far more gentle way of life. My life is such that it involves much travelling, and entertaining. I fear that this would have been too much for her to tend."

This declaration was a surprise to Lady Catherine, she had indeed expected Mr Darcy to make a stand in his wife's honour.

"You have been most deceitful Fitzwilliam," she said at last. "If, as you say, you have been thinking for some time, why did you not mention it in my presence. My poor Anne has been living under a falsehood of your promises."

"I have made no promises to Anne, aunt."

"No, that is true, but it was always understood Fitzwilliam, by all parties."

"I have been most wrong in my actions, aunt. I have lived in the hope that a younger, more sensible gentleman would capture your daughter's affections."

"This is not like you Fitzwilliam, to shirk your responsibilities. If what you say is true, then your thoughts do you much credit, but it doesn't alter the position of Elizabeth's unfortunate relations."

"Unfortunate is the right word, aunt. You have indeed an excellent mind. I cannot hold it against Elizabeth that her mother is of lowly birth. Indeed my marriage to Anne would have been most beneficial to all parties, but it would have been most ungenerous of me to force the issue, and cause her, and your excellent self, much discomfort. Her condition is such that the doubts are high of her ever being strong enough to bear the sons Pemberley needs to secure its future."

"And where are the signs that Elizabeth will bring a son to Pemberley. I have not received any information from that quarter?"

"It has been my choice to withhold the immediate start of a family. It is indeed no reflection on my wife. I wish to give Elizabeth time to immerse herself in the ways of Pemberley. It was my fervent hope, aunt, that you would be of great assistance in this matter."

"Why did you not explain this to me before Fitzwilliam, it would have saved much displeasure?"

"And have you think the worst of me, aunt? It would have served no purpose."

Lady Catherine allowed a slight smile to cross her face. "Does Elizabeth know she was second choice?"

Mr Darcy turned away, the smile on his face hidden from his hostess.

"This must be our secret, aunt. It would bring Elizabeth much pain if it became common knowledge. I will now have to rely on your discretion."

"Not a word will pass my lips Fitzwilliam. You have my promise."

"Thank you, aunt. I am deeply indebted to you. Now may we talk about the situation of Mr Wentworth and his sister?"

"Dear Edward. He is in desperate need of your guidance Fitzwilliam. The tragic loss of his parents has left him with only a sister as family. You, of all people should be able to understand his situation, having been in the same position yourself. I am relying on you to see that he is schooled in every aspect of both our estates."

"Is it your wish that he remains at Pemberley for a long duration, aunt, or would you like to see him settled in a property of his own?"

"I will leave it with you Fitzwilliam," replied Lady Catherine, "but I believe it will be in everyone's best interest to contain him within the boundaries of Pemberley until he has become accustomed to our ways. He has known no other life than the Far East since the age of eight. I leave his education in your hands," she stood up. "Now let us join the rest of the guests."

After dinner when all parties were gathered in the music room, Elizabeth was surprised, even alarmed to find Lady Catherine actively seeking out her company.

"Elizabeth, as you are well aware, I was most certainly not in agreement with your marriage to my nephew, but his explanation has brought new light to the matter. I admit now to the neglect of my duties towards you. From today forwards you may rely totally on my experience in the matters of Pemberley."

Elizabeth was shocked, she looked across at her husband, who smiled mischievously. No doubt he would explain this turn of events later, she thought.

"How you must have struggled these last few months Elizabeth," Lady Catherine continued. "Still it is a case of not owning up to one's own thoughts. The blame must fall directly at Fitzwilliam's door."

"Indeed there has been a great deal for me to learn," Elizabeth replied. "The responsibility of managing Pemberley in indeed very heavy. Mrs Reynolds has been of great assistance, without her guidance I would not have managed."

"Your worries are at an end now Elizabeth. I will travel to Pemberley with Anne tomorrow fortnight, and we will go through the duties together."

Elizabeth's heart sank, this was going to be far worse than the worry of broken relationships, she was sure.

Caroline Bingley was vexed indeed to see the two women talking so intimately. She wandered over in the hope of overhearing the conversation, but all she heard was Elizabeth's reply.

"Your Ladyship is very kind. I shall look forward to your visit with much pleasure."

"Eliza," Caroline smiled. "How nice to see you so well settled within the family. You have exceeded all my expectations."

"Thank you Caroline. If you will excuse me Lady Catherine I wish to talk with my sister," Elizabeth did not know how she managed to cross the room without screaming.

"O Jane, Mr Darcy has been talking to his, aunt. Of their conversation I know nothing, but the outcome is that she intends taking me under her instruction. She threatens to visit Pemberley two weeks from now."

"Lizzie, it is a great compliment that she wishes to visit you," Jane smiled at her sister's agitation. "Mr Darcy has indeed been clever if he has persuaded Lady Catherine to his way of thinking. I feared she would never talk to you again."

"In some ways I wish she would not, Jane."

"That is unkind, Lizzie. I know you do not mean it."

"How will I tolerate her interference? It is bad enough having her company for a few hours, but weeks of it, Jane. I am sure I shall not be able to bear it."

"I am sure you will win her over, Lizzie, you have the disposition.," Jane consoled her sister. "Who is the young gentleman playing the pianoforte with Mr Darcy's sister, Lizzie?"

"He is Mr Darcy's cousin. He and his sister have just arrived in England from the Far East. If I do not present Mr

Darcy with a natural heir, Jane, the estate will be entailed away to Mr Wentworth."

"He is a very good looking gentleman, and has many features of the Darcy family." Jane observed. "Is that his sister standing next to him? She is very pretty."

"Despite their reasons for being here, I must confess I find them very pleasing indeed." Elizabeth remarked. "He has an easy manner, with a great deal of merriment, and Miss Wentworth is quiet and agreeable."

"How long are they to stay with you at Pemberley, Lizzie?"

"I believe their stay will be of some duration. Mr Darcy spends much time with him, either in his study, or on the estate. O Jane, if only I could have a son, none of this would be needed."

"All this worrying will not be beneficial. You have only been married above nine months," Jane said. "It is really no time at all, Lizzie."

"But you have a daughter, Jane."

"I have been extremely fortunate, but you will too, Lizzie. I am sure of it, but you must try not to worry. It will not help. You are happy, are you not?"

"More than I deserve, Jane. Mr Darcy is very attentive, and takes pleasure in my company. Indeed he leaves my side but rarely."

"We have both been very fortunate in our husbands, Lizzie. Indeed I could not wish for a better one than Mr Bingley," Jane said, "but I must leave soon and attend to Mr Collins daughter. It is so sad that she should be left without a mother."

"Dear Charlotte," Elizabeth sighed. "Do you think she was happy with Mr Collins, Jane?"

"I believe she was content. I think she wished only a comfortable home, and Mr Collins did, I think, have a very high regard for her."

"I was surprised at the depth of his feelings. Truly, Jane, I believe he has not slept since Charlotte left us."

"He is very distraught. If only there was something we

could do to comfort him."

"Only time can do that, Jane. I do hope the funeral will not cause him too much pain."

"It will not be easy on his feelings I think. We will have to support him through this time, Lizzie."

"I am surprised Mary is taking such an interest in his condition," Elizabeth frowned. "to be this involved cannot be good."

"She has always favoured Mr Collins. I believe he is a great help to her in her learning," Jane reflected. "Mary is not like Lydia, Lizzie, she is only happy when she is reading, and Mr Collins indulges her in this matter."

"I am sure you are right, Jane. I am getting to worry like dear mama."

"Have you called on mama, Lizzie?"

"No, but I feel that I should do so on the return journey. O Jane I dread the remarks she makes to Mr Darcy. It is the cause of much discomfort to him."

"I fear mama's condition does not allow her much speech at this time. Mr Darcy will be safe I am sure. Now I must go, Lizzie. I will see you at the church tomorrow."

Charlotte's funeral was a very sorrowful affair. It was as much as Mr Collins could do to hold his feelings in check. There was a time when everyone thought he would collapse with grief, but Lady Catherine was at his side and gave every support needed. Sir William and Lady Lucas did their best to withhold their feelings, but Maria broke down completely. It was a painful experience to be seen indeed.

Elizabeth, whose grief was in great danger of overwhelming her was in much need of the support of her husband's arm.

"You must put every effort into your daughters welfare Mr Collins," Lady Catherine told him at the gathering afterwards. "She will need your support more than ever now."

"Your Ladyship has been kindness itself." replied Mr Collins. "Indeed I could not have born this heavy burden without your Ladyship's constant solicitude. My dear Charlotte has left an empty place in my life which I fear will never be filled."

"Time is a great healer, Mr Collins," replied Lady Catherine. "Your grief is at the moment too fresh for speculation over the future. Mrs Collins will be sadly missed by many.

"She will indeed," Mr Collins sighed. "If it had not been for the kindly benevolent assistance of our many acquaintances, I fear I would now be by her side. Indeed my life is now no more for living. The sun has departed my horizon."

"There will be no more talk like that, Mr Collins," snapped Lady Catherine. "My dear husband departed this life many years ago, and I have devoted my entire life to the raising of our dear daughter Anne. You, Mr Collins must do the same."

Jane stepped forward. "The parsonage is the place you should be at this moment I think Mr Collins. I am sure an hour or two of quiet reflection, will, I am sure, restore your sense of being, and adjust your mind to the responsibilities before you."

"You are right my dear cousin. My mind is not what it should be at this time."

"It is quite understandable, sir." Jane replied.

Mr Bingley, Jane, Mary, Sir William Lucas and his wife accompanied Mr Collins to the parsonage, while the rest of the party returned to Rosings Park.

The funeral had so upset Elizabeth, she went straight to her room. There was no way she wished to involve herself in conversation of any kind.

While Mr Darcy strolled in the garden with Georgiana, Mr Wentworth and his sister. Caroline Mr and Mrs Hurst retired to the drawing room with Lady Catherine. and her daughter.

"It is such a sad day for us all," Mrs Hurst commented. "I was saying to Mrs Darcy only yesterday, that I was not acquainted with Mrs Collins in an intimate way, but to be taken away at such an early age. It is indeed difficult to comprehend. Mr Collins, I fear will take much time to recover."

"He will find an inner strength Mrs Hurst I am sure, as I had to." Lady Catherine replied. "God has a way of bringing out strengths we were not aware we possessed. I shall make it my concern to attend to his welfare, and that of his daughter."

"Your kindness knows no bounds Lady Catherine," Mrs Hurst continued. "Mr Collins is fortunate indeed to have someone with your sense of loyalty."

Before anyone could answer, Caroline said: "Elizabeth's behaviour today was a slight to us all. To let her feelings be known, it is intolerable. Someone of her standing should have more regard for her position in life.

"The child was bereft, Caroline. We may be generous emough to allow her this one relapse," Lady Catherine answered.

Without intention, Mr Darcy found himself placed in a part of the garden where the voices from the drawing room carried with much clarity.

"I believe we have been generous enough," Caroline insisted. "Indeed her whole air portrays her descent. Her manners, Lady Catherine, leave so much to be desired, and her dress. Indeed it has no fashion at all. Do you not agree, sister?"

Mrs Hurst did not reply.

"How poor Mr Darcy must be regretting his decision to marry so much lower than his own company." Caroline was determined to make her point. "I believe it is the reason Mr Darcy does not show her to our society in town, as often as would be expected. Why she has not even given him an heir to secure Pemberley from entailment. I confess I cannot see what he sees in her. The attraction in the beginning, I admit. were her fine eyes, and she is different to our usual company. I suppose it amused him at the time, but these things do not last. Her relations have polluted the shades of Pemberley, and I am sure Mr Darcy will not tolerate it. The way she speaks to you Lady Catherine, I admire your forbearance."

"Elizabeth is now my nephew's wife Caroline," Lady Catherine stated. "He is indeed of such maturity to account for his own actions."

"But Lady Catherine, your anger knew no bounds when the marriage took place," Caroline would not let the matter drop.

"The deed is done, there is no more to be said on the matter." Lady Catherine was by this time most displeased.

"Well, I will never accept her into our society. Indeed our acquaintances are all amused by the situation. It is intolerable."

"That is enough, Caroline," ordered Lady Catherine. "I will not have such conversations in this house. Your private thoughts are your own. It will benefit the situation greatly, if you kept silent on this matter."

Mr Darcy's temper was at its highest as the words reached his ears. Caroline had certainly gone too far this time.

When he joined Elizabeth in her room, she could not understand his sudden change in manner. He was very unsettled, and paced the room a great deal.

"Is there anything offends you, sir?" she asked.

"The situation will be dealt with Elizabeth. Please do not concern yourself," was all he would say on the matter. He then left the room, closing the door quite violently. He was bent on securing Caroline Bingley's attention.

"Mr Darcy," she smiled sweetly as she met him in the hall. "This must be a very trying time for you, to keep all parties content. Indeed you look very out of sorts. Whatever can the matter be, sir?"

"I do have a matter that needs my immediate attention. Would you be so good as to stroll with me in the garden?"

Immediately she went to take his arm, but he managed to sidestep the action.

Elizabeth who had quickly followed Darcy out of the room, and was standing at the top of the stairs, was most perplexed. Whatever could be the matter that her husband wished to discuss it with Caroline Bingley? She returned to her room, and crossed over to the window where, she had a view of the garden. From her vantage position she could clearly see that they had stopped not far from the entrance. Mr Darcy, she observed was talking earnestly to Caroline.

"Miss Bingley! I found myself in the regrettable situation as to overhear your conversation with my aunt. Your feelings appear to be so strong on the matter of Elizabeth, I feel the only way forward is to exclude you from our company in the future. This is indeed a regrettable situation, as it will bring tension to my relationship with your brother, but it cannot be helped. I have indeed tolerated your company in the past for that sole reason alone, but now I fear you have gone too far in your insinuations. I will not have my wife slighted in this way. Your opinions are your own, and I urge you to refrain from uttering them in company in the future. I bid you good day ma'am." He walked swiftly away.

Caroline was in such a state of shock she could not utter a word and remained unmoved for several minutes, then she turned and rushed into the house, and straight to her room.

She did not appear for dinner, and as no-one had an idea what had become of her, Mrs Hurst went in search of her.

"Are you unwell Caroline?" she asked as she entered her sisters room.

"O Mrs Hurst, Mr Darcy has been so cruel. He insists he no longer wishes my company."

"What has been said Caroline?" Mrs Hurst was distressed indeed.

Caroline repeated the conversation that had occurred in the garden.

"Caroline your remarks have gone too far this time. His good opinion once lost, is lost forever. It is a great misfortune for your society."

"I only repeated what all society are thinking. To marry someone like Elizabeth, with her connections is unthinkable."

"Caroline, if Mrs Darcy has excluded you from his

company you have no-one but yourself to blame. Your words are born out of jealousy, and regret for the life you had intended for yourself. I cannot side with you in this matter Caroline. Mr Hurst relies on Mr Darcy's society for his amusement. He would not allow it, and in consideration of my own comfort and future, I would not offend him."

This was indeed another blow to Caroline. Her own sister turning against her. "But you agree with my thinking sister," she spluttered.

"They are married now, Caroline, and I accept Elizabeth as his wife. You, my dear sister should have learned to do the same."

"I shall talk to my brother on this matter," Caroline continued. "He will not let Mr Darcy treat me in this infamous manner."

"Charles, I am sure, will be most angry that you have put him in this position Caroline. Mr Darcy is his oldest friend. To cause discomfort between them will not lie well with him I am sure." Mrs Hurst turned and left the room before Caroline could reply.

"My sister is a little unwell this evening, she begs your forgiveness," Mrs Hurst explained as she returned to the drawing room. "She will not be joining us this evening."

"Is it anything serious?" asked Lady Catherine. "Can anything be done?"

"It is a slight headache, I believe. The emotions of the day. I am sure she will be fully recovered by morning." Mrs Hurst directed her answer to Lady Catherine, but her eyes sought out Mr Darcy.

He did not look up from the book he was reading, and his expression was unreadable.

The remainder of the evening was spent quietly.

Although Mr Bingley and Jane remained at Huntsford for several more days, Mr Darcy and Elizabeth left very early the following morning for Longbourne.

Elizabeth was much gratified to find her mother almost

returned to full health. Although her speech was slow, and at times indefinable, and her right side had restricted movement, she was in general of good health. She still kept her state above stairs, and it was with relief, that not even a glimpse of Mr Darcy did she have.

Chapter 6

As Georgiana and her two cousins had delayed their return to Pemberley until the arrival of Lady Catherine in two weeks time, Elizabeth looked forward to the sole company of her husband. This was a luxury rarely bestowed on them, making it all the more precious.

"Your aunt seems to have secured a change in her thinking," Elizabeth said as they travelled northwards.

"She has indeed," Mr Darcy smiled.

"And under your instruction I believe, sir."

"I admit a little deception was needed to avoid ongoing conflict." Mr Darcy continued to explain the contents of his conversation with Lady Catherine. "I fear I may unwittingly, have offered her an open invitation to visit."

Elizabeth smiled in spite of her own feeling on the matter. "My sister Jane suggested that you may have been very clever indeed in your handling of this matter. To be second best, does not sit well with me, sir."

"My dearest sweetest Elizabeth," he took her hand. "I am sure that you will now have many hours of pleasure in Lady Catherine's company."

"Your mischievous nature is in full flow I believe Mr Darcy."

"Under your instruction I believe," he replied and they both laughed.

"There is one more matter on which I wish to address you Elizabeth. His tone had taken on a serious note. "It regards Miss Bingley."

Elizabeth looked at him in surprise. "Caroline."

"I had the a most unfortunate experience when standing in the garden the day of the funeral. I overheard a conversation that was both unpalatable and unjust. On the result of which I had no option other than to exclude Caroline from our company in the future."

Elizabeth was shocked indeed, although the thought of never seeing Caroline again was quite enticing, she also knew what it would mean to the sister of Mr Darcy's best friend. "That was the only way forward, sir?"

"I am afraid it was Elizabeth. I will not have her vicious nature within your company ever again."

"Then her society will suffer much I fear."

"It will indeed. My only regret is that it will cause a rift between my greatest friend and myself."

"I am sure Mr Bingley will understand, sir. He is aware of her character."

"Let us hope so."

Over the following two weeks Pemberley was at its most peaceful. Mr Darcy spent many hours in Elizabeth's company, either strolling the gardens and groves or just enjoying the solitude that was so often denied them.

On Mr Wentworth's return, Elizabeth knew her husband would have to go into town for several weeks, and it was a prospect that she did not look on with pleasure. On her marriage to Mr Darcy she knew his many business interests would deprive her of his company freequently, so she would have to endeavour to bear the separation with much fortitude. Kitty, who had remained at the Bennett household arrived back a day after the other guests, and once again Pemberley was bursting with life.

"The house is indeed a credit to you Elizabeth," Lady Catherine announced after her first evening in residence. "Mrs Reynolds has indeed instructed you well."

"I thank you ma'am, your approval gives me much pleasure." Elizabeth replied.

"Yes, well, there are still a great many things that need attending to. We will make a start the minute Fitzwilliam departs for town."

"Thank you ma'am." Elizabeth answered with far more meaning than she felt. "I am indeed indebted to you for giving up your time to help me in this way."

"Never mind that. Pemberley has a standard to live up to, we must see to it that nothing goes remiss. I am very attentive to all these things." Lady Catherine continued. "Have you given any thought to the festive season at all, Elizabeth?"

"No ma'am," Elizabeth answered in surprise. "It seems a little early to be thinking of Christmas."

"It may very well have been in your past, Elizabeth, but there are a great many occasions to take in hand," Lady Catherine was now in full flow. "Have you given any consideration to the estate workers and their children? I doubt it very much. It has always been a great strength of the Darcy family to ensure their servants and estate workers enjoy a very congenial Christmas. Then, of course, there is the New Year's Eve ball. Now that, Elizabeth, is a very grand affair indeed. It has, in the past always been my concern to ensure that all arrangements were made, but this year I suppose you will want the responsibility yourself."

Elizabeth thought very quickly. "No indeed ma'am. If your ladyship could, on this occasion instruct me in the procedure, I am sure that when the task falls to me in future years, I will be far more capable of the organization involved."

Lady Catherine made a noise that was born out of self satisfaction. "Ahmm, well, at least you do not pretend to know it all. That is something. No doubt Mrs Reynolds would have seen you through well enough, but this is a new era for Pemberley. It now has a mistress, and it must be seen to have a mistress. Do you understand me Elizabeth? The whole of society will be watching you, and Mr Darcy must not be caused any embarrassment."

"God forbid ma'am, that is the last thing I would wish for."

"Then we are in agreement." Lady Catherine was in her element. "This year you will work under my instructions."

"As your ladyship wishes." Elizabeth sighed inwardly.

Mr Darcy left for town the following day and Elizabeth dreaded the prospect of having to entertain Lady Catherine and her daughter over the next four weeks alone. She turned to Georgiana for help.

"Lady Catherine is not so very difficult to handle Elizabeth," Georgiana said. "You just have to let her think she is getting her own way. That is all. Sow the seed of an idea and leave the rest to her."

"Easier said than done I think," Elizabeth frowned. "I would so much like to put my own personality into the Christmas festivities this year Georgiana, but I now fear that it will be taken out of my hands"

"Only if you let it Elizabeth. If you make a suggestion then I will back you. That way Lady Catherine will have to oppose the two of us."

"I am sure she is quite capable of that," Elizabeth laughed.

"I am sure she is, but if we both insist upon it, she will have to give way," she thought for a second or two. "Then of course we will have to allow her to have her own way to compensate."

"You, my sweetest Georgiana, have a mischievous mind, just like your brother."

"I am so happy you are here Elizabeth. This is, I am sure, one of the happiest years of my life," Georgiana hugged Elizabeth closely.

"Then you make me a very happy person. There was nothing I wished for more than to think of you as my sister." Elizabeth smiled.

Georgiana's face went into a serious expression. "I have seen the change you have made in my brother."

"For better or worse?" Elizabeth asked with concern.

"O for the better. He is now far more approachable Elizabeth, and he frowns so much less," Georgiana explained. "Since the death of our dear father, Fitzwilliam has spent much of his time alone in his study. It could not have been good for him."

"I am sure it was not Georgiana, but your father's death laid a very heavy burden on your brothers shoulders. To take on the full responsibilities of the Darcy estates was great indeed. Especially in someone so young."

"But now Elizabeth, he laughs so much more. It warms my heart to hear him, and I have you to thank. He would never have been like this if he had married cousin Anne."

"I do not think that was ever a serious thought in his head Georgiana. Caroline Bingley perhaps, but not your cousin Anne."

"Not Caroline, Elizabeth. My brother often says that she causes him discomfort with her conversation."

"That is all behind us now I believe," Elizabeth laughed. "Everything is as it should be, apart from Lady Catherine. Now that, you most certainly have to help me with." Both women laughed.

"I am sure we will manage Elizabeth. She really does have the future of Pemberley very close to her heart."

"Well that is one thing we agree on. Perhaps it is not such a lost cause after all." They laughed again and Elizabeth could not remember when she had been so content.

"Have you seen Kitty, Georgiana?"

"I believe she is at her desk writing a letter."

"She writes to mama, that is good."

"I think her letters are directed elsewhere Elizabeth," Georgiana coloured a little.

"Colonel Fitzwilliam?"

Georgiana nodded. "You are not displeased are you Elizabeth? I believe she likes him very much."

"I believe she does, and it pleases me very much. Mr Darcy also approves of the association."

"They make a very handsome couple."

"They do indeed, and it is all down to you Georgiana. You spent so much of your time, and energy making her what she is. She has a great deal to thank you for."

"I did very little," Georgiana blushed slightly. "She is a beautiful girl your sister."

"You have brought the best out in her Georgiana. Now, let

us go and face Lady Catherine together."

How Elizabeth held her temper during the next two weeks was entirely attributed to sheer will power. Lady Catherine had definite ideas on how Pemberley should be managed, and no way would she be sidestepped.

Georgiana to her credit, did her best, and in all fairness achieved a small amount of success, but the main points went to Lady Catherine.

Elizabeth did manage, after some persuasion, to convince Mr Darcy's aunt that a party for the village children was a matter very dear to her heart.

"Where would you wish to hold this occasion Elizabeth?" she asked.

"I thought the grand ballroom, as it would be large enough to accommodate a great many," replied Elizabeth.

"The grand ballroom," exclaimed Lady Catherine in horror. "Are you out of your mind. Think of the damage they would do."

"I am sure they will not. If we have enough amusements to keep them entertained, I am sure all will be well."

"Not the ballroom Elizabeth," she insisted. "Think of the floor, all those feet. We would never be able to use it again. It would be ruined. No I cannot give my consent."

"Then what would your ladyship suggest?" asked Elizabeth through gritted teeth.

"If you insist on entertaining the entire village, we shall have to restrict it to the hall. It is ample for what is required."

"As your ladyship wishes."

Georgiana tried to lighten the atmosphere. "I am sure my brother would approve, aunt. His mind is always open to different ways of involving the village people."

"As you wish Georgiana, I will not interfere, but the consequences of your actions will not rest in my hands. I will take no responsibility for any of it."

"Thank you, aunt," she looked across at Elizabeth and smiled.

The day progressed in roughly the same vein. There was much to-ing and fro-ing of ideas. Lady Catherine usually getting the upper hand, until, Georgiana tiring of the arrangements announced that she was going for a walk.

"Wrap up warm Georgiana," Elizabeth suggested. "This autumn weather is very damp indeed."

She watched her go with a heart longing to be with her. The thought of fresh air was very tempting indeed, but duty must come first. She turned her attentions back to Lady Catherine.

"Do you have a guest list from previous years ma'am?" she asked.

"We will make a new one Elizabeth. You must have acquaintances you wish to include."

This statement surprised Elizabeth, she had been convinced that her relations would not be welcomed by Lady Catherine at Pemberley. Especially at a time of great importance, such as the festive season.

"Thank you, ma'am, I am indeed obliged to you for your thoughtfulness," Elizabeth replied."I would like very much to invite my aunt and uncle Gardiner, and of course my sister Jane and Mr Bingley. My parents will unfortunately be unable to travel."

"Your list is very short, Elizabeth. Is that for my benefit?"

"No indeed, ma'am. My sister Kitty is already here, Mary will remain with Mr Collins, and the only other person that I would wish to invite is no longer with us."

"It still pains you I see to think of Mrs Collins."

"Very much ma'am."

"Your sister Jane is indeed a very sweet girl. Her concern for others does her much credit."

"She is the dearest person in the world to me. I miss her company very much indeed."

"Then we must ensure that her stay is of some duration."

"Thank you ma'am, you are very kind." Elizabeth was surprised at the gentle note in Lady Catherine's voice. "I would imagine Mr Bingley will wish to bring his sister."

"That Elizabeth remains to be discovered. He may feel that now Caroline cannot be invited he may wish to entertain them at Southview."

"Then my sister Jane will not be able to attend."

"Caroline is a silly gal, she should have had the presence of mind to keep her thoughts to herself. It has caused much discomfort to many."

The thought of Jane not being at Pemberley over the Christmas period saddened Elizabeth greatly.

"Shall we issue an invitation to Mr Bingley, Jane and Mr and Mrs Hurst and await their reply do you think."

"That is all we can hope for at the moment Elizabeth. I fear it will sadden your hopes greatly if your sister cannot attend."

"It will indeed. Caroline has never approved of my relationship with Mr Darcy, and will not accept it even now."

"She had hopes of securing his affections herself no doubt," Lady Catherine sniffed.

"I believe she did ma'am."

The door to the drawing room opened suddenly and Mrs Reynolds appeared. "I beg your pardon ma'am but it is Miss Georgiana."

"What is it Mrs Reynolds, what has happened to her?" exclaimed Elizabeth jumping to her feet.

"I am not sure ma'am. Ned the gamekeeper is bringing her in now."

The three women went into the hall where Elizabeth could see Georgiana being carried up the drive by the gamekeeper. It looked very much as though he was covered in blood, and was staggering badly.

"Someone help him," Elizabeth shouted as she ran out into the gathering dusk.

Two footmen relieved the gamekeeper of his heavy burden, and he immediately collapsed to the ground.

"Mr Daniels, what has happened? What has befallen Georgiana?"

"Gypsies ma'am," is all he could utter before unconsciousness overtook him.

"Someone get the doctor," she ordered as she ran back into the house to see what state Georgiana was in.

Her sister-in-law's clothes were torn and she was covered in dirt, but as far as Elizabeth could tell, the only blood on her was that belonging to the gamekeeper. Her eyes were closed and her face was ashen.

"Take her to her room," Lady Catherine instructed. "And see that Mr Daniels is attended to."

Kitty and Sophia Wentworth came running out to see what all the commotion was about, and were horrified to see the drama unfolding before their eyes.

"Is...is she dead?" Kitty asked in a weak voice.

"No, Kitty, but something has befallen her, we know not what as yet." Elizabeth replied, then turned and ran quickly up the stairs to Georgiana's room.

The doctor was not long in arriving, and he very quickly pronounced that, although Georgiana was not aware of her surroundings, there was no apparent injury that could have caused the condition.

"Then what has happened to her, Mr Williams?" Elizabeth was beside herself.

"Her appearance has all the indications of someone who has been molested Mrs Darcy. Her state of consciousness could have been brought on from the trauma."

"God forbid!" Elizabeth exclaimed, as she collapsed into a nearby chair. "Mr Darcy will never forgive me."

"I doubt if this was brought about by any of your doing, Mrs Darcy." the doctor consoled.

"I should have taken better care of her."

"She is a grown woman Mrs Darcy, she has the right to walk anywhere she may choose. Now was there anyone with her at the time?"

"I think not, but Mr Daniels the gamekeeper brought her home," explained Elizabeth. "He is indeed injured. Mrs

Reynolds has made him comfortable, but I am not sure in which direction."

"Did he explain the injuries Mrs Darcy?" the doctor asked.

"No, sir. The only word he uttered before passing out was 'gypsies'."

"Please do not distress yourself further, ma'am. I will go and attend to Mr Daniels and see if I can discover the cause of Miss Georgiana's accident."

Once the doctor had left to attend Mr Daniels and Georgiana was being made ready for bed, Elizabeth went in search of Lady Catherine.

"What are we to do ma'am?" she asked as she entered the drawing room. "The doctor is convinced that Georgiana has been molested. If she has been defiled Mr Darcy will be without all sense, and it is all my fault."

"How can it be your fault child. Try to compose yourself Elizabeth."

"I should never have let her out of my sight. Mr Darcy left her in my care and I have let them both down. He will never forgive me."

"We will concern ourselves with Georgiana's misfortune at present and worry about other matters later. Now tell me exactly what the doctor said."

For the first time ever Elizabeth was extremely pleased that Lady Catherine was in residence. "There are no physical injuries to report. She is indeed unconscious and he fears that this has been brought about by the shock she had received. O Good God, how could I have let this happen?"

"She should never have gone out walking on her own."

"You do it all the time Elizabeth. One was not to know that this would befall our dear Georgiana. I am indeed very distressed. Where is the doctor now?"

"He has gone to attend to Mr Daniels in the hope of procuring more information. What do you think can of happened?"

"It is highly likely that one of those travelling men, that

Mr Darcy welcomes to his land, have repaid him with this infamous crime."

"Mr Darcy! Should we inform him of the situation do you think?"

"We will await more information. The need to cause him pain may yet be avoided."

"With all my heart I pray for it. He will think nothing but ill of me if this is discovered."

"He will, under all conditions, have to be told. If we do not inform him of it ourselves. I am sure he will discover it from the servants. It is better coming directly from us."

"I am sure you are right Lady Catherine, but I fear the consequences of his displeasure."

"They will be great indeed," Lady Catherine replied.

Mrs Reynolds entered the room followed closely by the doctor.

"What news do you have?" Lady Catherine asked.

"Mr Daniels condition is grave indeed. He has suffered a stab wound to his chest that has resulted in a great blood loss. His survival is in the hands of the Gods."

"And Georgiana? Did you discover what had befallen her?"

"It appears, ma'am, that as she was walking she stopped to talk to one of the travelling men. He must have noticed the jewels she was wearing and decided to take them for himself."

"Was…was she…?" Elizabeth could not bring herself to say the words and the doctor picked up on her discomfort.

"I fear she was, Mrs Darcy, but not to the ultimate conclusion. If you understand my meaning."

"I do indeed." Elizabeth wanted to cry with relief.

"That is not to say that it wasn't attempted. Indeed it was. She was most fortunate that Mr Daniels happened upon the scene. The end could have had far-reaching consequences indeed."

"Thank you Mr Williams. What are your suggestions to my nieces needs at this time?" Lady Catherine asked.

"There is very little we can do at the present time your ladyship. A constant watch must be kept until she returns to us in mind. These cases have been known to take many weeks, or months even to resolve themselves."

"And Mr Daniels? What of his condition?"

"As I said before Lady Catherine, it is grave indeed. Mrs Reynolds has given me her assurance that she will send for me the minute there is any change."

"Would it not be beneficial to all parties if you remained in the house Dr Williams?" Elizabeth asked. "Georgiana may need you when she returns to us."

"As you wish ma'am. If it is a source of comfort to you, I will remain within calling distance."

"You are very kind, sir."

Once the two women were alone together Lady Catherine said. "Now Elizabeth, I think it is time to inform Fitzwilliam of what has befallen his sister."

"O yes, but I dread his reaction," replied Elizabeth. "He will be beside himself, and the consequences will be beyond all belief."

"Indeed they will," replied Lady Catherine, "but there is nothing to be done. Go to your desk and put pen to paper, I will check on dear Georgiana."

The letter was sent by express to Mr Darcy's address in town, and Elizabeth knew that it would not be long before his return.

Georgiana recovered her senses within the hour, but refused to speak to anyone. In fact her eyes had a vacant look about them that was indeed unnatural.

"Georgiana, it is Elizabeth. Can you hear me?"

She closed her eyes again.

"Please let me help you. Tell me where you are hurting."

"I think she hears you, Mrs Darcy, but is reluctant to speak. Thus happens very often in these cases. She has indeed had a very severe shock. It iwll take time. She will talk, I am sure, when she is ready."

"I am sure you are right, Mr Williams," replied Elizabeth. "Is your suggestion to leave her to herself until such good time?"

"I believe it is, Mrs Darcy. No good can become of pressure."

Elizabeth went back downstairs but could not settle, she paced the floor until Lady Catherine insisted that, if she could not sit down, then she should find something useful to do.

She was about to leave the room when a thought struck her and she stopped midway. "The man that accosted Georgiana, do you think he is out there somewhere, hurt? Do you think we should send someone to look?"

"I most certainly do not," replied Lady Catherine in a very indignant manner. "If he is hurt then he brought it about by his own doing. Let Mr Darcy see that he receives what is due to him."

Elizabeth felt a cold sensation run the entire length of her spine. She knew the gypsy deserved everything that was coming to him, and more, but the thought of Mr Darcy's wrath was something she did not want to contemplate.

She went back and sat with Georgiana. "Can you still not tell me where you are hurting?" she asked very quietly.

There was no answer. "I have no wish to distress you, but your brother will need to know. He is at this very moment on his way home, and will expect to receive some answers."

The reaction from the bed was sudden and violent. "You must not tell him Elizabeth. He must never know." she threw herself into Elizabeth's arms and sobbed as though her heart would break.

Elizabeth held the distraught girl until the crying subsided a little. "Do not distress yourself anymore. We only wish to help you Georgiana. If you can tell me what has happened, then I am sure all will be well. Mr Darcy will not attach any blame to you."

"Please do not tell him Elizabeth. I cannot bear it if he hears of this. I cannot live with his displeasure. Promise me Elizabeth that you will not tell him." Her eyes were full of pleading and it broke Elizabeth's heart.

"Your brother has already been informed Georgiana. He is at this moment returning to Pemberley."

"No…no, he must not be told." she was almost hysterical by this time.

"Please calm yourself my dear. to be this distraught is not going to help you recover. Come and tell me everything, and then we will decide what we are to tell Mr Darcy."

"Elizabeth, he cannot know. He will never forgive me, I am sure of it."

"There is nothing to forgive you for. What has happened was not of your undertaking. Now where were you walking when this happened?"

Georgiana told Elizabeth how she had gone down to see the new planting her brother had designed, and that there was a young man sitting on a fallen tree. She started to cry again. "O Elizabeth he sounded so polite, and gentlemanlike. He greeted me like any of our general acquaintances would."

"Take it slowly Georgiana, try not to distress yourself any further. Did you speak to him first?"

"O yes, my brother has always told me that they are to be treated with the utmost respect. They have been staying at Pemberley ever since my grandfather's day."

"What did you say to him?"

"I greeted him then started to walk away, but he spoke to me. He said that everything was all right, he was allowed to stay on the estate. I turned to tell him that I knew his residence was accepted, but he had moved a great deal closer. I stepped back very quickly and caught my foot on a branch. It was the cause of my falling to the ground." At this point her sobbing was out of control, so Elizabeth held her close until it had subsided a little.

"My poor dear sister, if only I could take away some of the pain."

"It was so awful Elizabeth. I keep seeing his face, and his breath was so offensive," she broke down again.

"Do you wish to rest for a while Georgiana? We can continue this conversation when you feel a little stronger."

"It is so hard Elizabeth. To recall it causes me much pain. It offends me to think of it."

"I know, but I am sure you will feel better once you have spoken of it. Did he offer to help you?"

"No,...no,...he,...he bent over me and stretched out his hand towards my neck. He said how my locket would look so much better on his sweetheart, I tried to stop him taking it. It was a present from my brother. He tried much harder to take it, but I moved my body away, across the ground. He stood up and smiled down at me, and then he started to take his jacket off. He said..." She was sobbing so hard now her words became distorted. "I cannot repeat what he said, his words were so disgusting."

"It is all right Georgiana, I can quite well imagine," Elizabeth tried to console her. "You do not have to explain."

"He...he said someone like me would never know what a real man was like, so he was going to show me, He said I had it coming to me because of the way I always looked down my nose at his sort. I was crying Elizabeth but he took no notice. He tore my Spencer from me and then tore my dress. His hands were all over my body, I felt so dirty." This time there was no stopping the body-racking sobs.

"That is enough Georgiana, you do not have to go on," Elizabeth herself was crying, and her heart was in torment for this gentle girl, who had been so cruelly abused.

She spoke again. "I closed my eyes so I would not have to look at him, and then his weight was lifted from me. I heard voices, then sounds like people fighting. I tried to see who it was but everything was spinning in my head."

"How much you have gone through. I will fetch the doctor to give you something to help you sleep. You will feel much better for it, I am sure."

"I do not want my brother to be told of this," she held on to Elizabeth's arm. "Promise me Elizabeth, you will not speak of this to him. I cannot see him, you must promise."

The pleading in her voice was like a vice on Elizabeth's heart, but she knew there was no way she could keep this from Mr Darcy. "Georgina," she spoke very softly but firmly. "It is not possible to keep something as horrific as this a secret. You have been wronged beyond all sense, and if I, do not tell him, someone else will, I am sure. It cannot be hidden."

"Do not let him come to me. I will not see him. I could not bear to see the look on his face."

"Do not distress yourself anymore. I promise I will not allow him to see you until you are more yourself. Now please let me call the doctor, so you may rest."

"You cannot make me see Fitzwilliam, Elizabeth," Georgiana said as Elizabeth left the room.

Within half an hour of the doctor administering a potion, Georgiana was sleeping soundly, so Elizabeth went down to relay the events to Lady Catherine.

"It is beyond comprehension," she exclaimed when Elizabeth had reached the conclusion of her conversation with Georgiana. "God forbid there are such people in the world. It is not to be tolerated. For a woman of my niece's breeding to be treated in such a manner. It is disgraceful. I blame Fitzwilliam for allowing those people to use his land. I cannot imagine what he was thinking of."

"I believe they come every year ma'am. Apart from a little poaching, there has never been any trouble before I believe. What do you think Mr Darcy's reactions will be?" Elizabeth asked, dreading the answer.

"Whatever he does will not be half enough," she almost exploded with anger. "They will I hope be many, diverse and of the severest kind. You, my dear, may count on it, and if you have any sense at all, you will leave this matter entirely in his hands. Did you mention in your letter the nature of Georgiana's discomfort?"

"No indeed ma'am. I simply informed Mr Darcy that his sister had befallen an accident, and although she was physically uninjured in body, her distress was of the severest kind."

"Ummph, well I must credit you with some sense at least," replied Lady Catherine. "Perhaps I have misjudged you in the past. Your handling of this whole affair has been without question."

"I thank you, ma'am. At what hour should we expect Mr Darcy do you think?"

"There will be no delays, his sole thought will be to attend his sister. It will surprise me greatly if he is not here by the morning."

"She refuses to see him ma'am, and I have promised to withhold his visits until she is more herself."

"You had no right to make a promise of that kind Elizabeth," Lady Catherine was most indignant. "If Fitzwilliam wishes to see his sister, and I am sure he will, nothing must be allowed to stand in his way."

"I fear his appearance will not help at this time, she is very distraught."

"Stuff and nonsense Elizabeth, the girl needs her brother at this time."

Elizabeth argued no more, it was a lost cause, but she knew if Mr Darcy forced his attentions on his sister, it would do more harm than good.

Although Elizabeth sat with Georgiana through out the night, not once did her eyes close. The fragile young woman slept evenly and quietly but Elizabeth's thoughts were with her husband. His rage, once he discovered the truth would know no bounds, his revenge would be complete.

Before dawn was breaking, she heard the sound of horses' hooves on the gravel, and quickly descended the stairs as to intercept Mr Darcy's passage through the house.

If he was surprised to see his wife in the hallway at this hour, it did not register. "What has happened to Georgiana, Elizabeth? Is she in bed? I must see my sister at once." His face was full of concern and worry.

"If you would be so good as to come into the drawing room, sir, I feel an explanation is needed at this time." Elizabeth was shaking with the thought of what Mr Darcy's reaction would be.

"What has happened, Elizabeth? Tell me at once."

As she related the happenings of the day Mr Darcy's face grew darker and more sinister. Temper flared in his eyes and colour to his cheeks. He was close to being out of control.

"To what extent did this assault go, Elizabeth? Tell me at once."

"The doctor is convinced that, although attempted, it did not reach the ultimate conclusion."

Mr Darcy physically relaxed a little. "Good God, Elizabeth, how could this be allowed to happen? Why was she walking alone in the grounds? She should have been taken more care of."

Elizabeth was close to tears, but she knew Mr Darcy's pain was so much worse.

"I must see her," Mr Darcy ordered.

"She will not see you, sir," Elizabeth pleaded. "Can you not see she is afraid to face you? She blames herself for what has befallen her."

"It is of no fault of her own. She has no reason to be afraid of me."

"I beg you, sir, give her time. She is much distressed. She will recover her senses and wish to see you very soon, I am sure."

"She is my sister, I will see her." He strode towards the stairs and Elizabeth ran after him.

He had nearly reached Georgiana's door when she caught up with him. She caught his arm. "I beg you, sir, do not do this. It will cause much harm."

He stopped and glared down at his wife.

"I cannot understand the meaning of this behaviour Elizabeth. She has no need to shut me out of her life. I have only her interests at heart," Mr Darcy was struggling with the reason for Georgiana rejecting him.

"At times of great emotion, sir, I find it is best to leave the person in question to themselves. Outside pressure from anyone will not help the matter."

"Your wife is right, Fitzwilliam," Lady Catherine, having been woken by the commotion stood behind them. "Georgiana has been through much today. If she does not wish to see you at this time, then you should be kind enough to respect her wishes."

"But she is my sister," Mr Darcy was perplexed.

"All the more reason to leave her be. The one person she will confide in is Elizabeth," Lady Catherine informed him. "I think it better that we leave things that way. She does not wish to see me either, and I can understand her feelings. She is hurt, embarrassed and in shock. A few days will make the difference I am sure."

Needing relief to his anger Mr Darcy turned on his heel and went back down the stairs, out of the front door into the early morning darkness. The two women exchanged glances, they both knew where he was heading.

Chapter 7

Mr Darcy, with a face resembling a thunder cloud walked directly towards where the gypsies had their encampment, but there was nothing to be seen. The caravans and horses had all disappeared, leaving only the ashes of a long extinguished fire. He kicked at the ashes in frustration, then scanned the surrounding area as best he could, looking to see which way they were headed. Although the moon was still quite bright, it was not sufficient enough to show up the tracks on the ground. He stood in deep thought for several minutes, before heading towards the planting area. What he hoped to find there was not at the moment apparent, but it helped him in his struggle to control his temper.

He could see clearly the log that the gypsy had been sitting on when his sister had emerged from the trees, and the area in which the struggle had taken place was also visible in the autumn moonlight. He felt physically sick and spun round on his heel in vexation. Then his eye caught the shape of a body lying at the edge of the clearing. Walking over he glared down at it, then with one hand he grabbed the man's shirt in his fist, raising the body at least three feet from the ground. He took in the man's features for several seconds before he threw it back down onto the ground with considerable force. Mr Darcy's face was contorted with fury.

He walked back towards the house, vowing to the night that he would track down the gypsies and make them pay for the action of their relation.

Elizabeth had, by this time returned to Georgiana's room. She heard her husbands footsteps approaching in the passage outside. They stopped as they reached the door, and she prayed that he would not enter. A few seconds passed, that, to Elizabeth seemed like a lifetime, and then she heard, to her relief the footsteps continue along the passage towards his own apartments.

Before he went down to breakfast, Mr Darcy went in search of his wife. Not finding her in her own room, he knocked very gently on Georgiana's door.

Elizabeth rushed across the room, and slid out into the passage before he could even attempt to open the door. Her heart ached for him as she saw how the news of his sister's misfortunes had ravaged the features of her beloved husband.

"My sister?" was all he said.

"She sleeps, sir."

"Be sure she gets every attention," he turned on his heel and strode down the passage.

Obtaining the information he needed from Mrs Reynolds as to the whereabouts of Mr Daniels, he went straight to his bedside. The gamekeeper was drained of all colour, his form lay still. His wife who had been sent for sat by the bedside. She immediately stood up on Mr Darcy's entrance.

"No, no. Pray do not disturb yourself," he spoke in a quiet voice. "Has his condition improved at all?"

"I fear not," Mrs Daniels replied. "The doctor fears the worst, sir." There were tears in her eyes.

"His actions to protect my sister, has indeed caused you much pain." Mr Darcy said softly. "He will now always have my sincere devotion. Be sure to obtain anything that will assist his return to health."

"Thank you, sir. May I ask how Miss Darcy is now, sir?"

"She sleeps," Mr Darcy stared down at the floor and sighed heavily. "Mrs Darcy is by her bedside."

He left the room, and without saying another word to anyone, he left the house. He had not slept at all, but his resolve to track down the gypsy family was strong enough to override any tiredness he may have felt.

After checking in which direction the caravans had travelled, he pointed his horse on the same course and rode with speed. He rode hard, his anger still as intent as when he had first heard what had befallen his sister. How much of the anger was attributed to the assault, and how much to the refusal of his sister to see him was unsure. His determination to find, and deal with his sister's abusers was overpowering all senses.

He rode for days, following tracks, asking questions, but to no avail.

Several villages had reported seeing the travellers, but of their sighting, there was none.

For over a week he roamed the countryside, following every lead he was given, but in the end, even Mr Darcy himself, had to admit the hopelessness of the search. If the gypsies did not want to be found he was sure that they could evade him. That this was probably not the best way to go about things was evident, but there were other ways. He had no intentions of relinquishing his responsibilities.

Meanwhile Georgiana's condition had not improved. Her distress was such that she would see no-one except Elizabeth.

"If I took her to Longboune for a while, would it help, do you think?" Elizabeth asked Lady Catherine one evening.

"Mr Darcy would not wish his sister to leave Pemberley, of that I am quite certain," Lady Catherine replied. "Her condition extends much too long and is distressing indeed. She still refuses to see Fitzwilliam, does she?"

"Yes ma'am, her condition is heightened I fear, by the thought of his displeasure. Indeed she speaks of little else, and nothing can be done to console her."

"Fitzwilliam has shown nothing but kindness to his sister," Lady Catherine continued. "Indeed it is most unfortunate."

"If only we knew where he was. His absence is close to a week now, and I fear for his health and safety."

"Fitzwilliam will not rest until he has completed his mission," Lady Catherine was sure of that. "The name of Darcy has been wronged, and he will, by his very nature be set on avenging the abused."

"Nothing I fear will alter what has happened," Elizabeth sighed, "and to add to it further by risking his own health is worrying indeed."

"There is nothing you can do Elizabeth, his course is set.

Mr Darcy, will I fear, defend Georgiana's honour to the death."

"O God forbid, this cannot be true." Elizabeth was now distraught.

"Do not distress yourself, child. The matter is out of our hands." Lady Catherine tried to pacify Elizabeth.

"If she still refused to see him when he returns, what is to be done?" asked Elizabeth.

"Fitzwilliam will insist on seeing her, it is his right," Lady Catherine declared. "Once contact is made, all will be as it should be. She needs her brother at this time, and he she."

"But it could do so much harm.Her distress is much indeed, and if she is forced to face him against her will, I believe her mind could be seriously damaged."

"Then we must ensure that the meeting is accidental. Once she is assured that her brother is not grieved with her, I am sure her recovery will be swift."

"If only this were the case, but she will not leave her room. How can the meeting be accidental?"

"We must find a way, Elizabeth. It is not beyond you I am sure."

Mrs Reynolds entered the room. "I beg your pardon ma'am, but Mr Wentworth has returned from town and wishes to see you."

"Let him come in," Elizabeth said. She had forgotten all about Mr Wentworth being left in town.

"Mrs Darcy, I am indeed confused. My cousin left town without a word to anyone. I awaited his return with much impatience, and when there has been no sign of him for above a week, I felt my only course of action was to return to Pemberley."

Elizabeth, who was at a loss as to what to say to Mr Wentworth looked across at Lady Catherine. How much information Mr Darcy would wish his cousin to have was unsure.

"Please sit down, Edward," Lady Catherine took over. "There has indeed been an unfortunate occurrence, which has sent Fitzwilliam away in another direction." She went on to explain the situation, and the reaction in Mr Wentworth was almost as severe as Mr Darcy's had been.

"Upon my word, this is abominable indeed. Why was I not informed at the time," he was pacing the floor. "My assistance could have been much used. Where is my cousin at this moment?"

"He is still away, sir," Elizabeth spoke for the first time. "we are not sure in which direction he has travelled."

"There must be tracks, show me where the gypsies camped," he sounded very angry indeed. "To be uninformed when I could be of assistance, it is offensive to me in the very least." This gentle, mild-mannered man was now strong of character, and authoritative.

"Edward," Lady Catherine said with a great deal of firmness. "You must understand the condition of our emotions at the time. We were all beside ourselves, and writing letters was not one of our main concerns."

"I apologize, aunt, my senses have been overridden by my feelings." Mr Wentworth said.

"It is perfectly understandable. Your reactions do you much credit. Now what do you propose by viewing the tracks?"

"Only that I may follow, and hope to assist my cousin on his quest."

"For two to go missing," Lady Catherine was put out. "It shall not be. It is Mr Darcy's honour he his defending. He does not need our help."

"I beg your pardon your ladyship, but it is the name of Darcy that has been abused," Mr Wentworth replied with much insistence. "I have the honour of carrying this family crest and therefore feel perfectly entitled to defend it."

Lady Catherine thought for a few seconds. "You are perfectly right Edward. Go do as you will, but I doubt very much, that there will be any sign left of the tracks after all this time and weather."

"If you would be so good as to inform me of the place in

which this abominable offence occurred, I will take my leave."

Lady Catherine turned away so Elizabeth said. "It occurred near the new planting area Mr Wentworth. I will fetch a servant to show you the way."

"There is no need Mrs Darcy. I know the area quite well. Please forgive my outburst, I was very much out of order." he bowed and left the room.

"I doubt he will be fortunate enough to discover Mr Darcy after all this time," Elizabeth speculated. "We have without forethought, offended his feelings I believe. It is with regret, that I admit, his residence in town had quite escaped my mind."

"Mine also," replied Lady Catherine, "but it cannot be helped. Where is your sister Kitty? I have not seen her these last few days."

"My sister and Miss Wentworth keep above stairs ma'am. I believe they feel that my time should all be directed in helping Georgiana to better health."

"She has a remarkable way of thinking, in one so young. It does her credit." Lady Catherine sniffed approvingly.

Lady Catherine's compliments about her family would have been warmly received, had they come at a more suitable time, but although they still pleased Elizabeth, their full meaning escaped her.

"If you will excuse me Lady Catherine, I wish to check on the health of Mr Daniels."

She made her way to the servant's quarters where Mrs Reynolds had prepared a bed for the gamekeeper. As she walked she wished with all her heart that she could confide in her sister Jane, but she knew it was not a prospect Mr Darcy would embrace. Jane, she was sure, would keep the information to herself, apart from imparting it to Mr Bingley, and of his involvement Elizabeth was not quite sure. At this moment she felt so alone. If only Mr Darcy would return.

She entered the room of Mr Daniels, and spoke quietly to his wife. "How is your husband today Mrs Daniels. Have there been any signs of recovery?"

"His sensible moments have been many ma'am," she replied. "Indeed I now have hope for recovery."

"I am very pleased to hear it. Are you being attended to with everything you need?"

"We are indeed ma'am. No-one could have been kinder. Has Mr Darcy returned yet ma'am?"

"I am afraid not Mrs Daniels," Elizabeth replied with a sigh. "It concerns me greatly."

"He must do what he feels is right, I am sure." The older lady put her hand on Elizabeth's arm. "You must not distress yourself ma'am. The master thinks the world of Miss Georgiana, and it must be hurting him deeply."

"He does indeed Mrs Daniels. I only wish there was something I could do to help in this matter. She still refuses to come out of her room."

"It is time she needs, that is all," Mrs Daniels smiled.

"Has your husband spoken of the occurrence at all?"

"Not really ma'am, he just repeats Miss Darcy's name, and keeps saying, 'not real gypsies,' over and over."

"What can he mean by that?" Elizabeth asked.

"Only that real gypsies would never harm anyone, I believe," Mrs Daniels explained.

"They camp here every year I believe," Elizabeth said. "Since my husbands grandfather was alive."

"They do ma'am, and they have never caused any trouble before, but they will not be welcome anymore. I am sure of that."

"Yes you are right. I fear Mr Darcy's revenge will be great."

"And so it should be. It is a disgrace what has happened here," Mrs Daniels spoke with venom

"Not real gypsies," Mr Daniels spoke from his bed, and Elizabeth went to his side.

"Can you tell me what your meaning is, sir?" she asked.

Slowly he opened his eyes, and as soon as he recognized his visitor he became agitated, and grabbed Elizabeth's hand. "Tell…tell the master…not real gypsies."

"What do you mean, sir, not real gypsies? Was it gypsies

that attacked Miss Darcy?"

Mr Daniels made a nodding movement then his eyes closed again.

"He is trying to tell us something Mrs Daniels. Have you any idea what it could be?"

"No ma'am. That is all he has been saying all day. I am sure it does not make any sense."

"If he should extend his message, would you be so good as to inform me at once?"

"At once ma'am."

Elizabeth returned to the drawing room, and relayed the conversation to Lady Catherine. "What can be made of it, do you think?"

"It is strange indeed," replied her aunt. "Most disturbing."

"Maybe he is saying that after this incident they can no longer be classed as true gypsies." Elizabeth speculated.

"After this incident they can have no class at all. Incarceration is all they are good for," Lady Catherine exclaimed. "The deepest and darkest hole will be more than they deserve."

"You could not speak more truth," Mr Darcy said as he strode into the room. His appearance shocked both women. His face was unshaven, his clothes soiled and wrinkled. Indeed he was hardly recognizable as the master of the house. "My sister, has she fully recovered?" he directed his question at his wife.

Elizabeth's joy at seeing her husband's return was tempered by his attitude. She wanted to run to him, comfort him, but she knew she could not.

"I fear not, sir. Her condition remains unchanged," Elizabeth replied. "Her refusal to see anyone, or to leave her room is implacable."

"This is not to be tolerated. Take me to her at once," Mr Darcy's anger was apparent.

"I cannot, sir," Elizabeth was close to tears. "I promised her I would not."

"You have no right to make such promises. She is my sister. I will see her," his face was dark with controlled anger.

"Fitzwilliam," Lady Catherine's voice rose over his. "Arriving in your sisters bedchamber attired as you are, would only serve to frighten her even more. A bath and a change of clothes will indeed make the difference."

Mr Darcy looked down at the clothes he was wearing as though it was the first time he had considered them. "Forgive me, aunt, I cannot understand my sister's feelings towards me. In the past I was the one she would turn to."

"No one can understand them, Fitzwilliam. Elizabeth will go and inform her of your return, and persuade her that she cannot refuse to see you any longer. Now go and attend to yourself."

"She will not see him ma'am, she is determined," Elizabeth said when Mr Darcy had left the room. "I have tried persusasion in every possible way, but it is fruitless."

"Then I will try," Lady Catherine stood up.

"No, ma'am," Elizabeth was in despair. "You know she fears your wrath as much as she does your brother's. I will go and explain to her that she can no longer avoid the prospect."

Lady Catherine sat back down. "If you do not Elizabeth, I fear Mr Darcy will go all the same."

With a heavy heart Elizabeth returned to Georgiana's room.

"Are you feeling any better?" she asked as she entered.

"I am well Elizabeth, as long as I remain here."

"You have to see people Georgiana. This is doing no good to anyone. Kitty and Miss Wentworth are missing your company, and Lady Catherine is most upset that you have no wish to see her."

"I cannot face anyone yet Elizabeth. I fear their contempt."

"For what reason. Nothing that has happened as been of your doing. Indeed I cannot see what there is to be afraid of. Everyone loves you very much, and your brother, who has just returned wishes to see you more than anyone. It is most distressing that you will not receive him."

"I will not see him. You promised Elizabeth. Please do not let him come to me." she pleaded.

"Georgiana, I can delay it no longer. He is insistent, and I fear if you do not agree, he will come anyway."

"He must not. I cannot bear it," she started to cry.

"Georgiana," Elizabeth had just had an alarming thought. "Is there anything you have not told me. Did something happen that you are afraid to tell of?"

Georgiana never spoke, she just sobbed loudly.

"My poor dear girl, please do not be afraid to tell me anything. Nothing can be so bad as it cannot be repaired."

"I have told you everything, Elizabeth," she said at last. " but can you not see I have disgraced the name of Darcy? My brother will never forgive me."

"That is being silly, Georgiana. You have done nothing, it is others who are to blame. It must be difficult for you, but truly, Georgiana, you have nothing to fear. Please trust me, your brother thinks only of you. You have not incurred his displease in any form. His only wish is that you are returned to health, and in his company."

"I cannot see his face Elizabeth. To see what I have done reflected in his eyes is more than I can bear."

Elizabeth stood up, she was determined to make Georgiana see sense. "You have been in this room too long Georgiana, your mind is not as it should be. Think of the kindness of your brother, and how he has loved you all your life. You cannot remain here forever. I cannot continue to sit with you day and night, my attentions are needed elsewhere. You must understand this Georgiana."

She was silent for some time and then she said. "You are right Elizabeth, but can it be delayed until tomorrow. I would wish to have some time to prepare myself."

"Of course you can," Elizabeth felt a great weight lifted from her shoulders. "Your brother will be so pleased to see you, I am sure."

"You will stay with me Elizabeth. I cannot go through

with it on my own."

"You know I will. Thank you Georgiana, you have made me a very happy woman." She kissed Georgiana lightly on the forehead and went back downstairs to announce her success.

"Thank the Lord for that," Lady Catherine said when she was told. "Her feelings will be much improved when the meeting has been attended to."

"I am sure it will. It is a great relief to me," Elizabeth said. "Do you think Mr Darcy will respect her wishes?"

"We will ensure that he does. What is one more night. A sound sleep for both of them will be most beneficial."

Mr Darcy, now looking more as he should be, joined the women for dinner and was given the news. "I still do not understand her reluctance to see me?" he said in a perplexed tone.

"She fears your displeasure, sir, that is all," Elizabeth explained.

"She has no need to. None of this was her doing. I am at a loss to understand her thinking. Am I that threatening in her eyes?"

"No indeed, sir. You are held so high in your sister's estimation she fears that she has brought shame on you, and is reluctant to bring it to your attention. She is still very young, sir, and cannot, as yet, fully understand your capacity for forgiveness."

"There is nothing to forgive. Have you not explained this to her Elizabeth?" Mr Darcy was now angry.

"I have indeed, sir, but she still fears she is at fault." Elizabeth was also getting upset.

"There is no point talking round in circles," Lady Catherine joined in the conversation. "Georgiana has agreed to see you tomorrow, that I hope will be the end of it. I am at a loss myself to understand fully what is in her head, but we must satisfy ourselves that she is now relenting. Your wife, Fitzwilliam has been Georgiana's constant companion these last two weeks, to the exclusion of all else. Her devotion to your sister's health showed no bounds, it must now be taking its toll."

Mr Darcy looked across at his wife, and for the first time noticed how this ordeal had affected her. "I have been selfish Elizabeth. I thought only of Georgiana and myself. Forgive me my dear I have treated you with less than respect."

"Your actions, sir were as they should be," Elizabeth tried to smile but without success. "It pains me greatly to see you both suffering so much."

"Then we will all feel better for a night's rest," said Lady Catherine with relief. "By this time tomorrow, all will be as it should be."

"I pray you are right, aunt," Mr Darcy replied. "Mr Daniels, does his health continue to improve?"

"I fear very little, sir," replied Elizabeth. "His words cause us much confusion. He repeats over and over, 'not real gypsies', we cannot understand to what he is referring."

Mr Darcy frowned.

"When I asked him if gypsies were responsible for Georgiana's misfortune, he nodded." Elizabeth continued.

"I will see him in the morning. Now if you will excuse me, I will retire." He left the room without another word.

Elizabeth, although exhausted, did not sleep that night. Her thoughts were with Georgiana. She prayed that her sister in law would not have second thoughts on her decision and refuse to receive Mr Darcy in the morning. She was sure that her husband held her responsible for the withdrawal of his sister's affections. It gave her much pain, but if relations were renewed, she was sure his good opinion of her would be restored.

Elizabeth dressed and went into Georgiana's room quite early. She wished to reassure herself that all was well, but the room was empty. The bed had been slept in, but of Georgiana there was no sign. She ran downstairs to check the rooms, but there was no-one to be seen. Her heart sank, Georgiana had run away, she was convinced of it. She had agreed too readily to the meeting with her brother, why had Elizabeth not seen it?

Quickly she ran back upstairs and checked Georgiana's room for any sign of a note, but one had not been written. She returned to her own room and sat very heavily on the bed, her thoughts racing. Georgiana could have hidden herself in any part of this large house. What was to be done? Standing up abruptly Elizabeth was determined to search every room, then she noticed a piece of paper lying just inside her door. Half of which was concealed beneath the carpet. She ran over and picked it up.

"O my God!" she exclaimed as she read it.

My dearest Elizabeth,

I know now that I cannot face the expression in my beloved brother's eyes. I have caused him pain that will not easily be healed. My actions have been such, that to face people is more than I can bear. You have been kindness itself to me my dear sister, and brought much happiness into my life, but my future now fills me with abhorrence. I cannot live knowing I have brought disgrace to the impeccable character of my dear brother. Take care of him, Elizabeth, he is the dearest person in the world to me.

Georgiana.

Elizabeth's first thoughts were to wake Mr Darcy, but she checked herself. Georgiana could not have gone far. If she could return her to the safety of the house before anyone knew she was missing, much pain could be avoided.

She threw the letter down on the bed, took up her outdoor coat, and ran down the stairs, out into the early morning darkness. Her only hope was of a place on the peaks, that she had often visited with Georgiana. It had become a favourite place for both of them, and Elizabeth was hoping that it was there that Georgiana had ran. Many times Georgiana had said she wished she could stay on the peaks forever. How long her sister in law had been gone, she did not know, but she prayed she would be in time. The autumn weather did not help in her orientation of the peaks. Mists were collecting in the valleys, and the rain was fine but heavy as she climbed the heights. She ran, stumbling as she went, time was of the essence. She must return Georgiana to Pemberley before anyone noticed she had gone. Several times she caught her foot and fell, but the pain did not register. So intent was she to discover the whereabouts of Georgiana, she did not comprehend the danger she was putting herself in.

A full hour she struggled against the weather, but there was no sign. The rain was falling much heavier now, and the wind had whipped itself up to almost gale force strength. It was getting increasingly difficult to keep an upright position. The rocks ripped at her boots, whilst the wind tore at her clothing.

The lake they visited together came into view, giving Elizabeth the urge to push forward. She tried to call Georgiana's name, but the wind tore the words from her lips. Breathless, wet and near exhaustion she climbed the final hill hoping against hope that she would now have a sighting of her sister in law. There was no sign. Elizabeth wanted to sit down and cry with the sheer frustration of it all, but she knew it would not help matters. She climbed down the slope, slipping and sliding on the mud until she was near the waters edge. Following the edge of the lake she carefully made her way round the rocks, hoping to see Georgiana round the next corner. She saw a flash of something white. It was Georgiana's dress, she was sure of it. Walking as fast as the ground would allow she scrambled over the rocks and through the water until she reached the rock on which Georgiana was sitting.

Without a word she ran to her and held her close, they both slipped to the floor with the force of the wind.

"Georgiana you have had me as I never knew myself," Elizabeth cried. "My poor sweet sister, what reason did you have to take such action? Come let us go back before either of us are missed."

"O Elizabeth I cannot go back, you know I cannot. How can I live knowing how I have caused my brother so much pain. You should not have followed me." The wind was ripping the words from their lips.

"Let us try to find a little shelter," Elizabeth shouted above the wind.

They climbed round the edge of the lake until they discovered a small cave that ran back into the rocks several yards. As they stepped out of the wind, it was like stepping out of a nightmare. Neither girl could speak for some time.

Finally Georgiana spoke. "Please do not make me go back, Elizabeth."

"We must. What else is to be done?"

"I cannot face it. It is beyond all endurance," Georgiana was crying bitterly now. "Leave me, Elizabeth, go back to my brother."

"I most certainly will not," Elizabeth was shocked at the suggestion. "We will go back together. Your brother will be beside himself with worry when he discovers your absence. He is not offended by anything that has happened, indeed he is not. I fail to see why you should think so."

"His honour, his reputation, they are now tarnished," replied Georgiana through her sobbing, "and I was the one to bring this disgrace to Pemberley."

Elizabeth was now shaking with the cold and wet. "Do you really think that is of any matter to your brother. All he ever thinks of is your happiness. His love for you is all consuming. To reject his affections and company is causing more pain than anything that has happened. Believe me Georgiana, this is true."

"You will never understand, Elizabeth, if you had been brought up in our circles you would see, what I say is true."

Elizabeth looked at Georgiana in surprise, and Georgiana realizing what she had said was even more surprised.

"O Elizabeth, I did not mean what I said. I only meant our family has more tradition. Truly I did. I would not offend you for the world."

"It is of little matter," Elizabeth said flatly. "If we continue in this state neither of us will live to keep up any tradition."

*****

Back at the house Mr Darcy was eating his breakfast, unaware of the drama being unfolded out on the peaks. His appearance was much refreshed after a full night's sleep, and his temper had subsided.

"It is unusual for Elizabeth not to be active at this time of day," Lady Catherine observed.

"Her concern for my sister has maybe made her tired. I have not disturbed her this morning."

"She has been of great assistance to Georgiana these past weeks," Lady Catherine continued. "I admit I may have been a little hasty in my appraisal."

"Are you softening your opinion towards my wife, may I hope?" Mr Darcy asked.

"My feelings at the time have not changed Fitzwilliam. Her connections are so far below our own, it is an unthinkable alliance. No more for that, the deed is done, and we must make what is best of it. I was speaking on a purely personal level. Her character I believe is not what I thought it to be that is all."

"Thank you, aunt," Mr Darcy replied solemnly. "Now if you will excuse me, I will go and see if my sister is ready to receive me."

Mr Darcy strode along the gallery with an eagerness to see his sister that overtook all other emotions. He tapped lightly on the door, but getting no response he knocked harder. Her refusal to answer his knock both angered and perplexed him. He tried the door handle, and to his surprise it was not locked.

"Georgiana, it is Fitzwilliam," he called out, but there was still no answer. He pushed the door open and was surprised, even shocked to find the room empty. Walking into the room he observed that the bed had indeed been slept in, but of his sister there was no sign. Thinking Elizabeth would know her whereabouts he sort out her room. On finding that empty as well, he was more annoyed than ever. His first thoughts were that Elizabeth had taken Georgiana to another part of the house, and the ploy of yesterday, delaying his visit had given them the chance to execute this plan. To go to such lengths as to avoid his company, it was ridiculous. These thoughts made him very angry indeed, and he was about to embark on a search of all the rooms when he noticed the letter on the bed. At first he thought nothing of it, then reconsidering the position he snatched it up.

The contents shocked and disturbed him greatly. He rushed out of the room and down the stairs.

"Mrs Reynolds have you seen my wife this morning?" he almost shouted the question at her.

"No, sir," Mrs Reynolds was most alarmed at her master's tone.

"My sister?"

"No indeed, sir. Miss Georgiana has not left her room for above two weeks."

He turned and strode into the breakfast room. "Aunt have you seen my sister this morning?"

"I have not, as you know full well."

He handed her the letter to read. "God forbid, what does this mean," Lady Catherine cried out.

"Get the servants to search every room in the house, even the cellars. I, myself will search the gardens. Elizabeth must have gone in pursuit of her, unless this was planned between them." Mr Darcy said as he left the room.

He had no idea how long the two women had been missing, and even less idea of where he should start looking. He searched the immediate grounds first, then further a field. The weather was such that he thought it impossible that they would be out in it, so he searched every building he came across.

Having no sight of either of them he returned to the house. "Have you any idea where they might be?" he asked everyone assembled in the hall. "Is there a place that she favours more than anywhere else? Miss Bennett, she must have confided in you at some point, you appear to spend a considerable time together."

"Elizabeth and Georgiana do spend a lot of time by the lake, sir," Kitty replied. "I have heard her say there is nowhere better on earth."

"They would not have gone on the peaks in this weather. Have sense child," Lady Catherine chided. "They are more likely to be sheltering in the village. Maybe Georgiana went there to secure a carriage to town."

"You could be right, aunt, I will go there directly and seek them out. Have you dispersed the servants?"

"They are at this moment searching every room in the house."

"I will ride to the village and if I see no sign, I will return here to see if there is news."

"You are wet to the skin Fitzwilliam, change your clothes at once." Lady Catherine ordered as he left the room. He either didn't hear her, or didn't take any notice, because a few seconds later they all heard the front door slam.

After an hour of searching there was still no sign of the two ladies, and everyone now was much concerned.

"They must have gone to the peaks," Mr Darcy said now beside himself with concern. "No-one in the village has seen any sign of them. "We will head out in the direction of the lake. If you hear any news, aunt send a man to inform us. There is no way they will survive if they are out in this storm."

"Mr Darcy, may I come with you?" Kitty had stepped forward. "I wish to help look for my sister."

"That is a kind thought indeed," Mr Darcy laid a hand on her shoulder. "I fear it would do more harm than good to be encumbered with some one who could not keep up. I am sorry, Miss Bennett, I cannot allow it."

"But I must, she is my sister."

Mr Darcy turned and walked out of the front door without another word.

Kitty started to cry, Mrs Reynolds was wringing her hands and Lady Catherine was pacing up and down.

"Stupid, stupid girl," Lady Catherine exclaimed. To run away when there is no need, It is distressing to say the least. She has put Fitzwilliam through much this last month. And for Elizabeth to go off without a word, it is grievous indeed."

"Lizzie would not go unless it was important," Kitty spoke through her tears. "I am sure she did only what she thought was right."

"You are probably right Miss Bennett, but to leave some instruction would have been most beneficial. Now stop your crying, it will serve no purpose."

*****

Elizabeth and Georgiana attempted to leave the security of their cave but the wind and rain were now so fierce Elizabeth was undecided whether or not to attempt it.

"We must try I think, Georgiana," Elizabeth decided. "Mr Darcy will, by this time be most concerned."

"You go, Elizabeth, I will never return to Pemberley," Georgiana said with feeling.

"This is not the time to play games Georgiana," Elizabeth had lost all patience. "We are going home together whether you wish to or not. There are many people there concerned for your welfare, and they do not deserve to be treated in this way."

"I will die rather than go back," Georgiana said stubbornly.

"And that is exactly what we will do, unless we can reach safety soon," Elizabeth was exasperated now. This stance of Georgiana's had gone quite far enough. She understood the girl's feelings, but it was now getting too much. "Do you really want me to die too Georgiana? Is this what it is all about?"

"O no, Elizabeth, I would not want any harm to come to

you. You are the dearest sister I could ever have, but can you not understand. To face my brother would be pain much greater than death. I have brought him so much embarrassment, he could never forgive me, even if he wished to."

"He has nothing to forgive you for. None of this was of your doing, it was an unfortunate occurrence. You are making far more of it than there is ever any need to be. I keep telling you Georgiana, your brother is not displeased with you. His anger is directed against the person who did this to you. Now come on we must try and reach safety."

They edged towards the mouth of the cave once more, and as they did so the wind whipped their clothing hard around their bodies. The lake had risen and was now starting to invade their sanctuary.

"We must go now Georgiana, or it will be too late," Elizabeth grabbed the girl's arm and almost dragged her with her as she stepped out into the water.

The wind, stronger than ever now, battered them against the side of the rocks, and Elizabeth had great difficulty manoeuvring herself and Georgiana around what was once the edge of the lake.

With extreme effort she managed to haul herself and her sister in law halfway up the side of the slope, before exhaustion over took her. She clung to a rock her heart beating so fast she thought it would burst, and her breathing was coming in great gasps. Through all her discomfort she refused to let go of Georgiana's arm. There was no way she was going to give her the chance to run away again.

If she had only known that, only a few hundred yards away Mr Darcy was battling against the same weather and heading in her direction, her efforts would have been reinforced, but she only felt alone, and helpless out there in the wilderness.

"Help me Georgiana," she pleaded. "I cannot do it alone."

Georgiana stared at Elizabeth for several seconds before taking her own weight, and then she started to climb the slope. Elizabeth thanked God for this change. her arms were almost pulled from their sockets by the exertion of pulling Georgiana behind her.

Mr Darcy, who was by this time behind the adjoining hill, tried in vain to shout to his men to spread out more, but the wind just threw the words back in his direction. His hat had long since disappeared with the wind, and his coat was being torn from his body with its force.

He tried desperately to scan the horizon for a sighting of his wife and his sister, but the rain was being blown with such severity it stung his eyes. Head down he battled towards the top of the incline. He was more than worried now. No-one, especially people as delicate as his two most beloved women, could possibly survive this weather. His heart was heavy as he continued his search. To make matters much worse, he did not know for sure that he was searching in the right direction, he just knew he had to find them.

Elizabeth and Georgiana, who had by this time, managed to reach the top of the incline thought they heard a shout, but could see no-one. They both collapsed onto the ground unable to go any further.

A farm worker, who was part of the search party, noticed the white material of Georgiana's dress, and waved frantically to Mr Darcy who was a hundred or so yards away.

"Over here," he tried to shout, but to no avail. He tried again, and this time Mr Darcy happened to be looking in his direction. Both men started to run at the same time.

Elizabeth scrambled to her feet, pulling Georgiana up with her. She could not believe the sight that met her gaze. Half a dozen or so men were all running in her direction. She wanted to burst into tears with relief, but she didn't have the energy even for that.

Georgiana, who had also seen the men suddenly pulled her arm away from Elizabeth's grasp. She stood and looked at her brother running towards her, then turned and ran back down the slope.

Mr Darcy shouted her name, but she either did not hear, or didn't want to, because she kept running.

Mr Darcy could not believe that she would do such a dangerous thing. He ran after her until they reached the edge of the lake. Georgiana had scrambled onto the top of a large rock.

"Georgiana, what are you doing?" Mr Darcy shouted. "Please come down, you do not have to be afraid of me."

"I cannot, forgive me," she screamed back. Then before anyone could stop her she hurled herself from the rock into the water.

Mr Darcy was rendered immobile with shock, but then he tore off his coat and boots, and without hesitation he entered the water after her.

Everyone watching were rooted to the spot. This sudden turn of events was not to be expected.

Elizabeth stopped breathing as the two bodies disappeared under the water. Her eyes never left the spot, until, a few seconds later they both reappeared. Georgiana with her arms flailing wildly, and Mr Darcy swimming towards her. Georgiana went under the water again and Elizabeth watched helpless as Mr Darcy dived to find her. It seemed an eternity before they were sighted again, this time much nearer the edge of the lake.

Half dragging, half carrying his sister Mr Darcy headed for a part of the shore line that was much shallower than the rest.

Two of the search party sprang into life and raced down to the waters edge to be of assistance. They lifted Georgiana free of Mr Darcy's grasp and carried her to safety. One of the other men removed his coat and wrapped it around the frightened girl.

Elizabeth half ran, half stumbled to where her husband was trying desperately to recover from his ordeal. She threw herself down on the ground, and cradled his head in her arms. With tears coursing down her face, her own condition forgotten she whispered. "O my love, I thought I had lost you."

He rose unsteadily to his feet, helping his wife up at the same time. They stood locked together for several minutes, while the wind and rain howled around them.

No-one was more pleased than Lady Catherine as the bedraggled party returned to Pemberley a little while later.

Kitty, who had been frantic at her sister's disappearance, ran out to help Elizabeth into the house. "O Lizzie, I have been beyond all sense," she exclaimed. "We were all so very sure that we had lost you forever."

Elizabeth did not have the strength to reply, she just patted her sister's arm and allowed her to help her inside.

All parties were packed off for warm baths, hot drinks and comfortable beds.

The following day found Mr Darcy and Georgiana much recovered, but Elizabeth remained in her bed chamber. The strain of the past few weeks, combined with her own cut and badly swollen feet made it impossible for her to stand.

Mr Darcy sat by her bedside. "My dearest sweetest Elizabeth, I owe you my sister's life. If it had not been for your constant attention to her welfare, she could have been lost to us forever. I am ashamed of my thoughts and what I have said. Please forgive me."

"It was you who saved her life, sir," Elizabeth smiled at him.

"I was only given the opportunity because of your own selfless actions. Had it not been for you my dearest wife, there would have been no-one to save." He took her hand in his, and his face became serious. "As much as I am indebted to you Elizabeth, you must not, under any circumstances, put yourself in so much danger ever again. I could not face life if I lost you now."

Elizabeth squeezed his hand. "Have you spoken with your sister yet?"

"I have not," he replied with a frown. "Indeed it puzzles me greatly why she should feel that she needed to act in this manner."

"She was frightened, that is all," Elizabeth said.

"Of me, her own brother?"

"Especially you, sir. You are more than a brother to her," Elizabeth explained. "Indeed she looks on you as a protector, a father figure. Her feelings are so strong on the subject of disappointment, she believes that she has let you down in the worst possible way, and has lost your good opinion forever."

"None of this sad affair was of her undertaking."

"Go and speak with her, sir. I am sure your resolve of this matter will be more than beneficial to all parties."

"Your generous nature never fails to warm my heart," he kissed her gently. "You are as beautiful on the inside as you appear to the world on the out." He left the room in search of Georgiana.

He found her sitting quietly in the music room, and it was a surprise to him to see her visibly shrink back in her seat as he entered the room. Not wishing to alarm her any further, he took a seat opposite. She looked so pale and fragile, he wanted to comfort her, but refrained from doing so.

"It offends me greatly that your fear of your own brother is stronger than the value you hold on your own life Georgiana," he spoke quietly.

Not hearing any response he continued.

"It is not in my nature, as you very well know, to ever wish, or indeed to be the cause of any distress to you. My only desire is for your comfort and happiness. To avoid my company when you are suffering so much pain, grieves me deeply."

"I could not face you, knowing I was the cause of so much discomfort to you, Indeed my heart is heavy with the burden of my guilt." Georgiana's voice was barely a whisper. Her head remained bent, and her position did not alter. "To bring shame to the name of Darcy was more than I could bear."

"None of it was of your undertaking Georgiana, can you not understand this? What befell you that day was grievous beyond all comprehension, and outside your control," Mr Darcy said. "What hurt me above all, my dear sister, was to be denied the opportunity of offering you my solace. It was a cruel blow indeed."

Georgiana suddenly threw herself on the floor at his feet. "I could not face the expression in your eyes, when you knew of my ruin and disgrace. To take your comfort, when I believed you had anger in your heart, was too much for me to carry."

Gently but firmly he lifted his sister to her feet and held her close. Her sobbing was such that it convulsed her whole body. Mr Darcy was filled with deep emotion for this poor distraught girl. Indeed his heart was in torment.

"My sweetest sister," he spoke into her hair. "My only wish is for your protection and happiness. It is my deepest desire that you should feel that you trusted me enough to turn to me in moments of distress."

Georgiana sat down on the settee. "I feel so ashamed of the way I have been acting. My motives have been selfish indeed, with no thought for the feelings of others. Can I ever expect your forgiveness now?"

"There is no forgiveness to be had. This infamous crime was none of your doing. It will be avenged I assure you, but blame, to you, can in no way be attached." Mr Darcy consoled her.

"Your kindness makes me humble. I do not deserve your generous nature, sir."

"Come Georgiana, let us put this where it belongs, in the past. You are now safe, and that is my only concern." Mr Darcy smiled at the fragile young girl by his side.

"Will Elizabeth ever forgive me do you think?" she asked. "I have caused her much distress, and her ordeal has been great."

"Elizabeth has only your welfare at heart. She has, I am sure, been suffering great strain these last weeks, but her gift of forgiveness is certain."

"But I owe her so much. I was the cause of much discomfort to her," she continued. "I could have been the instrument of her losing her life."

"That my dear sister, was grievous indeed. Your actions put many people in great danger. Elizabeth most of all. It was a very serious mistake, which I hope will never be repeated." Mr Darcy's tone was very serious. "I believe you owe Mrs Darcy a sincere apology."

"I will go to her at once." She held her brother close for a few seconds then turned to leave the room.

"Georgiana, I hope in the future you will trust me enough to seek my help," he called after her.

"I have learned a great deal over this time brother, and I promise to act in a more controlled manner in the future."

"That is all I ask Georgiana. It is now forgotten."

She ran straight to Elizabeth's room. "Elizabeth my brother has been so kind to me. He is so generous in his affections. I do not deserve it."

"Of course you do," Elizabeth was pleased to see her sister in law more as she should be.

"I had not the smallest hope that he would ever forgive me, but he is not angry with me at all." Georgiana explained.

"He has no reason to be. All he wanted was to help you Georgiana. You must not discard his company in the future."

"It was very wrong of me Elizabeth. I could not see it, and to think of the pain I have caused you. You are truly the best sister anyone could wish to have. Can you ever forgive me for my selfish actions?"

"It is as though it has never been. Just promise me that, in the future you will rely on your brother's judgement."

"I will Elizabeth, I promise. I will never cause either of you pain again."

"Then we will say no more, it is forgot. When I return downstairs I shall insist that you play for me. There, is that punishment enough?"

Georgiana laughed. "You are so good to me Elizabeth. I am so ashamed of what I said to you when we were on the peaks. I cannot believe I could say such a thing to anyone. Especially you Elizabeth."

"It is forgot Georgiana. We will speak of it no more."

For two days peace reigned at Pemberley before Mr Darcy spoke of his intention to return to town.

"I have sent a letter of apology to Mr Wentworth, whom I left without a word of explanation. He must, by now, be quite at a loss to what has become of me." Mr Darcy said.

Elizabeth shot forward in her seat. "O good gracious, I had quite forgotten. Mr Wentworth arrived here while you were away in the country. When told of our misfortune, he was most offended indeed that his assistance was not sort. He was very angry, and insisted on being shown the caravan tracks so that he could follow and help in the search."

"In what direction did he travel?" Mr Darcy looked concerned. "He has little knowledge of this land."

"Of that I am not sure. I believe, sir, that he did has you did, and followed the travellers wheel marks."

Mr Darcy smiled. "Am I never to have the pleasure of receiving all of my family under the same roof at the same time. When one returns the other is sure to go missing."

"It appears Mr Darcy that you have a very active family," Elizabeth laughed. It did her heart good to see that her husband had returned to good humour.

"Then what do you suggest I do Elizabeth? Shall I go to town, so that our cousin may return to Pemberley, or shall I stay in the hope of seeing him?"

"My wish is that you would stay here forever, sir," Elizabeth smiled.

"I would not suspend any pleasure of yours." he replied.

It wasn't long before Elizabeth had recovered well enough to join the rest of the party downstairs. Lady Catherine gave her a lecture on strong wills and the ills of being independent, but Elizabeth detected a note of softness in her tone. She wished to think this was the only way her aunt could find of conveying the fact that she was pleased everyone was safe.

"It was a fool thing to do Elizabeth, why you could all have been killed. No thought for anyone except yourself. You always were a selfish gal."

"Yes ma'am," Elizabeth said. "It was indeed a very foolish thing to do. It will not be repeated.

"I certainly hope not. I am not at all accustomed to this sort of behaviour," Lady Catherine rebuked. "Let us have some music Georgiana, This is indeed a very dull house.

Elizabeth smiled to herself. Lady Catherine was turning out not to be quite the dragon she had at first thought her to be.

"Georgiana has a great gift for music I think," Elizabeth said.

"She does indeed," replied Lady Catherine. "but I fear she is not in society enough at this time. A change of environment would be most beneficial, I am sure."

"You could be right, aunt. Is your suggestion to send her to town?"

"I shall be returning to Rosings in a few days, she may accompany myself and Anne. A change of scenery will be most beneficial. To enjoy Anne's company will bring her nothing but pleasure."

Although Elizabeth doubted the wisdom of this statement, she had no choice but to agree in principal. "It will have to be under Mr Darcy's agreement," she ventured.

"Fitzwilliam will see the benefits to be great. You can be sure of it my dear. He is after all to go to town himself, with Edward.

"I wonder what has become of Mr Wentworth?" wondered Elizabeth. "His absence has now been of some duration."

"His return will rest on the success of his journey, I am sure," replied Lady Catherine. "He is after all a Darcy and holds the family name with much pride. He will not return until this offence has been satisfied."

"Then let us hope it will be imminent your ladyship," Elizabeth said.

Chapter 8

Mr Wentworth, who had followed a very similar trail to Mr Darcy, was now over forty miles from Pemberley. His search had taken him through many villages, and he had met some very unsavoury characters, but his determination was not, in the least bit tempered. His sole aim was still to discover the whereabouts of the travelling family.

Several times, as Mr Darcy had done before him, he felt close to his quarry, only to be met with disappointment.

He was now entering a village that was far away from the usual carriageway, and he asked the same questions he had asked in previous villages, but this time the replies were different. His hopes were raised.

"They be camping up in Duckend Wood," one villager told him. "Tis their winter camping site, so it is."

"And they are still encamped there?" Mr Wentworth asked.

"Ay, sir, well um be last nite, to be sure."

Mr Wentworth tossed him a coin and then turned his horse in the direction the man had pointed. His hopes and temper raising with every turn of the road.

*****

When Georgiana was told of her impending departure for Rosings, she became quite disturbed.

"Are you insistent that I go Elizabeth?" she asked.

"Not at all. If it is your wish to remain here, or go to town, I am sure your brother will give his consent."

"Please do not think me ungrateful," Georgiana explained. "The festive season is but a few weeks away, and I would dearly love to help in the forthcoming arrangements."

"Then you shall," Elizabeth smiled at her, but was not convinced this was the true reason for her reluctance to travel with her aunt.

The disturbing thought that Georgiana had not left the house since her ordeal crossed Elizabeth's mind. She hoped with all her heart that her sister in law was, not now too frightened to visit the outside world.

"I think it would do my sister Kitty a great deal of good if you would accompany her to town for a few days Georgiana. Miss Wentworth, I am sure would be grateful for the change of society. They are both lacking in society, and you could be of help to secure some presents for the festive season."

"Do you wish it, Elizabeth?"

"I do indeed. Your help in that quarter would indeed relieve me of much concern."

"Then I will do it, for you," Georgiana smiled weakly.

"I thank you. It is indeed a worry to me no more. I shall now go and tell your aunt of our decision."

"Not accompany us!" Lady Catherine declared when informed. "Why ever not?"

"She is young ma'am, and wishes to see the new fashions in town, and to obtain gifts for family and friends."

"Uummph, well!" snorted Lady Catherine.

With sighing heart Elizabeth gathered all her courage together, took a deep breath and said. "Have you considered the possibility of remaining here at Pemberley until after the New Year ball ma'am? As all the girls and Mr Darcy are going to town, my lack of company will hang heavy indeed. Your ladyships continued residence here would bring me much pleasure."

"Your generosity is much indeed Elizabeth, but I regret I have to decline your offer," Lady Catherine replied. "There are a great many things awaiting my attention at Rosings. My presence there is long overdue."

"That is very sad indeed ma'am, but it cannot be helped," Elizabeth had great difficulty in stemming the overwhelming surge of relief that threatened to engulf her. "I shall, no doubt, find enough to entertain myself until everyone returns."

"It would do you no harm to go to town," Lady Catherine suggested. "You have not been seen enough in society since your marriage. Mr Darcy has a reputation to uphold. Besides you, yourself, would benefit from the change."

"I believe you are right ma'am. I will seek Mr Darcy's thoughts on this matter."

Elizabeth was making her way along the corridor in the direction of Mr Darcy's study, when she was intercepted by Mrs Reynolds.

"I beg your pardon ma'am, but I think you ought to know that Mr Wentworth has returned with a 'person'.

"A person?" queried Elizabeth.

"Yes ma'am," Mrs Reynolds explained. "I believe it is one of those travelling people."

"O good God!" exclaimed Elizabeth, her arms flapping wildly. "Where are they now? Does Mr Darcy know of their arrival?"

"Mr Wentworth went straight to the master's study, but the other one waits in the back room ma'am."

"Good Lord Mrs Reynolds, what are we to do? Mr Darcy will have no control of his temper, I am sure, and the consequences will be dire indeed."

"They will ma'am, and rightly so." replied Mrs Reynolds. "What poor Miss Georgiana has been through is a disgrace."

"It is Mrs Reynolds, but what good will come from it if Mr Darcy causes harm. It can only bring more concern." Elizabeth was beside herself. "Can we not stop the meeting between them?"

"It is too late Mrs Darcy. Mr Wentworth has all ready gone to my master."

"If Mr Darcy does something that cannot be undone, I fear matters will be very much worse."

"The master will take his revenge ma'am, no matter what else is said."

"I am sure you are right Mrs Reynolds, but it distresses me greatly." Elizabeth was now out of her mind with worry. She was lost as to which course to take. Mr Darcy must not be harmed in anyway, of that she was certain. "You say the gentleman is in the back room Mrs Reynolds?"

"He is, ma'am."

"Then I will go to him. Would you be so good as to ensure that Miss Darcy has neither sight or sound of our visitor."

"I will indeed ma'am."

When she entered the back room, the 'person'. was standing with his head bent, clutching his hat in his hands. He did not look up on her entrance.

"You are here to see my husband I believe?" she asked.

"Yes, ma'am."

"Can I be of assistance in any way?"

"No ma'am, my business is only with the master."

"I wish no harm to come to my husband," Elizabeth ventured.

"I have no wish to 'arm 'im ma'am. I am 'ere to put the story straight. That be all."

Silence descended on the room, and as Elizabeth could not think of anything else to say she turned to leave the room, almost knocking Mr Wentworth over in her haste.

"Mrs Darcy," he bowed. "I am very happy to see you again."

"Mr Wentworth, your return to us is most unexpected. Indeed we had no prior information of your arrival."

"My apologies, ma'am. I fear I was in no position to forward a letter of intent."

"No of course. Could I speak with you, do you think," Elizabeth asked.

Mr Wentworth followed her out of the room and closed the door behind them.

"I believe I know the subject of your meeting with Mr Darcy. May I be so bold as to claim your reassurance that nothing will befall my husband?"

"You may indeed, ma'am, but rest assured things are not as grievous as they first appeared to be."

"Thank you, sir, you have my gratitude."

Elizabeth felt a great weight lift from her heart as she quickly left the corridor in the direction of her room. She had no wish to converse with anyone on this subject or any other matter. As she climbed the stairs she noticed Mr Wentworth and his 'guest', heading towards Mr Darcy's study.

On entering the room the two men found Mr Darcy pacing the room, his face contorted with the anger he was feeling.

"This is a grievous act indeed that has befallen my sister," he almost spat the words out. "I cannot believe, after the patronage my family have shown to you over many years, you repay them with a crime so despicable it evades description. Is there one good reason why I should not horsewhip the lot of you, and may I say take pleasure in the punishment. To even see you in my sight offends my eyes."

The man stood just inside the room, turning his hat round and round in his hands. He did not speak.

"Speak man, before the control of my temper is lost. I demand, and will have revenge for what has befallen here."

"This be a sad day for my family Mr Darcy, to be sure it is," the man spoke at last. "I would cut off me arms rather than hurt a 'air on the heads of any one of you. To be sure I would. It was not of me family's doing this assault on your sister. Indeed it wasn't."

"Are you trying to tell me that none of your family had anything to do with my sister's misfortune?" Mr Darcy was close to losing control. "Damn you man, do not lie to me. I have my gamekeeper's word that it was one of the travelling men in the garden that day. Now tell me at once which of your family did this despicable thing? Why if you had nothing to hide did you leave my land in such a hurry? Speak man."

"We was ignorant of what had happened here, sir," replied the man. "T'was not till this gentleman came to our camp that we heard of it, and we were all grieved to be sure."

The man explained the best he could that his family had left the estate not knowing of the incident. They had had no knowledge of what had befallen Georgiana. When Mr Wentworth had arrived at their camp site in a dreadful rage, they were indeed very much at a disadvantage as to what was amiss.

"I asked all me family 'bout it," the man continued, "but they be at the same loss I be. And none of 'em would lie to me. I can tell if um be lying caught um out before, they wouldn't do it again."

"If you are lying to me, I swear on my sister's life I will tear you limb from limb with my own hands," Mr Darcy thumped the desk. Then he sat down in the chair with every appearance of a broken man.

"My friend here informs me, Darcy," Mr Wentworth spoke for the first time, "that there was a traveller of knives on the area about that time. He says he visited the camp and spent an evening with them."

"Is this true?" Mr Darcy was on his feet again. "Tell me man, what was his appearance?"

"He be young, sir, dark hair, bad skin," the man explained. "Come to think, sir, he never gave his name."

Mr Darcy's mind flashed back to the man lying in the plantation. The image was clear.

"You have never seen him before?" Mr Wentworth asked.

"No, sir, never."

"Then you must forgive me," Mr Darcy said. "I have been most unjust with my thoughts of your family."

"No 'arm bin done, sir. I would lay down my life for the Darcy's to be sure," the man said. "If any one of my kin had done this to the missy I would have settled the score me self."

"I believe you would," Mr Darcy was greatly relieved. "There was a body lying in the plantation close to where you were camped. It was devoid of life. This action was due to my gamekeeper, Mr Daniels, who happened upon the scene. He now lies under my roof, his life in the balance."

"I am grieved to hear that, sir. If there is anything me family can do, we will be more than happy to do so."

"Your kindness is generous indeed. I am ashamed of my thoughts."

"We would have all thought the same," the gypsy replied.

"You have no need to avoid the Darcy estates in future. I

will be glad to welcome you back anytime you wish to visit."
Mr Darcy felt decidedly humble.

"Thank you, sir. I be most relieved."

"Make sure our guest has enough brandy to keep out the
cold this winter Edward," Mr Darcy said. He turned to the old
man. "I can only hope of your forgiveness. My thoughts
towards you have been grievous indeed."

"All past now, sir," the man replied as he left the room.

Mr Darcy sat for quite some time after Mr Wentworth and
the gypsy had left. If he had happened on the encampment
that night, he was fully aware that he would not have asked
questions first. He had been lucky indeed that they had not
come within his sights.

By the time he joined the rest of the party in the drawing
room, his good humour had returned.

"Elizabeth would like me to take her sister and Miss
Wentworth to town for a few days, and she has offered to
accompany us, if you approve." Georgiana said as Mr Darcy
took a seat.

"I am not sure I should let anyone of you out of my sight
ever again." he smiled.

"They are seriously lacking in society, sir," Elizabeth
joined the conversation, "and as you will, yourself be in town,
I think little harm will come of it."

"In that case, you have my consent." he replied.

The rest of the evening was spent in pleasant harmony,
and Elizabeth was more than happy that things, at last had
returned to normal.

Mr Wentworth and his sister spent a great deal of time
entertaining Kitty and Georgiana with stories of their travels,
and they, in their turn amused their guests with recitals on the
pianoforte. Elizabeth and Mr Darcy caught up on their reading,
whilst Lady Catherine, gave her opinion on the younger parties
amusements, with much emphasis.

Two days later Lady Catherine departed for Rosings,
threatening to return in two weeks, while the remaining party

set out on their trip to town.

Kitty was very much overawed at the standard of society in town, but was delighted beyond all words when, at a party given by one of Mr Darcy's friends, she enjoyed the company, once again of Colonel Fitzwilliam.

To Elizabeth's surprise Caroline Bingley did not make an appearance. Mr and Mrs Hurst were among the party, but of their sister there was no sign.

"Mrs Darcy," Mrs Hurst came to sit by Elizabeth. "How nice to see you in town. Your family are all in good health I hope."

"Except for my mother Mrs Hurst, my family are well. I thank you," Elizabeth replied.

"I must congratulate you on the transformation of your younger sister Elizabeth," Mrs Hurst continued. "She is indeed turning heads."

"She is indeed, but I have Georgiana to thank for it. She has tutored Kitty in the ways of society most excellently."

"Such a sweet girl Georgiana. Do you not think so Elizabeth?"

"She is one of the dearest people. Her company brings me much joy."

Mrs Hurst turned to Elizabeth and laid a hand on her arm. "I am grieved indeed that Caroline has lost the good opinion of Mr Darcy," she said. "It is of her own doing I know, but Elizabeth she is distraught, She refuses to come out into society, at any time. She will not receive company, and stays within the confines of our house."

"It is a sad state indeed Mrs Hurst, but it is not for me to influence my husband on his judgement of this matter."

"My brother, Elizabeth, is very much put out. He quite understands, as well as we all do, that Caroline was very seriously out of order with her conversations, but I am of the opinion, that she has now learned the error of her ways."

"I am sure she has Mrs Hurst, but my husband's good opinion once lost, is lost forever."

"Then it is grievous indeed. I fear she will remain a recluse. Lost to society forever."

"If you will excuse me Mrs Hurst. I must speak with Georgiana." Elizabeth rose and crossed the room. She had no reason to speak with her sister in law at this time, but she had less wish to continue the conversation with Mrs Hurst. It had been some time now, and under the instruction of Lady Catherine, that she did not interfere with her husband's decisions. If he chose to avoid the company of certain people, it was not her place to intervene.

"O Elizabeth, I had forgotten the pleasure company brings me," Georgiana said as Elizabeth joined her. Although, I have not seen Caroline in this assembly."

"I believe she is a little unwell at present," Elizabeth replied. "I am happy though that this gathering is bringing you pleasure."

"I hope it is nothing serious that ails Caroline."

"I am sure it is not. Mrs Hurst informs me that Caroline, at this time, prefers her own company."

Although Georgiana refrained from asking any more questions, her expression remained puzzled.

"Mrs Darcy," a very handsome young man bowed to Elizabeth. For a few seconds she was quite puzzled as to who it was, but then she remembered their meeting at Southview.

"Mr Randal, I am delighted to see you in society. I trust you have settled back into your ancestral home."

"We have indeed Mrs Darcy, and I must say that society in your country is far superior to what we have been used to." He looked at Georgiana.

"Mr Randal," Elizabeth said. "May I introduce you to Mr Darcy's sister. Georgiana, this is Mr Randal, he has come to live near my sister Jane."

"I am most happy to make your acquaintance Miss Darcy. May I be so bold as to engage you in the next two dances?"

"Thank you Mr Randal, I would be delighted."

Elizabeth smiled to herself as she noticed the impression

this handsome young man had made on Georgiana.

"I was hoping to engage Miss Darcy in a dance, but I can see I have been outwitted." Mr Wentworth had joined Elizabeth. "Can you tell me who the gentleman is Mrs Darcy?"

"His name is Randal, Mr Wentworth. He and his elder brother have come to live in England from France. Their ancestral home is in the same county as Mr Bingley and my sister Jane."

"Then, like myself, he is new to society."

"He is indeed."

"Then if you will excuse me I shall go and engage my sister."

Elizabeth watched from the safety of her chair as her three charges danced to the familiar music of her single days. It had been little over a year since she herself had looked forward to the sole activity of these gatherings, but now she knew she would be happy to spend her whole life within the confines of Pemberley.

Many acquaintances sought out her company through out the evening, so it was nearing the close of the party when Mrs Hurst managed to gain her attention again.

"Mrs Darcy, I have no wish to cause you discomfort," she said. "but I am most concerned for my sister's sanity. Indeed this unfortunate occurrence has had a most alarming affect on her very nature."

"Much as I would wish things to be different Mrs Hurst, it is not in my power to change my husband's wishes." Elizabeth was a little put out by the continued pleading, but she had to reluctantly admire the loyalty Mrs Hurst was showing for her sister. "If Mr Bingley wishes to approach my husband on this matter, I am sure he will do so in his own time. It is indeed out of my control."

"This is not like you Elizabeth, to refuse to help a friend," Mrs Hurst rebuked.

"Your sister Mrs Hurst, has in the past caused me much embarrassment and discomfort. I did not see any sign of aid on your part during this time." Elizabeth spoke more sharply than she intended.

"You are right Elizabeth, my sister does not deserve your generosity. Forgive me for bringing the matter to your attention." she curtsied and quickly walked away.

Elizabeth was left feeling a little discomforted. It was indeed unfortunate that matters had reached this conclusion, but they were none of her doing. Caroline had, indeed brought about her own circumstance.

The ladies enjoyed their visit to town very much, but Elizabeth was greatly relieved when Mr Darcy suggested that they all return to Pemberley the following day.

Kitty, however was not keen to leave Colonel Fitzwilliam's company. On hearing they were to return to Pemberley she immediately went into a depression of spirits.

"Kitty you must not let the world know that Colonel Fitzwilliam's company affects you in this manner. It is very unladylike to take on so." Elizabeth instructed.

"O Lizzie, I know what you say is true," Kitty sighed. "but I enjoy his company so much it distresses me greatly to think of losing it."

"Then make the most of this evening, Kitty. Go put on your prettiest dress, so that he will remember you when you have left town."

"Do you think he will, Lizzie?"

"I am sure of it. He pays you much attention as you are very well aware."

Kitty hugged her sister then ran up the stairs to do as she had been advised.

Elizabeth's advice did not work. In fact Colonel Fitzwilliam actively avoided Kitty's company that evening by bringing with him a lady of his own.

"Lizzie, I am at a loss to understand Colonel Fitzwilliam's actions this evening," Kitty cried once they had returned home. "His look did not even search me out, and who was that he brought with him?"

"It is puzzling indeed," Elizabeth said as she comforted her sister. "I know not of the answer, but I am still convinced he likes you very much Kitty."

"That cannot be so, Lizzie. If it is as you say, then he would not have brought a partner this evening."

Elizabeth had no answer. What Kitty said was indeed true.

"I wish I had never come to Pemberley. I would never have met him then," she sobbed.

"There is a sensible answer to this, Kitty, I am sure. Dry your eyes, it pains me to see you suffering. I will seek Mr Darcy's thoughts on the matter. Maybe his companion was his sister or cousin."

"Do you think that is possible, Lizzie?" asked Kitty with hope in her eyes.

"I do indeed. I will do my best to discover the truth. Now go to bed, we have an early start in the morning."

If it had been his sister, Elizabeth thought, he would have had no reservations in introducing her to his company. Indeed she had no idea what his intentions were.

Their return to Pemberley heralded delight for Elizabeth. Her sister Jane, Mr Bingley and their daughter had paid a surprise visit.

"Lizzie, I am so pleased to see you," Jane hugged her sister. "I hope we are not taking advantage of your hospitality. Mr Bingley has urgent business with Mr Darcy, so we travelled in the hope of surprising you, and as you have not seen my dear Charlotte for a while, we thought to make this a special visit."

"My dear Jane, you are always most welcome," Elizabeth smiled happily. "I do not see enough of you. I miss your company very much indeed. Lady Catherine is insisting upon it that your stay at the festive season is of some duration."

"What has happened to bring about this turn of favour, Lizzie?" Jane laughed. "Not that I am indeed happy to comply with her wishes."

"I have had to learn to temper my emotions, Jane, as you instructed. Believe me, my dear sister, it has not been at all easy."

"I believe you. Lady Catherine is not, as I recall, the easiest of women."

"Let me change my outdoor clothes, Jane, then we can converse at length. I have very much to acquaint you with."

While the women had been talking, Mr Bingley was a little way off conversing with Mr Darcy. He strode over to meet Elizabeth.

"Mrs Darcy, I am very pleased to see you again. May I say you are looking very well indeed."

"I am, thank you, sir," replied Elizabeth. "It is indeed a pleasure to have you stay."

"I thank you. Are you in command of all the amusements to be held at Pemberley this festive season?"

"Lady Catherine has indeed been a great help. Without her continued assistance, I should indeed be at a loss."

Mr Bingley looked a little puzzled at this turn of events. "I am very happy to hear it," he said at last. "Lady Catherine is, I believe an authority on these matters."

"She is indeed, sir," Elizabeth laughed.

"Please excuse me, Mrs Darcy. I have urgent business to discuss with your husband."

As Elizabeth took her leave of her brother in law, she had no doubt as to what the subject of his urgent business was all about.

The two men retired to the study.

"Look here Darcy," Mr Bingley said when the door had been closed. "I know my sister Caroline has caused much irritation to both you and Elizabeth, but to exclude her from your society, it is dire indeed, sir."

"Bingley, I have no wish to cause unpleasantness between us. You are indeed my oldest friend, but your sister's attitude towards my wife, cannot, and will not be tolerated." Mr Darcy explained. "She has indeed been most offensive, I myself have overheard her conversations and they have been very unpleasant indeed."

"This is most distressing," Mr Bingley sighed. "I

understand your opinion fully, Darcy, and indeed respect it, but Caroline is in much distress. She refuses all society and will not leave the house. At most times she confines herself to her own room, it is most unsatisfactory."

"It cannot be helped, Bingley," Mr Darcy was adamant. "I will not have my wife slighted in this way, and to be made feel uncomfortable in her own home."

"Darcy, you of all people should understand that your marriage to Elizabeth destroyed Caroline's hopes of becoming mistress of Pemberley. I am sure her temper is regulated by this event."

"I am sure it is, Bingley, but I have never encouraged your sister in that direction. It escapes me that she should think it would be so."

"We have been constant companions for many years now," Mr Bingley said. "It is quite understandable that my sister would have had designs in that direction."

"None of which were promoted by me." Mr Darcy was adamant.

"I understand your feelings towards my sister Darcy, and I must say she has actively encouraged them, but it distresses me to see her suffer in this way."

"Bingley," Mr Darcy said firmly. "How can I continue to receive your sister in to my company, when her sole intention is to cause Elizabeth discomfort?"

"You are right Darcy," replied Mr Bingley sadly. "I have indeed asked too much of your most generous nature."

"No, no, Bingley. It is a sensitive subject, and I quite comprehend your feelings." Mr Darcy soothed. "It is not my wish that this matter should cause unpleasantness between us, but I have Elizabeth's comfort to ensure."

"You are perfectly right Darcy, as always. In your position, I am sure I would have acted in the same manner," Mr Bingley replied. "We will converse no more on this subject."

"Does this mean that we will be deprived of your company throughout the festive season?" Mr Darcy asked.

"I fear it does. I cannot abandon Caroline to herself at this time."

"Elizabeth will be very sad indeed," Darcy frowned deeply at the distress of his old friend. "It is not in my character to have a change in my opinion, as you very well know, but I will consult with Elizabeth on this matter. If she is prepared to receive your sister at Pemberley, I am sure this situation can be resolved."

Mr Bingley's face lit up with relief and pleasure. "Darcy, I cannot tell you how much this means to me. I am indeed indebted to you. It has troubled me greatly. You are very generous indeed, my sister does not deserve your good opinion."

"She most certainly does not," Mr Darcy smiled at his friend. "I am prepared to accept your sister back into our society for the sake of our friendship Bingley, but if this occurrence is ever repeated, her exclusion will be complete."

"And rightly so. I, myself will instruct her on this matter. Mrs Bingley will be delighted with the news. It is far more than either of us could have ever hoped for. To be deprived of Elizabeth's company, would be grievous indeed. she holds her in great esteem, as you well know. You are, Mr Darcy, a most excellent friend, and my gratitude is great indeed."

"You forget Bingley, we have yet to secure Elizabeth's consent," Mr Darcy smiled at his friends elation.

"Her generous nature falls little short of your own Darcy. I am confident she will relent."

"Let us pray she does. Now let us go and join the ladies."

While the men had been talking, Elizabeth had been acquainting Jane with recent events. Although she was careful not to mention Georgiana's misfortune.

"Do you think Kitty is in love with Colonel Fitzwilliam, Lizzie?" Jane asked with some concern.

"I am sure she is, Jane. Her manner discloses it in every way."

"And Colonel Fitzwilliam, do you think he is love?"

"A week ago I would have had to say yes, but his behaviour at the dance was so against his character," replied Elizabeth sadly. "Indeed, Jane, she was most upset, and I was at a loss to explain it to her. I must consult Mr Darcy on the matter and see if I can gain an explanation from him."

"Poor Kitty, I do hope things resolve themselves. Now tell me, Lizzie, what has brought about this generous nature of Lady Catherine."

"I am not sure," Elizabeth laughed. "At one time she even complimented my family. It is indeed difficult to explain. She has been most helpful without pressure."

"Perhaps she is sorry for what she has done," Jane said. "To be deprived of Mr Darcy's company must have been the reason for much pain."

"It was indeed I think, but she still believes him to have married beneath his station in life."

"It is very generous of her to accept it, Lizzie. I fear she would be a formidable enemy."

At this point Jane's baby started to cry. "O Jane, I have been so selfish, taking all your time for my revelations. I have not even asked how motherhood is suiting you?"

"She is the dearest child, Lizzie. Her birth has brought much joy to both Mr Bingley and myself."

"You are so lucky, Jane. Am I never to be allowed the joy of giving Mr Darcy a son and heir?"

"You worry too much, Lizzie. I am sure all will be well in time." Jane consoled her.

"I wish I had your conviction, Jane. It is well over a year now and there is no sign." Elizabeth sighed heavily.

"To spend time with Mr Darcy alone is most beneficial, Lizzie. Indeed when a child is born, a relationship changes."

"O Jane, everything is all right between you and Mr Bingley, is it not?" Elizabeth was most concerned.

"Of course it is, Lizzie, he is the dearest man," Jane laughed. "No, what I intended to imply, was that a mother's thoughts are divided. You, at this moment may give Mr Darcy your full attention, while I, my dear Lizzie, have to think of Charlotte as well."

"She is so very sweet, Jane. I am indeed envious." Elizabeth spoke with feeling.

"You too will know the joy, I am sure." Jane took her sister's hand. "It pains me to think of the joy our dear friend Charlotte has lost, Lizzie. Mr Collins was indeed suffering when I left Huntsford."

"Yes, Charlotte's death affected him very deeply indeed." Elizabeth sighed. I miss her, Jane, she was a very good friend."

"Do you think Mr Collins will marry again, Lizzie?"

"I do not know, but I think it unlikely. He was very fond of Charlotte."

"Lady Catherine will be of great service to him I am sure." Jane mused. "It would not surprise me if she undertook to care for his daughter's welfare."

"I am sure she will."

The two men entered the room at this time.

"Have you two been hatching plans to cause me discomfort?" Mr Darcy asked as he took a seat.

"No indeed, sir," Jane laughed. "Lizzie has been telling me about the plans Lady Catherine has for the festive season."

"They will be many, I am sure," Mr Darcy replied.

Mr Bingley went to sit near his wife, and the look that passed between them, was an assurance that all was well between himself and Mr Darcy.

The unfortunate situation had not been discussed with her sister, as the discourse was between Mr Darcy and Caroline."

"And this is the cause of much happiness I take it?" Mr Darcy rose and peered down at the infant Bingley.

"Mr Darcy, may I have the pleasure of introducing you to my daughter Charlotte." Mr Bingley said solemnly, and everyone except Elizabeth laughed. The look on Mr Darcy's face as he took in the baby's features disturbed her very much indeed. His expression had softened, and his eyes had taken on a dreamy quality.

Why had she not conceived? It was the one thing that marred an otherwise perfect relationship. Mr Darcy to his credit had never once, approached the subject, but Elizabeth knew it must be in his mind.

Throughout the evening Elizabeth could not shake off the feeling of failure that threatened to overwhelm her. Her continued state of wife and not mother was of great concern to her.

"Lizzie, will you not play for us this evening?" Georgiana asked. "It has been some time since we have had the pleasure of hearing you play."

"You play so beautifully yourself, Georgiana, it makes my efforts look very ill indeed." Elizabeth tried to smile.

"You play beautifully, my brother has always said so," Georgiana coaxed. "Please play for us."

"If you insist upon it, I will, but only one," Elizabeth crossed to the piano forte. Her rendition of a ballad reflected her mood, and Jane watched her with concern.

"You must not worry so much, Lizzie," Jane said as Elizabeth returned to sit beside her. "I know what is in your heart, and it will only make matters worse."

"It distresses me so, Jane. Indeed I fail to understand my condition."

"Please, Lizzie, I beg of you, do not take on so. You are worrying for nothing. All will be well in time I am sure."

"I wish I was more like you, Jane. God is repaying your goodness most generously."

"He is indeed. I am sure I could not bear anymore happiness."

Elizabeth smiled at her sister. She was so happy for her.

Jane and Mr Bingley remained at Pemberley a further two days, and were only allowed to depart on the promise of a longer stay over the festive season. This assurance they gave with pleasure.

Their carriage departed down the drive as another one arrived with the daily post.

"You appear to have another letter from your father Elizabeth," Mr Darcy said as he looked through the letters.

"Two in the same amount of days, he must have serious news to report."

"He must indeed, so much correspondence is most unusual," she took the letter he handed her with a slight frown.

"O my goodness me," she exclaimed as her eyes took in the news. "I cannot believe it."

"It is not bad news I hope?" Mr Darcy asked.

"I do not think so. It is better I think if you read it for yourself," she handed back the letter.

My dearest Elizabeth.

It is with some sadness on my part that I have to convey to you that Mrs Bennett has now returned downstairs. She has at last recovered her nerves, and I fear greatly for my sanity. I have to admit though, Lizzie, I have missed them. They have been my old friends for some time now, and their absence was disturbing. Think of me from now on my dear, as my time will be spent more in the study, than in the drawing room.

We have in the past spoken of the sport we occasionally give our neighbours. Well, dear Lizzie, we now have a new one, that I fear will keep them all amused for some time to come.

A letter arrived by yesterday's post from your cousin Mr Collins. Its contents caused much amusement to Mrs Bennett. He informs us, my dear Lizzie, that he wishes to marry your sister Mary. Her goodness, since the death of his dear Charlotte, has given him much comfort, he says, and he is convinced of his continued happiness with my daughter. Lady Catherine is in complete approval, as she stated on her return from Pemberley.

Well, Lizzie, what do you make of this turn of events? If I marry any more of my daughters off to unsuspecting men, I fear Mrs Bennett will have nothing to live for."

Your loving father.

"Well, this is news indeed," Mr Darcy smiled as he handed back the letter. "What are your feelings on this matter Elizabeth?"

"She has always favoured, Mr Collins, sir," Elizabeth replied. "I think it may be a very good match indeed."

"Then everyone is happy."

"I believe they are, sir, although it is such a short time after the death of poor Charlotte, I doubt very much if Sir William and Lady Lucas will approve."

"He has a daughter to care for, Elizabeth. I believe he is seeking to secure her future."

"I am sure you are right, sir."

"Then let us invite them for the Christmas festivities. I am sure Lady Catherine would consider it a very generous gesture on your part."

"Mr Darcy, I firmly believe your mischievous nature is now firmly established." she laughed up at her husband.

"I had the best tutor my dearest Elizabeth. I hope you are now not regretting the lessons you have taught me?"

"No indeed, sir."

"When Elizabeth imparted the news to Kitty, it did not have the desired affect she had hoped for. In fact she burst into tears and ran to her room. Elizabeth followed her with much concern.

"Are you not pleased for your sister, Kitty?" she asked.

"Of course I am, Lizzie, but it only leaves me. Will I never find someone to love me as Mr Darcy loves you?"

"I am sure you will, Kitty," Elizabeth consoled her. "You are not yet one and nine, it is very young to be getting so distressed over this matter. You have several years of enjoyment before this thought will be of any concern."

"But, Lizzie, all my sisters will be married, and I will be very much talked of."

"Of course you will not. Mary is older than you by above a year, and as for Lydia's marriage! Do you really wish to marry as she did, in haste, and have her concerns."

"No, of course not, but it is so unfair."

"I believe this news has arrived at a very unsuitable time for you Kitty dear. You are, I think still distressed over Colonel Fitzwilliam's actions at your last meeting."

"You are right, Lizzie, I am sure. Did you inquire from Mr Darcy of the relationship between them?"

"I am afraid I have no information to impart at present, but I will, as soon as it is convenient, ask his opinion." Elizabeth had not lied to her sister as such, but she had indeed sort out the information from her husband. His reply had been quite evasive.

"She is of no relation, I believe," was all he would say on the matter.

"Come, Kitty, let us go down and design our list for the festive season. I am sure Colonel Fitzwilliam will consent to be our guest on that occasion, then you may ask him for yourself."

"Will he come, Lizzie, do you think?" she brightened a little. "What if he should bring her too?"

"She will not be invited, I assure you. There, now dry your tears, we have no wish to let Georgiana and Miss Wentworth know you are out of spirits."

"I shall write to Mary, and wish her happiness," Kitty said solemnly. "I am happy for her, Lizzie. Truly I am."

Elizabeth hugged her sister, then they both returned downstairs.

Before Elizabeth could enter the drawing room, Mrs Reynolds appeared. Her face was pale and drawn.

"Mrs Reynolds, what ever is the matter?"

"It is Mr Daniels, ma'am, he is with us no more. Would you be so good as to inform the master?"

"Of course I will. Poor Mrs Daniels, she was so certain that he was in the stages of recovery. What exactly happened Mrs Reynolds?"

"He just faded away Mrs Daniels said. The doctor says he never made up the blood he had lost, and didn't have the energy to fight."

"Mrs Daniels, where is she now?"

"I believe she has gone to her home, as to inform the children ma'am."

"I will visit her directly," Elizabeth said. "Go and rest Mrs Reynolds, I fear this news has upset you greatly."

"It has indeed ma'am. Mr Daniels and myself have been at Pemberley for many years together."

On sharing the news with Mr Darcy, Elizabeth was concerned for his reaction. His face visibly paled, and his stance became unbalanced.

"Good God," he spoke after a few seconds. "This is grievous indeed. To give his life for my sister, it is beyond all bounds of loyalty. Where is his wife now?"

"I believe she has gone to her children, sir." Elizabeth replied.

"Then I will go to her immediately. Pray do not speak of this in the presence of Georgiana. I will speak with her directly myself."

"Very good, sir."

Once he had left the room Elizabeth sank down into one of the chairs. Was there to be no end to the distress that had recently befell this family? First her mother, then dear Charlotte. Georgiana's misfortune, and now this. That was apart from Caroline's condition, and that of Kitty. Elizabeth was sure Jane did not have to contend with such misfortunes.

It was over half an hour before Elizabeth joined the rest of the party in the music room

"Lizzie, Georgiana has promised to take Miss Wentworth and myself to St James's Palace when we are next in town. This is so generous of her, is it not?"

"It is indeed," Elizabeth was pleased to see her sister's return of spirits.

"Now there is a great deal to be done if we wish to enjoy this coming festive season. You can both help me with the placement of our guests at the table, and the guest list for the New Year ball must be checked. There are a great many, and I am sure three pairs of hands will dispense with them much quicker.

"Do you think mama will be well enough to visit us, Lizzie?" Kitty asked. "And what about Lydia? I would love to see Lydia again."

"I doubt very much whether Mr and Mrs Wickham will be joining us Kitty. They are, I believe, going to Longbourne."

"Then they could all travel here together. I long to see my sister again." Kitty said.

"If you wish to see Lydia, Kitty, you will have to spend Christmas with mama. Although she is a little better, she is not yet fit enough to travel such a distance. You would not wish to put her through discomfort, I am sure."

"Of course not, but it would be nice to have all the family at this time."

"Maybe next year, Kitty. Now let us attend to our duties."

Chapter 9

Three days before the festive season itself, all Elizabeth's favourite people arrived. Her aunt and uncle Gardiner, Jane with Mr Bingley and their daughter.

"Aunt, it is so good of you to come," Elizabeth kissed her aunt with warmth.

"You look well, Lizzie. Marriage suits you I think," her aunt smiled at her favourite niece.

"I believe it does," Elizabeth laughed. "Mr Darcy is at this moment in town, but his return is imminent. I have so much to acquaint you with, aunt, I fear I may take up your entire evening."

"Then it will be a very pleasant one, I am sure."

Elizabeth loved her aunt and uncle, they were the dearest of people. It was with much pride she listened as Mr Darcy conversed with Mr Gardiner on topics above her understanding. To have one set of relations that did not embarrass Mr Darcy was of great worth. Indeed if it had not been for the holiday she had spent with them in Derbyshire, she was convinced her marriage would never have taken place. Her debt to them both was great, and Mr Darcy's opinion of them was extremely high.

During the evening Elizabeth informed her aunt of the forthcoming marriage of Mary to Mr Collins.

"This is news indeed Elizabeth," Mrs Gardiner exclaimed. "It is a little soon after losing dear Charlotte I feel, but he does have a child to consider."

"These are my feelings too, aunt, but Mr Darcy has convinced me that the child's welfare is paramount."

"Do you think Mary is aware of the responsibilities she is undertaking, Lizzie?"

"I believe she has always favoured Mr Collins, and this is the outcome she had hoped for I think."

"Then let us wish them well. Have you seen them since the engagement has taken place?"

"No, but Mr Darcy insisted that they be invited to Pemberley for Christmas," Elizabeth laughed. "He has, I fear, aunt, developed a very mischievous nature indeed."

"And all under your instruction I am sure," her aunt replied. "Jane looks very well, Lizzie. Motherhood suits her I think."

"It does indeed. I am so pleased to see her so content. She deserves all the happiness in the world."

Mr Wentworth passed at this moment. "Mr Wentworth, may I introduce you to my aunt, Mrs Gardiner."

"I am delighted to make your acquaintance," he bowed low.

"Mr Wentworth is recently arrived in this country, aunt. His life, I believe has been spent in the Far East."

"How interesting. You must find our climate here very different," Mrs Gardiner suggested.

"I do indeed ma'am, and my cousin Mr Darcy assures me I have not as yet experienced the worst of it."

"No indeed, the peaks can be quite savage at this time of year," Elizabeth's aunt smiled.

"If you will excuse me ma'am, I must take possession of a delivery that has, at this very moment arrived."

"He is a very nice young man, Lizzie. How long is he to stay at Pemberley?"

"For some duration, aunt. He is, in the event of Mr Darcy not having a son, the heir to Pemberley. Mr Darcy spends a great deal of time schooling him in the matters of the estates."

"This is a little premature, Lizzie," her aunt said with a frown. "Your marriage has been but a year, surely there is no reason to believe that there will not be a son?"

"Thank you, aunt, but if anything should befall Mr Darcy before that event can take place, the estate has to be secure."

"I understand, but it causes you concern I see, Lizzie."

"A little, aunt. If only I had Jane's good fortune, and had a child of my own, the future of Pemberley would be without question."

"This is troubling you, my dear Lizzie?"

"I am ashamed to say it is, aunt."

"Surely it is a little early to be of concern?"

"That is what my sister Jane says, aunt, but I know there are people who have expected news in that quarter for many months now. I cannot understand my condition."

"And this sort of behaviour will not help at all," Mrs Gardiner said with some emphasis. "Truly, Lizzie the more you worry, the less prospect of you achieving your wish. Believe me, Lizzie, I know. I was married above three years before my first born arrived."

"I always believed that to be design, aunt," Elizabeth spoke with feeling.

"Indeed it was not. So determined I became to give Mr Gardiner a child of his own, I jeopardized my very wish. As soon as I had resigned myself that it was not a blessing I would receive, it came about. So now, Lizzie, put it from your mind. Enjoy the life you have now. God will provide in time."

"You are so kind, aunt, but I fear it is not that easy."

"You must try, Elizabeth. Worrying will not help the situation."

"I will try, aunt, I promise."

"Mrs Darcy," Mr Bingley had joined their company. "I do hope I am not interrupting."

"Indeed you are not, Mr Bingley," Elizabeth smiled up at him. "I was just discussing with my aunt the engagement between my sister Mary and Mr Collins."

"It is good news indeed," Mr Bingley replied. "May I be so bold has to claim your attention."

"You may indeed," Elizabeth replied.

"I will go and speak to your sister Jane, Elizabeth," Mrs Gardiner said as she rose from her seat.

"Mrs Darcy, I wish to extend my deepest gratitude over the position of my sister Caroline. She has I fear, in the past caused you much distress, and I have spoken to her at length on the subject. I have her assured promise that nothing of this nature will ever befall you again."

"It is all forgot, I assure you Mr Bingley. Caroline has

indeed brought about her own discomfort, but I am sure she has learned much from her actions. If Mr Darcy wishes to accept her back into his society, then I have no objection."

"She is indeed a different person, Mrs Darcy." Mr Bingley's face was a picture of relief. "It offends me greatly that she has put Darcy in such a position he felt he had to exclude her from his society.

"It is unfortunate indeed, Mr Bingley, but I am sure Mr Darcy has it no longer in his mind."

"His forgiveness is more than she deserves. You are both very dear friends."

"We are brother and sister now, Mr Bingley, we should have no discomfort between us, but you still seem a little troubled. Is there something else that offends you, sir?"

"My dear Mrs Darcy, you do indeed see my mind," he sighed deeply. "Well…can I just say…it is just that. Well, Caroline will be arriving tomorrow…"

"I will treat her as though it has never been. You may be assured I will cause her no discomfort." Elizabeth felt for this gentle man who was trying to do right by all parties.

"Mrs Darcy, how can I ever repay the kindness you are offering? Indeed, your generous nature is more than I deserve."

"Do not think again on this matter, sir. It is forgot by all parties."

"I thank you, ma'am."

As he walked back to where his wife was sitting he was a much relieved man.

"May I say what a warm welcome you are extending to everyone, Elizabeth," Mr Gardiner said as he took the vacant seat next to her. "It pleases your aunt very much that her two favourite nieces have been most fortunate."

"We have indeed, uncle. My happiness is more than I deserve," replied Elizabeth with a smile. "I was just telling aunt Gardiner of the engagement between my sister Mary and Mr Collins."

"Really, this is a surprise," Mr Gardiner was visibly surprised. "When is the wedding to take place?"

"Early in the New Year I believe."

"Well, well who would have thought it. Young Mary hey, well I never ." Mr Gardiner chuckled to himself. "I must confess I never thought that she would ever marry."

"No, nor I uncle, but she did always favour Mr Collins. I believe they will make a very good match."

"On reflection, I think you might be right, Lizzie," Mr Gardiner continued. "My sister Mrs Bennett must indeed be delighted."

"She is indeed," Elizabeth laughed. "To my father's consternation, it has stimulated her to relinquish her state above stairs and return to the drawing room. I believe."

"That is most fortunate, and if Kitty should marry too, no doubt it will encourage my sister to visit the village and tell all her friends."

"Indeed it may, sir."

They both laughed.

"There is much gaiety radiating from this quarter of the room," Mr Darcy had returned from London and was standing beside them. "I hope it is at no-one's expense?"

"No indeed, sir," Elizabeth was most pleased to see her husband. "I was just acquainting my uncle with the forthcoming nuptials."

"I am delighted for them both," Mr Darcy replied. "Everyone should marry. I highly recommend it."

"I am pleased to hear that, Mr Darcy," Mr Gardiner said. "My niece has certainly benefited from the experience. I have never seen her look so radiant."

"I thank you, sir. I believe Pemberley has taken her to its heart. It has most certainly had a more lively atmosphere since Elizabeth arrived. This house seems to be full of very attractive ladies most of the time. I indeed have no complaints. Now, shall we have some music Elizabeth? I am sure our guest would approve."

Georgiana was persuaded to give a recital on the pianoforte, and was soon accompanied by Mr Wentworth. The evening continued pleasantly in the same vein, until tiring of music the guests involved themselves in various games.

"This is a very happy house Mrs Darcy," Sophia Wentworth expressed her pleasure. "I believe I could live here happily forever."

"You are very kind Miss Wentworth. I believe Mr Darcy would be more than happy with that arrangement" replied Elizabeth. "I must confess when I first moved to Derbyshire, the thought of a house as large as this was daunting indeed, but now I believe I love Pemberley above all buildings."

"You are most fortunate. Mr Darcy has great regard for you I believe."

"I am indeed," laughed Elizabeth. "I can honestly say that I am truly happy."

The following day Mr Wentworth requested that Elizabeth, Georgiana and Kitty accompany his sister and himself to his own drawing room. They had a gift for them he explained, and he hoped it would meet with their approval.

"We may have been too bold in our assumptions," he said. "If our gift to you offends in any way, please do not feel any regret at refusing it. Your hospitality has been beyond our wildest hopes and we felt we would like to give something back in return."

The women were interested but puzzled as they followed him to his apartments.

It seemed, as they entered the room, that it was completely filled with materials, silks and jewels of every description.

"I took the liberty of securing some fabrics from India. I hope you approve," he sounded very unsure of his gift.

Kitty squealed with delight, and Georgiana could not believe her eyes.

"They are really beautiful," Georgiana exclaimed. "Are they for our pleasure?"

"They are indeed, Miss Darcy," Mr Wentworth smiled at

her. "Beautiful cloth for a beautiful lady. Every lady in the house shall have a share."

"I have never seen anything as fine as this," Kitty found her voice at last. "Look at the colours, Lizzie, and they are all so soft."

"Indeed they are magnificent," Elizabeth said. "Mr Wentworth you have been most kind. These gifts must I fear have cost you dear."

"Your hospitality has been above the call of duty Mrs Darcy, you have accepted us as part of your family. I have been most comfortable in your home. I could not have wished for better."

"You are most welcome Mr Wentworth, but your tone suggested that your visit is drawing to a conclusion," Elizabeth asked puzzled.

"I feel my full time presence under Mr Darcy's roof would not be beneficial Mrs Darcy."

"To whom, Mr Wentworth?"

"To myself. I believe this festive season will convince me that I have made the right decision. Now, please choose at your leisure," he indicated the fabric. "If you will excuse me I have business with my cousin." he bowed and left the room.

His attitude caused Elizabeth much concern. Was he not happy under Mr Darcy's roof? It could not be so. Every hospitality had been offered him.

The pleasure of her two sisters soon pushed the thoughts to the back of her mind. Mr Wentworth and his sister had been most generous with their gift. It was more than possible that there was enough material here to clothe half of Derbyshire.

"Is all this really for us, Lizzie?" Kitty asked in amazement.

"I believe it is Kitty," Elizabeth laughed at her sisters delight. "Surely you will find something here to catch the eye of Colonel Fitzwilliam."

Time was forgotten as the four women together with Jane and aunt Gardiner, admired the gift they had been given. It was not until Mrs Reynolds came to the apartments, to inform them of Mr and Mrs Hurst and Caroline's arrival, that Elizabeth realized how the time had flown.

"I will come directly, Mrs Reynolds. Please apologize for me to our guests." She turned to Jane.

"This is a wretched beginning, Jane, Caroline will think I am avoiding her company with some purpose."

"Do not take on so, Lizzie. I am sure Caroline is just relieved to be invited here. She will not slight you again. I have Mr Bingley's word on it."

"I did not mean that, Jane. I had planned to meet her at the door, that is all."

"Then hurry, Lizzie, you may yet avoid offence." Jane laughed.

Caroline stood behind Mr and Mrs Hurst, which in itself was unusual. Her face was pale and solemn, her head bent a little.

"Mr and Mrs Hurst, Caroline. I am so pleased you could join us for the festive season."

"Mrs Darcy, we are delighted." Mr Hurst said. "I hope Darcy has plenty of sport for us?"

"I am sure he has, Mr Hurst."

"Caroline, I am pleased to see you. Please come through to the drawing room," Elizabeth had decided to treat Caroline as though nothing offensive had ever happened between them. "I will send for refreshments. It is indeed cold at this time of year."

"The snow on the peaks is a sight indeed," Mrs Hurst observed.

"I believe winter can be as exciting as the spring," Elizabeth agreed. "My only regret is that it makes walking difficult."

"You always were a good walker Elizabeth, as I remember." Mrs Hurst reflected.

"I confess I enjoy it very much. Now shall we go through?"

"Mr Randal and his brother are hard on our heels I believe, Mrs Darcy. It was most kind of you to invite them to your home at this time."

"They are new to our society Mrs Hurst, and lack the knowledge of our society. They will be most welcome. Ah here is Georgiana," Elizabeth was much relieved to see her sister in law.

Once Mr Randal and his brother had joined them everyone retired to the drawing room.

"This is a most magnificent house, Mrs Darcy," Ross Randal said as he gazed round at the well-proportioned room It has been with Mr Darcy's family for many generations I believe."

"I believe it has, Mr Randal. May I introduce you to Miss Darcy. Georgiana is Mr Darcy's sister, sir."

"We are happy to make your acquaintance Miss Darcy." he bowed then introduced his brother. James Randal was most impressed with Georgiana's beauty and had difficulty taking his eyes off her.

With the rest of the introductions made everyone settled into little groups, each discussing their own choice of subject.

"Caroline, I missed you when we were in town. Are you now fully recovered?" Georgiana smiled at her guest.

"Thank you, Georgiana, I am now quite well."

"Mr Wentworth and his sister have just given us a gift of some beautiful fabrics from India," Georgiana explained. "You would not believe the colours, Caroline."

"Then you must show them to me when you are able," Caroline replied.

"It is good to see you so animated, Georgiana, you appear very happy indeed."

"Oh, Caroline, it is a joy to be here with my brother and Elizabeth. She is so good to me. I am very lucky."

"I am very pleased for you."

"Lady Catherine and her daughter will be joining us shortly," Elizabeth joined in the conversation. "She brings with her Mr Collins and my younger sister Mary. They are to be married in the New Year."

"So soon?" Caroline had spoken without thinking. She dropped her head. "Forgive me Eliza. I did not mean to interfere."

"Not at all Caroline, I am of the same opinion, but Mr Darcy has convinced me the wisdom of it. It must be difficult indeed for Mr Collins to raise a daughter on his own."

Caroline was greatly relieved. "It must indeed. It was a very sad occasion when Charlotte was lost to him."

"It was Caroline. I miss her very much, but I am sure Mary will make him a good wife."

"They have Lady Catherine's blessing?" Caroline asked.

"It appears so, but we will find out to what extent when she arrives."

Caroline smiled for the first time since her arrival. Elizabeth was not sure if she preferred the old Caroline. This new one lacked spirit, and appeared frightened to voice an opinion on any subject. She hoped that her guest would in time relax. She said as much to Jane.

"I am sure she will, Lizzie. Once her fear of meeting Mr Darcy again is overcome, she will be herself again I think."

"I do hope so, Jane. This character of Caroline's does not suit her."

"Does nothing please you, Lizzie?"

"I did not mean it in that way," Elizabeth said with a frown. "Her behaviour is so different, something in the middle would be suitable I believe."

"I was teasing you, Lizzie. You are getting to worry like dear mama."

"God forbid. I must attend to it at once." They both laughed.

Caroline was in conversation with Georgiana when Mr Darcy entered the room, and did not notice. The expression on her face when he appeared in front of her was fear indeed.

"Caroline, I am most pleased you could join us at this time. You are in good health I see."

"I…I am, sir, thank you."

"I am glad to hear it. Please relax and enjoy your stay. My wife and Lady Catherine have many amusements for our pleasure, I believe."

"I thank you, sir."

Mr Darcy turned on his heel and walked away, a faint smile on his face.

Elizabeth was starting to regret the change she had made in him. He had taken to the mischievous side of his nature a little too well.

"Lady Catherine, Miss de Burgh, Mr Collins and Miss Bennett," Mrs Reynolds announced from the doorway.

"It is very good of you to come, aunt," Mr Darcy bowed in greeting. "Anne, Mr Collins, Miss Bennett. You are most welcome. May I be so bold as to congratulate you on your forthcoming marriage, Mr Collins."

"Your kindness is most gratifying, Mr Darcy. Indeed I have been most fortunate. Lady Catherine has been most gracious in her concern for my future happiness. She has bestowed upon my dear Mary and myself, her blessing." Mr Collins, head down in respect was about to embark on a monologue of gratitude but Mr Darcy interrupted.

"Lady Catherine, if you could allow me a few moments of your time."

They moved to one side of the room, so Mr Darcy could explain the presence of Caroline, the death of Mr Daniels and how they were keeping the information from Georgiana.

Mr Collins was still in conversation with Elizabeth.

"Mrs Darcy, this is most gracious of you to invite both Mary and myself into your home at this time. It is indeed an honour that I would have in no way expected."

"We are to be brother and sister, Mr Collins," Elizabeth replied. "The festive season is for all the family. I am very pleased for you both. I hope your marriage is as happy and contented as my own." She turned to Mary. "Mary, I am delighted you are settled in your affections."

"Mr Collins has, I believe, seen the benefit my company can

bring to his future life." Mary said seriously. "His misfortune in his previous marriage was grievous indeed, but we must think only of the future, and that of our daughter. It is my destiny, I believe to bring comfort to Mr Collins at this time."

"But are you happy, Mary?" Elizabeth was a little concerned.

"Happiness is a state of mind, Elizabeth," Mary replied. "With sufficient effort one may develop whatever emotion is required of them. Mr Collins and myself share interests that will insure our marriage is both satisfying, and stimulating."

"Then I wish you all the happiness in the world, Mary. Have you visited mama and papa yet?"

"My parents have been good enough to invite us to take part of the New Year with them." Mary explained.

"Then you will have much to converse with Lydia on," Elizabeth suggested.

"I doubt very much that Lydia and myself are of the same opinion. Her approach to the marriage state, and that of motherhood are far different from my own."

"I believe you are right, Mary. Now come let me introduce you to the rest of the party.

Mary's attitude to life had always been confusing to Elizabeth, but she was convinced that her sister, and Mr Collins, would find much to give them pleasure in each other's company.

Colonel Fitzwilliam was the next to arrive, and Elizabeth noticed that Kitty watched with anticipation to see if he brought his own company. He did not.

"Darcy, this is most generous of you," he exclaimed on his entrance. "To be invited to Pemberley at this time of year is indeed an honour."

"Fitzwilliam, you are always welcome as you very well know," Mr Darcy smiled.

"But your status has now changed, Darcy. I must not be so presumptuous as to take for granted my welcome."

"You will always be welcome Colonel Fitzwilliam,"

Elizabeth smiled at his jesting nature.

All guests were now assembled, and it was Elizabeth's concern to ensure that they were all entertained at all times.

"Elizabeth is there anything of an outstanding nature that needs attending to." Lady Catherine asked.

"I would be most grateful for your ladyship's attention to many things," Elizabeth replied with a sigh. "We have indeed many guests under our roof who will need constant stimulation and amusements."

"Then I will make sure they are not disappointed."

"There is one point that I wish your ladyship's assistance," Elizabeth frowned. "It concerns Mr Wentworth. He has implied by his tone, rather than suggestion, that he is not solely contented under Mr Darcy's roof. It is indeed distressing, as every hospitality has been extended to him. If your ladyship would be so kind as to discover the nature of his intentions, I would be most grateful."

"I will indeed," Lady Catherine exclaimed. "If something offends Edward I wish to know of it. He has not as yet familiarized himself enough with this country and society to enable him to set up on his own."

"I very well may be of the wrong impression, but his conversations all seem to be in the past tense." Elizabeth explained.

"Leave the matter with me, I will attend to it."

Over the course of the evening Lady Catherine held her conversation with Mr Wentworth, and Kitty with Colonel Fitzwilliam."

Elizabeth was amused to see that James Randal spent a great deal of time in Georgiana's company, and Ross Randal spent his with Mr and Mrs Hurst and Caroline. Mr Wentworth was the quietest person there. He stood to one side as though he felt out of place, it was a concern indeed.

"Mr Wentworth," Elizabeth said. "Are our entertainments not to your liking, you seem a little discomforted?"

"No indeed, Mrs Darcy, everything is most satisfactory."

"The dancing will start shortly, I hope you are going to partake of the music."

"I am sure I will, Mrs Darcy."

Elizabeth walked away still not convinced that everything was as it should be.

Caroline was also a concern. Although she talked a lot she rarely moved from the chair she was sitting in.

Elizabeth could stand it no longer. "Caroline are you not fully recovered from your indisposition. Your manner is of some concern to me?"

"I am Eliza, a little out of spirits this evening," she replied. "I shall be more myself tomorrow I am sure."

"That gives me comfort Caroline. Georgiana has been anticipating your arrival with much pleasure. She was a little discomforted that she did not see you when she was in town."

"Our new neighbour is indeed paying her a great deal of attention. I have not known her to hold company so much."

"She does indeed seem to be enjoying herself."

"And Colonel Fitzwilliam also spends much time with Mr Darcy's cousin."

"Yes indeed." Elizabeth was cross with herself that she had not noticed this change in Colonel Fitzwilliam's behaviour. Poor Kitty would certainly be at a loss to account for it.

"Kitty please try to smile, it is not good that you look so sad." Elizabeth said as she went and sat next to her sister.

"O Lizzie, Colonel Fitzwilliam has only danced with me once. He prefers the company of Miss Wentworth this evening. I am convinced that he does not favour me any more, but I was so convinced."

"It is strange indeed. You held a conversation with him earlier, Kitty, did he not give you an impression then?"

"No, he was very offhand. He talked of subjects that were of no concern to me." Kitty was most aggrieved. "I cannot account for his behaviour at all."

"I will see what I can do to acquaint you with his change of manner, but try to look content, Kitty. It is not wise to convey your feelings to the outside world."

"I cannot help it, Lizzie. I truly believe Colonel Fitzwilliam is the most amiable man of my acquaintance."

"I am sure he is, Kitty, but to show him your concern, is not in your best interests."

Later in the evening, Elizabeth noticed that Colonel Fitzwilliam was in deep conversation with Mr Darcy. She could not overhear what was being said as they had retired to the furthest corner of the room. His manner appeared to be serious in the extreme, it puzzled Elizabeth.

"Darcy, I cannot contain my feelings any longer. This evening is indeed causing me much pain." Colonel Fitzwilliam stated with much anxiety. "Mrs Darcy's sister, Miss Bennett is controlling my every affection, and in doing so is causing much distress to my parents."

"This is indeed serious, Fitzwilliam," replied Mr Darcy. "Can you not persuade them to your intentions?"

"I cannot, Darcy. As the younger son of the Earl of Matlock, it is expected that I should marry Lady Emily Montague. To bring our two estates together would be most beneficial in my parents estimation."

"I am sure it would, but to marry for material gain when it is not required, would not bring you contentment I am sure."

"Indeed it would not. I have tried in vain to arouse feelings of interest in Emily, but her points of view are so outside my own. I have no wish to distress my parents, but I cannot do as they wish. Miss Bennett is the dearest person I have ever had the pleasure of being associated with. You know I like lively conversation Darcy, and Miss Bennett is indeed spirited."

"She takes after my wife in that quarter I believe," Mr Darcy smiled. "Surely, Fitzwilliam, your two brothers will marry well and enhanced the family estate?"

"There is nothing at this moment to imply that they are even considering the possibility of marriage. Father most of all is quite determined that I should marry Lady Montague. What am I to do, Darcy? It does indeed give me much anxiety."

"I have noticed the change in you Fitzwilliam," Mr Darcy was now serious. "What are your father's intentions if you should go against his wishes?"

"He has threatened nothing as yet, but it is sure to cause a rift, that will never be healed I fear."

"To live a life of grief in order to please your parents is not agreeable to any party. Can your brothers not speak on your behalf?"

"I admit I have not asked this of them," admitted Colonel Fitzwilliam. "I have at present only implied the suggestion that a marriage of my father's choosing was not to my design."

"Then they have no knowledge of your intentions as such?"

"I have not had that courage, Darcy. My father's temper is great as you are well aware."

"Then my opinion is to be honest and explain your feelings. He will not, I believe wish to lose a son over this matter. If you were the first born it would indeed be a different matter, but has you are the younger, I can see no reasonable objection."

"If only it were that simple, Darcy," Colonel Fitzwilliam looked very downcast. "I long to dance with Miss Bennett, and indeed tell her of my feelings, but to raise hope that she is of the same opinion, will be of no avail to either party."

"If your heart lies with Miss Bennett, Fitzwilliam, I suggest that you follow it. Your father will. I am sure return to your way of thinking in the future. If Miss Bennett is not worth fighting for, she is not worth having."

"Good God, Darcy, you are right," his face became hopeful. "It will cause a devil of a stink at the time, and my name will never be mentioned in the family home, I am sure."

"Seek the comfort of your brother's opinion, Fitzwilliam. If he will agree to side with you, I doubt your father will risk losing two sons."

"God, Darcy, you are most discerning. I will do as you say. I am sure you are of the right order."

"Then go to it, Fitzwilliam. I am convinced of your success."

"I will indeed, directly on my return, Meanwhile I shall engage the beautiful Miss Bennett in a dance."

Mr Darcy watched as he crossed the room in the direction of Kitty. He was surprised at the change in her countenance as he approached. The feelings on both sides, he was sure, were of equal regard.

"Once Colonel Fitzwilliam had left Mr Darcy's company, Elizabeth went to inquire if anything was amiss."

"Quite the contrary I assure you Elizabeth. Colonel Fitzwilliam is now assured of his way in life."

"I am glad to hear it," Elizabeth replied, a little disconcerted with Mr Darcy's lack of information. "It was just that he appeared to be much discomforted."

"I believe he was."

As Mr Darcy would be no further drawn on the subject, Elizabeth reluctantly spoke of Mr Wentworth's gift."

"It was extremely good of him to think of us in this manner," Mr Darcy agreed. "I must confess he has turned out to be a most agreeable gentleman indeed."

"Is his schooling reaching a conclusion, sir?"

"There are a great many aspects of the estates that he has not yet been acquainted with, but he is an excellent student. To what does your question tend?"

"He appears to be tiring of our hospitality, sir," she replied with a frown. "I cannot understand his feelings."

"If this is true, Elizabeth, it is grievous indeed. In what respect was his concern?" Mr Darcy was alarmed at Elizabeth's suggestion.

"I may be causing alarm for no reason, sir," Elizabeth replied. "It is more in his general manner, than in the spoken word. Although he did mention that this festive season would seal his judgement. I have asked Lady Catherine to try and ascertain what the problem may be."

"I will speak with him myself. If there is concern of any sort, my wish is to clear it up directly."

Apart from a few minor misfortunes between the guests

the evening ended very happily indeed, with Caroline and Kitty playing a duet of seasonal carols while Mr Randal, his brother and Colonel Fitzwilliam looked on. Some of the guests even attempted a vocal accompaniment, which was very festive indeed.

The following day, being Christmas was spent with much food, wine and gaiety. Elizabeth could not remember when she had spent a more enjoyable Christmas.

Colonel Fitzwilliam had now turned his full attention on Kitty, which gave her much pleasure. Mr James Randal spent a great deal of time in Georgiana's company, while the older Mr Randal took delight in the company of Mr and Mrs Hurst and Caroline.

Caroline was more of her true character on Christmas Day but without the snide remarks, and the rest of the guests were just happy to be with congenial company.

Elizabeth sought out Lady Catherine's company. "Have you discovered the reason for Mr Wentworth's discontent ma'am. I do observe that he is even more melancholy today than in previous times."

"There does not seem to be a reason for it Elizabeth," she sighed. "He seems delighted with all his relations. I cannot make it out at all. I must confess my questions took a turn for the direct at one point, but to no avail. He was inquiring from me the possible houses available, but would not say why. I suggested that he would do better to stay under Mr Darcy's roof while he was under instruction, but he just said his sister required a house of her own."

"This is most distressing, as Miss Wentworth told me herself, that she would be happy to remain at Pemberley forever." Elizabeth frowned. "Mr Darcy is most offended that he wishes to reside elsewhere. It is perfectly understandable if Miss Wentworth would wish her own house, but I fear if Mr Wentworth insists upon it, it would be very lonely for his sister, as she has not, as yet, enough society to occupy her time."

"At what point did Mr Wentworth's conversation concern

you, Elizabeth?"

"It was while he was showing us the gift he had brought. He was speaking in the past tense. I inquired if he was happy at Pemberley, and he replied by saying his full-time residence would not be beneficial. I was quite at a loss to understand his meaning."

"It is most distressing," Lady Catherine frowned. "Could it be that he is homesick and pining for the Far East?"

"It is possible, ma'am. I confess I cannot make it out at all."

The subject was dropped as neither of the two women could explain the situation.

"I hope the party for the village children will go well." Elizabeth said.

"No doubt it will pass with much inconvenience to everyone." Lady Catherine replied. "I have to attend, I suppose?"

"I would deem it an honour if your ladyship would distribute the presents. The village people hold your ladyship in much esteem, and I am sure it would be a great delight for them to accept such a token from you yourself."

"Then I will do it for you Elizabeth," her tone has brisk but Elizabeth knew that she would be delighted to perform this task.

In fact, the party went off without incident. Everyone enjoyed the magnificent table that was laid out for their consumption, and were more than grateful for the presents that were bestowed upon them.

Mr Darcy put in a short appearance to wish everyone a happy Christmas, and Jane and Mr Bingley spent a great deal of their time entertaining the children.

Mr and Mrs Gardiner were a great help, but Mr and Mrs Hurst together with their sister Caroline made little effort to join in.

Caroline did, however, consent to play the pianoforte for a chorus of seasonal carols that ended a very enjoyable afternoon.

Chapter 10

With the festive season behind them, the New Year Ball was the talk of the house. Lady Catherine, having been given full rein by Elizabeth was in total charge. Her powers of organization were second to none. Everything was done immediately she spoke, and done to perfection. No way would she tolerate second-rate attempts.

Elizabeth had to admit to herself that her aunt was arranging things with far greater ease than she herself would have done. To give Lady Catherine credit, she made sure that Elizabeth was involved with every aspect.

"Next year you will be doing this alone Elizabeth, so it is best you know in advance the arrangements."

"Thank you ma'am, you are most generous. May I congratulate you on the ease in which you have arranged this ball."

"It comes from many years of experience Elizabeth. Attention to detail, that is the main point."

"I will remember, aunt." Elizabeth smiled.

"Your sister Kitty, Elizabeth, she does not look as though she is enjoying the preparations."

"No indeed, ma'am. I will go and speak with her, and discover what is ailing her."

Elizabeth knew exactly what was ailing Kitty. Colonel Fitzwilliam had returned home directly the festive season had finished, and she was missing his company.

"Kitty you really must keep your emotions to yourself. Everyone is concerned for your temper," she said as she sat beside her sister.

"I am sorry, Lizzie, it is just that Colonel Fitzwilliam has gone away without a word of his returning."

"He will be back for the ball Kitty as you very well know."

"He did not say so, Lizzie, and what if he brings that woman with him again. I am sure I could not bear it. It isn't even as though she is very pretty is it?"

"Not as pretty as you, Kitty, I am sure. Now please smile, Kitty, I have many concerns of my own at the present time."

"Elizabeth, may I say how comfortable you have made us feel this visit." Mrs Gardiner had joined them.

"Thank you, aunt. I believe it has gone very smoothly."

"It is as though you have been mistress of Pemberley for many years, Lizzie. Mr Darcy should be extremely proud of you."

"You are very generous, aunt, but Lady Catherine has been of great assistance."

"She has forgiven you for depriving her of a son in law then, Lizzie?"

"I believe so, aunt, although I think it is more acceptance than forgiveness," Elizabeth laughed. "I believe her thoughts are turning to Mr Wentworth and her daughter Anne."

"Really that is surprising," Mrs Gardiner frowned slightly.

"What makes you say that, aunt? He is a very handsome gentleman, and his fortune is great indeed."

"Maybe so, Lizzie, but I think his partner would have to be a little more entertaining, would she not?"

"I see what you mean, aunt, but if Lady Catherine has set her heart on him, then he will have to be a very strong character indeed to dissuade her."

"I cannot imagine him to settle for less than his heart's desire, Lizzie. I do not believe that it will be Miss de Burgh, his favour lies a little closer to home I think."

"I do not understand what you mean, aunt," Elizabeth frowned. "He is only recently in this country and has many acquaintances to make before he settles down."

"Regard waits for no-one, Lizzie, as you should be well aware."

Elizabeth could still not understand the meaning of her aunt's words, so she made a mental note to observe things more closely.

******

The evening of the ball arrived and the house was filled with music, people, laughter and dress colours in every shade.

Elizabeth and Mr Darcy started the ball by taking part in the first dance, and Elizabeth could feel every eye in the room upon her.

"It is like living in a glass bottle, Jane," she complained to her sister a little while later. "Everyone is expecting Mr Darcy to announce the arrival of a son and heir, or wondering why I am not with child."

"Lizzie, I am sure they are not," Jane laughed at the anxiety in her sister's voice. "You are making far too much of the subject I think. I am sure no-one has said anything in my presence."

"Of course not, Jane, they whisper behind their feathers."

"Lizzie that is not so, you are being unfair. I am sure they are only interested in how you fit in at Pemberley."

"I am sure you are right, Jane. I just feel that everyone is staring at me that is all."

"Then it is because you are the prettiest woman in the room," they both laughed.

"Are you travelling to Mary's wedding next week, Jane?"

"Mr Bingley is insistent that we go. He feels Mr Collins needs the closeness of his family at this time I believe."

"Do you think Lydia and Mr Wickham will make the journey?" Elizabeth asked.

"I think not," sighed Jane. "Their situation does not allow for journeys such as these. His regiment will be expecting his return."

"If only she had not married in such haste, Jane. I am sure she would have found a more suitable match."

"She is in love I believe, Lizzie. Mr Wickham, to her is the most handsome man she has ever seen."

"If only she would realize his true character. I am sure she would not have the same feeling then." Elizabeth speculated.

"Then we had better hope she does not. She is now married to him remember. To discover his true nature now Lizzie would only bring grief."

Elizabeth gave her sister a quizzical look, then realizing she was jesting, she smiled. "O, Jane I do wish my disposition was more like yours."

"Mrs Darcy, you have done us proud once again." Mr Gardiner said as he passed close by.

"Thank you, uncle. It is indeed a very fine ball, and for that we have Lady Catherine to thank. Her efforts to attain this level of pleasure have been great indeed."

"Then she is to be congratulated. Her efforts have not been in vain I believe."

"Her help has indeed been generous," Elizabeth said. "I confess my feelings towards her in the past have been most unjust."

"Praise indeed, Lizzie, but have no fear. I believe her reputation was much deserved at the time."

"I believe it was, sir."

Elizabeth was amused at one point, to observe Mr Darcy dancing with Caroline. His face showed much amusement, whilst hers was reserved and concerned. His mischievous side was very much to the fore at this time she feared. She smiled to herself then crossed the room to talk with Mr Wentworth who was standing alone.

"Mr Wentworth, is the ball to your taste, sir?"

"It is indeed, Mrs Darcy."

"I have not had the pleasure of seeing you dance this evening. Are you not inclined to dance?"

"I regret it is not one of my favourite sports, and I decidedly lack a partner."

"There are many pretty ladies in the room, Mr Wentworth, maybe you are spoilt for choice."

"You could be right, ma'am."

Elizabeth was most concerned at Mr Wentworth's attitude. He did not appear at all to be enjoying the amusements.

"Mrs Darcy, I must confess it is a delight to see my sister enjoying herself once again." Mrs Hurst spoke as Elizabeth passed by. "I must extend my gratitude to you for your dealings with Caroline. You are generous indeed."

"Not at all Mrs Hurst," Elizabeth smiled. "If Mr Darcy is prepared to extend his forgiveness towards your sister, then I have no objections."

"I admit Mrs Darcy that her actions were grievous indeed towards you, but I truly believe they were born out of resentment for your relationship with Mr Darcy. She has indeed nursed a hope for many years, that she would, at some point, become his wife."

"I quite understand Mrs Hurst, but shall we now put it firmly in the past. To continue this trend would be of no worth to anyone."

"You are right, Mrs Darcy," Mrs Hurst changed the subject. "I was delighted to hear of the engagement between your sister and Mr Collins. Your mother must be beside herself with pleasure."

"I am sure she is, ma'am, although I have not spoken with her since this happy event was announced."

"Is the wedding to take place soon, Elizabeth?"

"Within the week, I believe."

"And your mother. will her health allow her to attend?"

"I am sure my father will ensure that her attendance is possible. If you will excuse me, I wish to talk with Lady Catherine." Elizabeth said, and moved quickly away. Although she was prepared to accept Mr Bingley's sisters into her home, she could not help but have reservations towards them. There was something in their air that was most displeasing.

"Lady Catherine, you have indeed made the New Year ball a success, everyone is complimenting your arrangement." Elizabeth said.

"You are very kind, Elizabeth," she replied bristling with pride. "I see Fitzwilliam has taken Caroline Bingley for his partner this turn. Is all well between them now?"

"It is. I believe for the sake of his good friend Mr Bingley, that my husband has accepted Caroline back into his society."

"Uumph, well, I would not have had it so. Her behaviour has been insulting to us all."

"I believe she has learned a lesson she will not forget too quickly, ma'am."

"Mark my words, Elizabeth, no one changes their personality. It is only time, you will see."

"I pray you are wrong, ma'am. If the situation is repeated, I fear Mr Darcy will not forgive again."

"I should hope not. It is not to be tolerated. I myself, would certainly not have welcomed her back into my society."

"Lizzie," Kitty spoke as Elizabeth passed close to where she was sitting, "Colonel Fitzwilliam has not arrived as yet. Can it be that he has no intention of returning?"

"O Kitty dear, I had not noticed, forgive me," Elizabeth was a little alarmed. "He made a promise to be here, indeed his invitation was accepted very readily."

"Then I do not understand," Kitty looked for all the world as though she was going to cry. "It can only mean that he wishes to avoid my company."

"That is silly, Kitty, he has no wish to avoid you I am sure. Why do you not go and talk to Miss Wentworth or Mary? I am sure Mary will have much to divulge, she is after all getting married next week." As soon as Elizabeth had spoken she knew she had chosen her words wrongly. Kitty's eyes filled up and were about to turn into tears."

"Kitty, I know you are upset, but please do not show me up by crying in front of all these people. Go upstairs and refresh your face. There are many reasons why Colonel Fitzwilliam is not here. He could have family business, or has just left it late to travel. He will be here shortly I am sure."

Elizabeth was not as sure as she sounded. It was indeed very unusual for Mr Darcy's cousin to not attend the main event in the estates year. She went in search of her husband.

"Colonel Fitzwilliam is not in attendance, sir. Do you know what ails him?"

"I have no idea, Elizabeth. It is probable that his family wish him with them for the New Year celebrations."

"I am sure you are right, sir, it is just that his invitation was accepted."

"He may have unexpected pressures put upon him, that make it impossible for him to join us."

It was no point pursuing this line of conversation, as Colonel Fitzwilliam's whereabouts were not known to any of the guests.

Several dances and conversations later everyone raised their glass to welcome in the New Year.

"May we always be as happy as we are this evening Elizabeth," Mr Darcy smiled down at his wife.

"I thank you, sir. I truly believe we will be."

The dance came to an end a little while later, and the guests that were staying overnight, gathered in the music room.

"Georgiana, I hope you have enjoyed this evening as much as you had anticipated.?" Elizabeth asked. "You seem to have claimed the attentions of the younger Mr Randal most of the evening. Do you like him Georgiana?"

"He is very nice, Elizabeth, I am sure he will settle well within our society." Georgiana replied without much enthusiasm.

"And there was me thinking you were of the same opinion as he is," Elizabeth laughed lightly.

"His company is very entertaining, but I have no particular regard for him."

"You are young, Georgiana, there are many years yet that you may enjoy the company of handsome men without thought of serious connections."

"But am I not too young, Elizabeth?"

"Of course not." Everyone's attitude was most concerning for Elizabeth. Colonel Fitzwilliam's absence, Mr Wentworth's solitude, Kitty's despair, and now Georgiana. The whole situation was most disturbing.

"Mr Darcy," she said sadly as she went to join him. "The situation between our younger sisters and friends is causing much concern."

"In what way, Elizabeth?"

"They each have a regard for each other that, I fear, will not suit them all."

"I do not have the pleasure of understanding you Elizabeth."

"Mr Randal has a regard for your sister, which is not reciprocated. My sister Kitty craves the attention of Colonel Fitzwilliam, who, I believe tends his favours elsewhere, and our guests Mr and Miss Wentworth are not at all enjoying the amusements."

"This is indeed a sad situation my dear, but I have caused much unhappiness in the past by arranging other people's affairs, I have no wish to enter that domain again."

Elizabeth smiled as she remembered Mr Darcy's opposition to her sister Jane and Mr Bingley.

"I must admit however Edward's countenance is causing me much concern. I shall speak with him in the morning and see if I can discover his displeasure."

"Darcy, this has been a most excellent evening," Mr Bingley announced as he crossed the room towards them. "Upon my word, I cannot think of an evening that I have had so much pleasure."

"I am glad to hear it."

"Mrs Darcy, will you be travelling to your sister's wedding in our company? I believe Mr Darcy has business in town that prevents his presence." Mr Bingley asked.

"He does indeed, Mr Bingley." Elizabeth smiled. "It would give me much pleasure to travel with you. I would like it very much."

"Then you shall."

"Your presence here, until your departure for Longbourne, would give Elizabeth and myself much pleasure Bingley. It is below a week, and I am sure the ladies have much to talk of."

"That is a splendid idea," Mr Bingley beamed with pleasure. "I shall go and tell Jane at once."

******

Not long after breakfast the following day Mr Darcy and Mr Wentworth retired to the study.

"Edward, your disposition is causing myself, and my wife much concern. You appear to be much dissatisfied with our hospitality."

"Good gracious, no," Mr Wentworth was adamant. "Your attentions have been most generous. Indeed I have no injury in that direction."

"You are not happy, Edward. I have heard talk that you are wishing to reside elsewhere. This is of much concern, as your knowledge of our society is not well enough established, to afford a circle of your own friends. Your life I fear would be quite solitary."

"I find myself in a situation that is out of my control, and my continued presence here, will, I fear end in offence."

"In what way?"

"It is a subject on which I cannot converse with anyone."

"There is nothing on which you cannot approach me, sir. Anything that you say in this room will ever be repeated elsewhere. You may be assured of my secrecy."

"Your honour is renowned, sir, but my disposition is of such a personal nature, that it can only be attended to by myself."

"That leads me to believe it is a matter of the heart, sir."

Mr Wentworth started to pace the room. "I have no wish for you to think ill of me, sir. Your goodness throughout my visit as been beyond all hopes, and to repay you with offence, is something I cannot bring myself to do."

"I assure you cousin there is nothing that will cause offence, if I have previous knowledge."

Mr Wentworth stopped pacing and stood with his back to Mr Darcy deep in thought.

"It obviously weighs heavy on your mind Edward," Mr Darcy offered. "If there is any attention I may give to the matter, that will relieve your suffering, I am much inclined to do so."

The young man whirled round on his heel. "Forgive me Darcy, I have a regard for your sister that, believe me is all consuming. My struggle to overcome this affection has been to no avail. Indeed I find I cannot think of anything else, and my continued presence under your roof will only cause pain to everyone."

Mr Darcy was most taken aback. "My sister Georgiana?" he spoke with surprise. "Is she of the same opinion?"

"I have not spoken with her on the subject. I have made it my intention to remain at a distance. Now you see how my feelings may cause offence."

Mr Darcy was quiet for some time. "I have no objection to the match in principal," he said at last. "Indeed you are a fine gentleman, and in a position equivalent to my own, but my sister's happiness is my sole concern. She has believed herself to be in love before, and I am afraid to say it came to a very unsatisfactory conclusion. I will not have her feelings discomforted in any way again. The fact that you have not already approached her on this subject does you much credit. Have you hopes of her returning your affection?"

"I do not know. I feel she likes me well enough, but as for further regard, I have not had the presumption to aspire."

"This situation must be attended to," Mr Darcy frowned deeply. "I must ask your permission to set my mind to it over the next few days. If my permission is given for you to speak with her on this subject, will you give me your assurance that nothing will be said to give her pressure of any kind."

"Upon my life, Darcy, you have my deepest assurance that I would do nothing to cause Miss Darcy discomfort in any way."

"Very well, I will give it my most serious consideration, but my immediate feelings are, that my sister is far too young to be contemplating this sort of attachment. If, after due consideration, my conclusion is not favourable, then your residence elsewhere will be immediate."

"Your generous nature is more than I deserve, sir. You have my most sincere promise that no distress will be caused to your sister."

"Thank you, Edward."

Mr Darcy pondered on this new turn of events quite some time. His sister was still very young to be making such a commitment, but much as it concered him, he knew that her feelings would, in the end, prevail. He wondered if he should speak with her on the subject, but if his cousin had not displayed his intentions, Georgiana would be most confused with his conversation.

At length his decision was to seek Elizabeth's thoughts on the matter.

He did not get the opportunity to speak with his wife alone until the following afternoon.

"Elizabeth, I have a matter that would benefit from your advice," Mr Darcy said.

Elizabeth knew by the tone of his voice that this was a subject that affected him deeply. "If I can be of assistance in any way, sir, I would be more than happy to do so."

"It concerns my sister Georgiana."

"Georgiana? Is she unwell, or unhappy, sir?" Elizabeth was most surprised.

"No indeed. In fact, I believe it is just the opposite." Mr Darcy paused for several minutes before continuing. "I was wondering if she had shown, in your presence, any form of attachment to any particular person?"

Elizabeth frowned deeply. "No-one is apparent, sir. Does she confide in you about her particular favours, sir?"

"Certainly not, well, not at this present time." Mr Darcy's expression was one of much concern. "No, I was of the opinion that one gentleman was seeking her favours. That is all."

"Would it be beneficial to the situation if I sought her opinion on this matter, sir?" Elizabeth suggested.

"I believe it may, but do it with discretion Elizabeth. I have no wish to open suggestions of any kind."

"You may put your trust in me, sir." Elizabeth replied.

"Thank you Elizabeth. I have faith in your judgement."

As Mr Darcy left the room, Elizabeth remained seated, a puzzled look on her face. Her mind was thinking of the many acquaintances that passed through her life, and wondered to which one Georgiana could be attracted. Providing it was not Colonel Fitzwilliam, she believed all would be well. To favour him would bring heartbreak to her sister Kitty. That situation was one she did not wish to find herself.

After a short while, she decided that the only possible candidate for her sister in law's affections, was the very dashing, younger, Mr Randal. He did indeed spend much time with Georgiana, and she, in her turn, seemed to favour his company.

She stood up decisively, speculating was to no avail. She would seek Georgiana's thoughts on the matter.

A beautiful ballad floating down the corridor from the music room told Elizabeth that Georgiana was doing what she enjoyed most.

"Elizabeth," she spoke as Elizabeth entered. "Where is everyone? There is not a soul to be seen."

"Miss Wentworth and her brother have gone into the village, and I believe Kitty is in her room." Elizabeth smiled. "Are you feeling lonely?"

"No, not at all. It just seemed very quiet. That is all."

"Did you enjoy the ball last evening, Georgiana?"

"O yes, it was a great success. I do believe yourself, and Lady Catherine excelled all previous years."

"Thank you Georgiana, you are most kind." Elizabeth paused. "Mr Randal took up many of your dances I believe. He is a very handsome man, is he not?"

"He is indeed. His sense of humour is very much to the fore."

"Do I detect a note of favour in your address, Georgiana?"

Georgiana became serious. "O no, Elizabeth. I mean he is a very nice man, but, with the ladies, I do not think he could be trusted."

Elizabeth smiled. "You are probably right. He does indeed turn the heads of every female."

Georgiana lapsed into silence, so Elizabeth ventured. "You have no favourite among our acquaintances then Georgiana?"

"No," she replied, a little too quickly, and the colour in her cheeks gave away her secret. "I am still very young."

"And in love I believe." Elizabeth was guessing, but the result was instant.

"O Elizabeth, how did you know. No-one else can tell, can they? I have tried to hide my feelings. How did you discover it?"

"I too, am in love Georgiana," Elizabeth laughed. "and you are showing the classic signs. Does he have the same regard for you?"

She crossed the room and sat beside Elizabeth. A puzzled look crossed her face. "I do not know, I have not given him any indication of my feelings. Indeed his company is quite new to our acquaintance, but I cannot stop thinking of him Elizabeth. His conversation were many but now, his manner is distant. I believe he is in awe of my brother."

Elizabeth was most confused. The only new acquaintance was Mr Randal, and Georgiana had all ready stated that he was not in favour. "How do you intend to solve this situation Georgiana?" Elizabeth asked. "If you show him no encouragement, how can he tell how you feel."

"What can I do Elizabeth? I have no wish to appear forward."

"Can Kitty be of any assistance in this matter. Maybe she could discover his true feelings?"

"I have thought of talking with his sister, but our acquaintance has been of such a short duration. She may be offended by my thoughts."

Mr Wentworth! Georgiana was in love with Mr Wentworth.

'How could I have been so blind' Elizabeth thought. Of course, that was why he wished to leave Mr Darcy's house. Everything now became clear.

Elizabeth took a few seconds to calm herself down after this shock revelation. "How can anyone not love you

Georgiana. You have the sweetest disposition."

"You are very kind Elizabeth, but the feelings I have for my cousin are of a different nature." Georgiana looked so forlorn Elizabeth's heart went out to her.

"If you want my opinion Georgiana, I believe he likes you very much." Elizabeth smiled. "His gift of fabric and jewels, were, I am sure, for your benefit."

"Do you think so Elizabeth," Georgiana's face lit up, then just as suddenly collapsed into a frown. "No, he wished only to thank us for our hospitality. Why should he look at me, when there are more attractive ladies to be found?"

"Georgiana, you are truly beautiful," Elizabeth laughed at her sister in law's confusion. "Besides love has nothing to do with appearance Georgiana. It is an attraction between two people that can not be explained."

After a few seconds of silence, Georgiana continued. "Elizabeth, may I ask you something?"

"Of course, anything."

"If I found myself attracted to some-one, how do you think my brother would look on the situation."

"It would depend entirely on the gentleman in question, I believe." Elizabeth replied. "Your brother thinks only of your happiness. Now, come, let us cheer ourselves up. Play me a nice piece of music."

While Georgiana played Elizabeth mused over this new information. How would Mr Darcy look on a match between his sister and Mr Wentworth? His cousin was indeed of the same social standing as Mr Darcy himself. He was attractive, intelligent, and very respectful of society. Georgiana could do a lot worse, Elizabeth decided.

When she imparted this information to Mr Darcy, he was silent for quite some time. Then he said. "He is of the same opinion I believe."

"Have you spoken with Mr Wentworth on this subject, sir?"

"I have indeed." Mr Darcy replied. "My concern was for his displeasure at being under my roof. When I approached him on the subject it became apparent that my sister was the cause of his wish to reside elsewhere."

"Why should that be, sir?"

"His concern was that his attentions towards my sister would offend me."

"That was thoughtful indeed."

"Georgiana is very young. To make a commitment of this nature, she must be very sure of her feelings. What is your opinion on the matter?"

"On reflection, sir, I believe they would make a very good match. They are both of such a taciturn disposition, they will do very well together."

"I believe you are right, Elizabeth."

"May I be so bold as to suggest you talk with your sister on this matter, sir," Elizabeth ventured.

"You think she would not take offence at my interference."

"Certainly not. She has much regard for Mr Wentworth. Her concern is that he does not return her favour. By enlightening her of his feelings, will bring much joy I am sure."

"Then I will go to her."

As he left the room Elizabeth smiled to herself. Yes. they would do very well together she was sure.

*****

"Georgiana, I wish to speak with you on a delicate matter." Mr Darcy announced as he entered the music room.

Georgiana stopped her recital and crossed the room towards her brother. "Is there something wrong, sir."

"No, Georgiana. I had occasion to talk with our cousin Mr Wentworth yesterday morning. His manner had been a concern of mine for some time. He did not appear happy with our hospitality, I wished only to know why."

"And did you discover the cause of his discomfort, sir."

"I did."

"Is it something we have done that offends him/"

"His concern was more personal. He has a deep regard for

you, my dear sister, and he was of the opinion that it would offend me."

"Are you offended, sir?" Georgiana asked, delighted with this turn of events.

"Not at all. Concerned but not offended."

"Your concern is for me, sir?"

"It is indeed. Your feelings towards Edward, are they of the same strength?"

"I believe Mr Wentworth to be the best person I have ever met. Indeed, he has brought a great deal of happiness into my life. My regard for him is of such a strength, it frightens me."

Mr Darcy looked at his younger sister with a mixture of emotions. "You are still very young, Georgiana. I wish only for your happiness, and must be sure of the depth of your feelings. Edward is indeed a fine gentleman, and I believe he will take great care of you, but this is a lifetime commitment. I do not wish to have the concern of you choosing your partner in life wrongly."

"If Mr Wentworth has as much regard for me as I do for him, sir, there will be no happier couple in the whole world."

"Then I shall give him my permission to speak with you on the subject."

"You are truly the best brother anyone could wish for." Georgiana kissed Mr Darcy on the cheek as he turned to leave the room.

When the ladies had retired for the night, Mr Darcy remained in the drawing room in the company of Mr Wentworth.

"I have had the opportunity to speak with my sister on the subject of your regard for her." Mr Darcy said. "It appears Edward that she is of the same opinion as yourself."

Mr Wentworth could hardly contain his emotions. "Darcy, can this be true? Can I dare to hope that she will look on me as a suitor?"

"I think you may, sir."

"You have my eternal loyalty, sir. I shall take the greatest care of her. I assure you."

"You will indeed Edward, or you will answer to me. My sister is still very young, and very precious to me. If I hear she is discomforted in any way, my temper will know no bounds."

"My feelings towards your sister, sir are so ardent, her happiness will always be my main concern."

"Then you have my permission to approach her." Mr Darcy said.

"I am deeply indebted to you, sir."

*****

The following morning Mr Wentworth approached the music room, where he knew Georgiana practiced every morning.

"Mr Wentworth," she coloured a little as he entered the room. "Did you enjoy the ball the other evening? Indeed I did not see you dancing."

"My preference to a partner was not available to me, ma'am."

Georgiana blushed even deeper.

"I have spoken with your brother, Miss Darcy, on the delicate nature of my feelings towards you. I have indeed struggled to keep them under control, but my regard for you is so fervent, it overrides all my other senses. May I dare to hope that you have a regard for me, that in any way mirrors my own?"

Georgiana looked at the young man standing so unsure in front of her, and smiled shyly.

"You may indeed, sir. My wish, for many weeks now, was that you would look on me with regard."

"My dearest, sweetest Georgiana, you have made me a very happy man." His smile lit up his entire face. "Would you do me the greatest honour of all and agree to be my wife?"

"I will, with all my heart, sir."

"Your brother has agreed to my approaching you with my proposal, but I must speak with him again and ascertain he has no objection to our marriage."

"When he knows the extent of my happiness, sir, I am sure he will have no objection to offer."

Mr Darcy, although saddened by the loss of his sister, wholly embraced the situation. Mr Wentworth was a gentleman of happy manners, and a generous nature. His fortune was close to that of his own, and he was sure Georgiana could not have made a better match. When he conveyed the outcome to Elizabeth she was overjoyed.

"I hope their marriage is as content as ours, Mr Darcy." she said.

"That, my dear, is a very high standard to achieve." Mr Darcy smiled and kissed her lightly on the cheek.

Before the engagement could be conveyed to anyone else, Colonel Fitzwilliam entered the room.

"Fitzwilliam," Mr Darcy smiled. "You are a little late for the ball, it ended in the early hours of the morning above three days ago."

"My regrets are many, Darcy, but I have the most amazing news. Miss Bennett has agreed to be my wife. What do you say to that, sir?"

"I am delighted for you, Fitzwilliam. When did this happy occurrence take place?"

"I was fortunate enough on my arrival to encounter Miss Bennett in the garden. Having sought the agreement of both my parents I was then free to extend to her my true feelings."

"I am pleased everything has turned out well for you," Mr Darcy said.

"I followed your advice, Darcy, and arranged the alliance of my brothers. It turned out as you predicted."

Elizabeth did not understand the tone of this conversation, and was surprised that Mr Darcy had prior knowledge of the situation between Colonel Fitzwilliam and Kitty, but she was too excited to dwell on the prospect too much.

"Colonel Fitzwilliam, this is happy news indeed." Elizabeth was beside herself with joy. "Kitty will be so happy. Have you secured the agreement of my father, sir."

"I am sorry to say I have not, but I will travel to Longbourne immediately and hope to secure it."

"I am sure there will be no objection, sir. Kitty's happiness will be his main concern."

"I hope you are right, Mrs Darcy." Colonel Fitzwilliam was indeed a very happy man.

"Kitty, I am so happy for you," Elizabeth ran to her as she entered the room. "Have you told Jane the good news yet?"

"Not as yet, Lizzie," Kitty smiled. "Colonel Fitzwilliam has yet to obtain papa's consent, but I am so happy, Lizzie. I did not think it was possible to be so."

"You are a very lucky girl, Kitty," Elizabeth hugged her sister. "I wish you both all the happiness in the world."

"Thank you, Lizzie. I am sure I cannot believe it. Lydia will be much out of sorts when I write to her, I am sure."

"Do not crow over your sister, Kitty, she has many concerns in her marriage I believe."

"With all your sisters settled Elizabeth," Mr Darcy laughed. "I fear your mother will be at a loss to occupy her mind."

"She will indeed, sir, but my father will have many visits to make. This I believe will enhance his life considerably."

"It will indeed. He is welcome at Pemberley when ever he chooses, you must assure him of that. Your mother too must visit. I believe she has not had the pleasure of seeing Pemberley for herself."

"She has not, sir, and much looks forward to it I believe," Elizabeth said but without zeal. The thought of her mother under the same roof as Mr Darcy for many days still filled her with foreboding. She felt guilty for her feelings, but they would not be repressed."

"We also have happy news to extend to you," Mr Darcy said. "My sister Georgiana is to marry my cousin Mr Wentworth."

"Good God, Darcy, this is news indeed." Colonel Fitzwilliam was delighted. "I had no idea the match was taking place."

"It was a secret that was kept from all of us, but the outcome is happy indeed." Mr Darcy smiled. "My wife and I are delighted for them both."

"Then we can have a double wedding, Lizzie," Kitty squealed in delight. "Just as you and Jane did."

"You must consult with Georgiana on that subject." Elizabeth laughed.

"Lizzie, this is wonderful news Kitty brings," Jane said. "Mama will be so happy. I am sure it will bring much recovery to her health. Do you not agree? And Miss Darcy too, it is such a surprise. I am so happy for them both."

"Kitty is a very lucky girl, she could not have chosen a more amiable partner. Colonel Fitzwilliam is one of the most pleasant people I have ever met."

"O he is, Lizzie. I am sure she will make him a good wife." Jane said. "When is Miss Darcy to marry, has she spoken of it?"

"Not as yet, but I am sure it will not be long." Elizabeth sighed happily. "We now have three weddings to attend. Poor father will be much distressed with all the talk of gowns and lace."

"Yes indeed, but he will be most content to see all his daughter's settled and happy I think."

"It will be a great relief to him. To have five daughters, all unmarried, must have lay heavy with him." Elizabeth laughed.

"Kitty did not say when she hoped the wedding would be. Did she tell you, Lizzie?" Jane asked.

"I am afraid not, Jane, she has yet to obtain father's consent."

"But he will give it. Surely he can have no objection?"

"Do not look so worried, Jane, I am sure father will agree, but Kitty cannot talk of the wedding until he has confirmed it."

"No indeed. I am so happy for her, Lizzie, and Miss Darcy too. We have been the most fortunate of families."

"I am sure you are right, Jane," Elizabeth smiled and then

a frown came to her face. "Mr Darcy wishes I invite mama to stay at Pemberley, Jane, but I confess I have no high spirits over the thought."

"That is not like you, Lizzie. Surely it will do mama much good to be invited into Mr Darcy's home."

"I am sure it would, but her comments, Jane, they cause Mr Darcy much discomfort."

"I do not think mama will cause too much distress, Lizzie. Her speech has not yet returned in full. You will be safe I am sure," Jane assured her sister. "If her stay causes you too much distress, I am sure Mr Bingley will welcome her to Southview."

"I should not think so ill of mama, Jane, but I do feel concern for Mr Darcy's discomfort."

"I am sure mama will not embarrass you, Lizzie. She is, I am sure, more concerned for her own state of health. And Kitty's marriage will also give her something else to consider. Do you think Kitty will marry at Longbourne or will she remain here at Pemberley? Here is Georgiana, we must go and congratulate her."

"Georgiana, I am so happy for you," Elizabeth hugged her sister-in-law. "It is much of a surprise you give us. I was sure your intention was in another direction."

"Oh, no, Elizabeth, Mr Wentworth has always been high in my regard."

Georgiana smiled with happiness.

"Mr Randal will be much put out, I am sure," She turned to Mr Wentworth. "May I congratulate you, sir, on your good fortune. Georgiana is, in my opinion, the most generous natured."

"She is indeed, ma'am. I am indeed a very happy man."

"My sister Kitty is also to be married to Colonel Fitzwilliam, so we have a double celebration," Elizabeth said.

"I am delighted to hear it. He is a very amiable gentleman, I think."

"Kitty is to marry as well?" Georgiana was most surprised.

"I am so pleased for her. She did indeed favour Colonel Fitzwilliam above all others."

"She did indeed. Have you decided when your wedding will be, Georgiana?" Elizabeth asked.

"I will talk with my brother on the matter," Georgiana replied. "I hope it will not be long."

******

Mary's wedding was a quiet, sober affair. No frills or flowers, just Mary as Elizabeth had always known her.

Mr Collins on the other hand was deliriously happy.

"Mrs Darcy, I confess I am the most fortunate of men," he said with exaggerated pleasure.

"I am pleased to hear it, Mr Collins. My sister does indeed look beautiful today."

"She does indeed, and so able in the care of my daughter, Mrs Darcy. Her presence in my home has been of the most beneficial kind."

"My sister Mary has many qualities, Mr Collins. I am convinced she will make you a good wife."

"She will indeed cousin Elizabeth, and when you unite this happy event with the benevolent patronage of Lady Catherine de Burgh, you will see, I am sure, that my life at Huntsford is blessed indeed."

"You are indeed most fortunate Mr Collins," Elizabeth smiled.

"I believe Lady Catherine has spent many weeks with you at Pemberley, cousin. You must indeed feel honoured that her benevolence extends to assist you."

"I do indeed Mr Collins," Elizabeth smiled. "I find myself deeply in her debt. Lady Catherine's company has indeed enhanced my life at Pemberley

"When you look back and discover that her feelings were most discomforted on your marriage, this new turn of events must seem very favourable indeed." Mr Collins gave a sly smile.

"Lady Catherine wished Mr Darcy to marry her daughter Anne, Mr Collins," Elizabeth was most affronted. "When it did not take place her pride was offended, that is all. Now if you will excuse me, I must attend to mama."

Mrs Bennett, who throughout the service, remained in a chair, now stood a little unsteadily by her husband's side.

"O Lizzie, I am so happy, four daughters married, we have been lucky indeed. And Kitty to marry soon."

"Indeed we have, mama, but please do not over tire yourself, you are not fully recovered I am sure."

"O stop fussing, Lizzie, you always did fuss so."

"I am just concerned for your health mama."

"What do you think of the engagement of your sister Kitty, Lizzie?" Mr Bennett asked. "He seems an amiable enough sort of fellow."

"He is father. She could not have chosen a better partner. I am convinced of their happiness together."

"All my daughters settled, well, well, who would have thought it," Mr Bennett chuckled.

"Mama, Mary looks very pretty today," Jane said excitedly. "She has made a good alliance, I think."

"You could be right, Jane," Mr Bennett answered for his wife. "I am sure Mary and Mr Collins will have an interesting life together, but how will she fit in with Lady Catherine do you think?"

"I believe she will have considerably more to say than dear Charlotte dared." Elizabeth laughed.

"She will indeed. I would not like to predict a winner if a confrontation were to occur." Mr Bennett speculated.

"Do not even imagine it, father," Elizabeth gasped. "The outcome would be grievous indeed."

"I am sure Mary would not do anything to offend Mr Collins," Jane argued. "Besides, Lizzie, Lady Catherine seems very attentive towards her."

"Yes, Jane," Elizabeth laughed, "but we do know Mary a little better I think."

Jane looked despondent.

"Have you heard from Lydia father?" Elizabeth asked.

"O yes," Mrs Bennett cheered up at the sound of her favourite daughter's name. "She and dear Wickham are enjoying life very much. She writes to tell us that they are moving to better accommodation."

Elizabeth frowned, this was not good news. She looked at her father who signalled by his expression, that he was of the same opinion.

"Where are they moving to mama?" Jane asked.

"O I do not know, Jane. I never did like them up north. Their friends cannot be the same as in Colonel Foster's regiment. She had many friends there you know, who liked her very much, and she liked them too."

"I am sure she did mama, but to change regiments again so soon. It cannot be beneficial. If they could only settle, I am sure their life together would be more comfortable."

"O stuff and nonsense, Lizzie." Mrs Bennett scoffed. "She is young, plenty of time to settle down."

"I am sure you are right mama," Elizabeth agreed, not wishing to upset her mother any further.

"Come now, let us go and join the rest of the party. I am sure Mary and her new husband wish to be on their way back to Huntsford." Mr Bennett suggested as he helped his wife across the churchyard.

"O cousin," Mr Collins approached Mr Bennett. "Your daughter brings me much happiness, and she is indeed a godsend to my dear daughter. I was convinced the moment I stepped into your home, that my future happiness lay with one of your daughters."

Elizabeth was quite put out that Mr Collins could have forgotten her dear friend Charlotte so soon.

"You are very kind, sir," Mr Bennett replied. "I am sure Mary will be of much comfort to you."

"I am delighted you are happy Mr Collins," Elizabeth could

no longer hold her tongue. "but it is a sad circumstance indeed that brings about this union."

"Yes indeed, Mrs Darcy," Mr Collins had the grace to look abashed, "but my dear Charlotte, I am sure, would wish me to find happiness."

"You are right, Mr Collins," Elizabeth reflected. "She would indeed."

"And now my dear cousins," Mr Collins continued. "If you will permit me, I shall return to Huntsford with my new family. Lady Catherine will, I am sure be delighted that the situation has returned to its proper state."

"She will, Mr Collins," Elizabeth curtsied and moved away.

A few moments later the carriage carrying Mr Collins and his new bride departed for Kent.

"Are you to join us at Netherfield, Lizzie?" Jane asked.

"I will, Jane, but first I must spend a little time in mama's company."

"Then I will stay too," Jane replied.

"There is no need," Mrs Bennett joined the conversation. "I shall rest now. You have no idea how much I suffer, and now I only have Hill for company. Go, go to your posh houses, do not think of me."

"Mama, we are much concerned for you," Jane was put out with her mother's attitude. "Lizzie and I will stay and keep you company."

"As you wish, I do not want to be a burden to anyone." Mrs Bennett continued. "And another thing, Lizzie, a whole year you have been married, and not once have you extended an invitation to your poor mother. Ummph, well now you think you are too important for the rest of your family I suppose."

"Not at all mama," Elizabeth blushed slightly. "I have had a great deal to contend with at Pemberley, it takes much knowing. It is far larger than Longbourne, and there is much to learn."

"It is of no matter. Indeed I have no wish to travel so far."

"Mama, you are welcome anytime time you wish to visit, but your health is of much concern at present." Elizabeth was stalling and she knew it. "When you are fully recovered, Mr Darcy will be happy to receive you into his home."

"I have no wish to go anywhere I am not wanted," Mrs Bennett had no intentions of giving up this conversation. "You have no need to worry. I have many places where my company will be most welcome. If it was not for your father visiting Netherfield when Mr Bingley first moved to Hertfordshire, you would not be where you are today, my girl. But no, all that is forgotten now you have got your own way. You always were selfish, Lizzie. I am sure Mary will welcome me to Huntsford."

"Mama," Elizabeth was exasperated. "Why do you take on so? You know what you say is not true."

"O yes, yes it is. A whole year and no invitation. Everyone is talking behind my back, sniggering and saying your own mother is not good enough for you these days. Well they are probably right. I would not like to think I was the cause of embarrassment to my own daughter's."

"You may come to Pemberley when ever you wish, mama," Elizabeth was feeling very guilty now. "Come in the spring when the weather is a little kinder."

"O yes, mama," Jane suggested. "You can spend some time with, Lizzie, then come to me. Mr Bingley will be so happy to see you, I am sure."

"Well I may come to visit you, Jane," Mrs Bennett was much enjoying the situation. "Mr Bingley is at least agreeable, but some of his friends do not deserve the good fortune they were born with."

Elizabeth sighed heavily. Whether Mrs Bennett visited Pemberley or not, she knew that there would never be any good feeling between her mother and Mr Darcy.

Elizabeth remained at her parent's home for a further two days until her return to Pemberley. There she was greeted by much excitement and all conversation was of the forth coming nuptials.

She felt a little sorry for Miss Wentworth, who must have been feeling decidedly out of place.

"It will be just the two of us for company in the future I think," Elizabeth said to Mr Darcy's cousin.

"I am so happy for them, Mrs Darcy. They have chosen well I think," She smiled softly. "My brother has, since the moment he met Miss Darcy, been much in favour of her company."

"It was never spoken of in my hearing," Elizabeth said in a puzzled tone.

"My brother would not offend Mr Darcy by paying attention to his sister; he felt it could only bring dishonour and shame upon us if Miss Darcy did not feel the same way."

"He should have spoken of it sooner, we were all concerned for his disposition these last weeks." Elizabeth said. "You say his affection started on his arrival?"

"He always favoured Miss Darcy, and when she suffered her misfortune I believe it was more than he could bear. It was then, I believe that the strength of his feelings became apparent to him."

"Well I am glad everything has turned out the way it should be. Georgiana is very happy, you may be assured of that."

"They will make a very handsome couple do you not think?" Miss Wentworth asked.

"They will indeed. I believe they have decided to share their wedding day with Kitty and Colonel Fitzwilliam?" Elizabeth said.

"It will be a proud day for my brother. I have never seen him so happy."

"Then we shall all be one big happy family, although I have no idea how long Georgiana and your brother will wish to remain under Mr Darcy's roof."

"I hope it will be for some duration," Miss Wentworth replied. "Truly I cannot think of a time when I have been so content."

"Then let us pray it continues."

There was no containing the happiness in the house during the following few weeks, and Mr Darcy found himself caught up in all the excitement.

"To have all our sisters married Elizabeth, is fortunate indeed." Mr Darcy said.

"It is, sir. My father is very proud to have his five daughters settled in such happy circumstances."

"It must be a great relief to him, I think."

"It is indeed, sir."

*****

A week before the wedding was to take place, Mr and Mrs Bennett arrived at Pemberley.

"Mama, I am so pleased you have come at last." Elizabeth said as she greeted her mother.

"If it had not been for the wedding of my dear Kitty, I doubt if you would have extended this invitation at all my girl," Mrs Bennett stated.

"Please mama, you know that is not true."

"It is of little matter," Mrs Bennett looked up at the imposing facade of the building. "So this is where you call home now, is it, Lizzie. Well, you have had more good fortune than you deserve."

"Yes, mama." Elizabeth sighed, dreading the days that were to follow.

"Mr Bennett, Mrs Bennett, you are most welcome at Pemberley." Mr Darcy had now joined the group. "I hope your journey was without incident?"

"It was indeed, Mr Darcy. I thank you." Mr Bennett bowed in greeting.

"Your health, Mrs Bennett. I see that it is much improved," Mr Darcy said.

"No-one knows what I suffer, and to be forced to travel all this way, it does me no good at all," she replied.

"Then you must rest, to ensure you are healthy enough to enjoy the celebrations ahead." Mr Darcy suggested.

"Rest, how can I rest when my daughter Kitty needs me so much. I doubt I shall get a moments rest until I have returned to Longbourne. I see no reason why she could not got married from her place of birth, like the rest of you."

"She wishes to share her wedding with Mr Darcy's sister mama." Elizabeth was losing patience with her mother all ready.

"That may be so, Lizzie, but there is no thought for her poor mother who had to get out of a sick bed to travel so far."

"Shall we go inside and enjoy some refreshments?" Mr Darcy suggested.

Elizabeth felt for her husband who, despite his considerable help in the past, was still the object of dislike to her mother. She admired the way he tolerated her mothers insults.

"Jane will be here directly," Elizabeth said as they sat in the drawing room. "I believe she is bringing dear Charlotte with her."

"That is good," replied Mrs Bennett. "Jane is a good girl, always has been."

"Mr Darcy, your sister is to share my daughters wedding day." Mr Bennett tried to turn the conversation.

"She is indeed, sir," Mr Darcy replied. "Her choice of husband is our cousin. He has only recently returned from India, where he has spent most of his life."

"A foreign gentleman," Mrs Bennett exclaimed. "What ever next."

"He is not foreign mama, he has only lived abroad. That is all." Elizabeth was exasperated with her mother.

"It is the same thing," insisted Mrs Bennett. "What is wrong with the English gentlemen? There are many nice gentlemen in the regiment. I am sure Lydia could have found her a nice young officer."

"I am sure she could," replied Elizabeth. "Ah, here is Jane."

"Mama, it is lovely to see you.," Jane said as her entered the room. "See how Charlotte has grown since your last meeting."

Whilst Mrs Bennett made noises at her grandchild

Elizabeth confided in Jane.

"O Jane, mama has been here less than an hour and has already been more than offensive towards Mr Darcy."

"You worry too much, Lizzie, I am sure Mr Darcy is more than capable of dealing with mama." She turned towards her mother.

"Mama, why don't you come upstairs while I put Charlotte down for a rest?" she asked.

Elizabeth silently thanked her sister as the two women left the room.

"Mr Bennett, this is indeed a proud time for you I believe." Mr Bingley greeted his father in law.

"It is Mr Bingley. Five daughters all married. It takes some believing I think."

"And all in happy circumstances I believe."

"Let us hope so, Mr Bingley. Of four I have no concerns," Mr Bennett sighed.

"Pray tell me, sir, your youngest daughter, Mrs Wickham, is she settled now," Mr Bingley enquired.

"I doubt she will ever be settled, Mr Bingley, but just for the moment the storm has abated."

"I am pleased to hear it." he turned his attentions to his friend. "Darcy, this is a time of much pride for you I think."

"It is indeed, Bingley. I have never seen my sister Georgiana so happy."

"She could not have chosen a better husband," Mr Bingley suggested.

"I believe not." Mr Darcy smiled.

Over the following few days there was much coming and going at Pemberley. The house was decorated as never before. The flowers sending a heady perfume throughout. Food, wine and music flowed in abundance, and apart from Mrs Bennett, everyone was in high spirits.

Elizabeth did her best to keep Mr Darcy and her mother apart, and to her relief, on the few occasions they did meet, Mrs Bennett's conversation was at least tolerable.

Mr Darcy had been gracious enough to relent, and allow Elizabeth to invite her younger sister Lydia to Kitty's wedding. On the subject of Lydia's husband, however, he was adamant. "Mr Wickham will never set foot in this house Elizabeth. That is my final word." Elizabeth could not blame him, Mr Wickham had been the cause of much distress in Mr Darcy's life."

"O Lizzie, this is a very large house, you are so lucky," Lydia announced on her arrival. And to think dear Wickham and myself have to struggle every day."

"You would not have to struggle so much if you did not visit the shops so often Lydia. Your condition is of your own making." Elizabeth rebuked her sister.

"You are so cruel, Lizzie, and so is Mr Darcy. To refuse to allow my dear Wickham to travel to Kitty's wedding with me. It was most unfair."

"After the way your husband has treated Mr Darcy, Lydia, I am surprised he even allows his name to be mentioned." Elizabeth was cross with her sisters attitude.

"You are just like him, Lizzie. You never used to be this cruel. Now you are rich you should be more benevolent towards your relations. Where is Kitty?"

"I believe she is with Jane and mama in the drawing room."

Throughout the evening Lydia continued to compare Lizzie and Jane's life to her own, to the great consternation of the other guests.

Her aunt Gardiner, who had refrained from expressing an opinion, was now so exasperated by the situation, she could no longer hold her temper.

"Lydia, you are most ungrateful. If it had not been for the generous nature of your sister's, and their husband's your life would be very much poorer. I can not believe you can be so selfish. It is your sister Kitty's wedding day tomorrow, can you not, for once, put her happiness first?"

Lydia was about to reply but thought better of it. She sat heavily down on the settee next to her sister Jane with a sulky look on her face.

Elizabeth felt sorry for the way Lydia's life had turned out, but she was so headstrong, she would not be advised.

*****

The spring morning of the wedding dawned bright and clear. Georgiana and Kitty were in a much nervous but excited condition.

They both looked beautiful in their wedding gowns, and Mr Darcy felt extremely proud as he escorted his sister to the chapel in the grounds of Pemberley.

"You are most fortunate, Georgiana," Mr Darcy smiled down at his sister. "Your cousin Edward is a fine young man. I believe you will be most content."

"I am sure I will, sir. I cannot remember when I have been so happy. I am sure I do not deserve it."

"You deserve every happiness in the world, Georgiana. I shall miss your company very much."

"We have no intention of leaving Pemberley," Georgiana said in surprise. "I am sure I will see you every day."

"Then I too am delighted." He kissed her lightly on the forehead then taking her arm he proudly led her inside the chapel.

"Your sister, sir, has never looked more beautiful." Elizabeth told her husband.

"Nor yours, my dearest Elizabeth."

"I wonder what mama thinks of the arrangements? She has, after all had very little to do with this day.

"I believe she is more taken up with the wedding of her daughter, than thinking to cause you any discomfort Elizabeth." Mr Darcy observed.

"I believe you are right, sir. It is indeed a good time for her to make a visit. She does look a great deal better I believe."

"She does indeed."

"Lizzie, Mr Darcy this is a proud day for us all," Mr Bennett said as he approached them. "Five daughters all married, who would have believed it."

"Colonel Fitzwilliam will make your daughter a good husband, sir. He has been my friend all his life and I can vouch for his character."

"You are probably right, Mr Darcy, he does indeed seem to bring pleasure to my daughter."

"Lizzie, O Lizzie, Kitty looks so beautiful, does she not?" Mrs Bennett had now joined them. "And to think above a year ago all our daughters were still at Longbourne, and now they are all settled." She waved her arms about in excitement.

"We have been most fortunate, ma'am." Elizabeth smiled at her mother's pleasure.

"Mr Darcy," Mrs Bennett's tone changed as she turned to acknowledge her son in law. "You have been very good to my girls, I thank you."

"The pleasure was all mine, I assure you." Mr Darcy bowed in acknowledgement of this rare compliment, "I am happy to see that you also have returned to health."

"No-one knows how I suffer, but I would not embarrass Kitty by complaining on her special day," Mrs Bennett explained. "Your sister, Mr Darcy, is a very pretty girl."

"She is indeed. I am very proud of her. I believe both ladies have made a very good alliance."

"I understand that your sister will be staying at Pemberley after her marriage, Mr Darcy," Mr Bennett said.

"She will indeed, sir. Mr Wentworth is not as yet familiarized enough with our country to establish his own society."

"It must be a great comfort to you to have your sister settled so close." Mrs Bennett suggested.

"It is indeed. I would miss her company very much."

During the gathering afterwards Mr Darcy spoke of his observations to his wife.

"I believe, Elizabeth, that there may very well be two more weddings to be attended in the not too distant future."

"I do not understand your meaning, sir. To whose wedding are you talking?"

"Look around you my dearest. Our cousin Miss Wentworth is very much taken with the younger Mr Randal, while the older brother is showing much regard for our friend Caroline Bingley."

Elizabeth was most surprised, but as she watched she was more and more convinced that her husband could be right.

"I feel we will have much congratulating to do in the future, Elizabeth." Mr Darcy smiled.

"I fear I have not been so observant of late as is my usual character, sir. My mind has been involved on another matter closer to my heart."

Mr Darcy looked at his wife with concern. "My dearest Elizabeth, is there something that concerns you?"

"On the contrary, sir, I do believe that there will be congratulations of our own later this year," Elizabeth smiled shyly at her husband.

Mr Darcy looked down at his wife in confusion. Then as the realization of her words occurred to him, his face took on a look of sheer pride.

"Can this be true, my love?" he asked in delight.

"When Lady Catherine and my parents are invited here together, I believe we can announced that an heir to Pemberley has at last arrived, sir."

He did not speak again, but the emotions that crossed his face were the ones that Elizabeth had almost given up hope of ever seeing. A new chapter was about to begin for Pemberley.

The End